CUT TO THE FEELING

BIG BOYS, SMALL SPACES
BOOK 2

A.J. TRUMAN

M.A. WARDELL

For anyone who's ever been told they're "too much" or "not enough." You're exactly the right amount for someone.

A NOTE FROM THE AUTHORS

Cut to the Feeling is our love letter to classic rom-coms. Writing it, made us wish we lived in Nora Ephron's New York City, and we hope you feel the same. We kept thinking of our favorite NY stories when writing (When Harry Met Sally, You've Got Mail, The Goodbye Girl), and we hope we captured that feeling here.

This work is an open-door romance intended for mature audiences. The characters in the story are consenting adults, and there is explicit, on-page sexual content, explicit language, and adult situations.

Cut to the Feeling is a low-angst story, but here are the few content warnings in case they're helpful:

Mentions of car accident, mention of death by car accident, mention of death of a sibling, an excessive number of Carly Rae Jepsen references, a dog who was supposed to be a side character but fully stole the spotlight, sexy times on a stairwell, exploration of beard kink, a swearing parrot, and forehead kisses for good boys (of dog and human varieties).

For signed paperbacks, merchandise, more information, and updates, visit us at:

www.ajtruman.com

www.mawardell.com

All our best,

A.J. and Matt

ONE

BRYCE

SURE, men are lovely, but does anything top spending quality one-on-one time with your dog?

Especially when that dog is the size of a miniature horse and there's so much more to love. Bobo clocked in at one-hundred-twenty pounds at his last checkup—on the high end for a Bernese Mountain Dog. We're both in our Big Boy Era. He stands just over two feet tall, and much like his dad, he tends to command the attention of those around him.

"C'mon, Bobo! You already peed on that tree. No need to belabor the point." I give his leash a gentle tug as we continue down the street, and Bobo breaks into a determined trot. Busy New Yorkers part for us, which is understandable since it appears a fluffy Seabiscuit is coming right for them. "We want to get these home to Anthony while they're still warm!"

Heat emanates from the bag of cardamom buns in my other hand.

Bobo's gait quickens as we get closer to our apartment building. One woman jumps out of the way and shoots me a look, and I mouth "sorry" to her.

I didn't know he would get this big—I study the intricacies of music video choreography, not dog breeds. When Anthony and I first brought the relatively small puppy home at six weeks, we had no idea how large he'd grow. Looking back, the fact that he had paws the size of dinner plates probably should've raised some suspicions. By the time Carl, our super, realized how massive Bobo would become, he was already smitten.

Another few blocks of charging down the sidewalk and smiling awkwardly at annoyed glances and we arrive at the Bigby. We live on the sixth floor. Of a walk-up. Now comes the real test of cardio endurance.

We love most of our neighbors. Marsh and Data downstairs are hashtag gay goals. Marsh is a fantastic cook; Data loves to treat me to brunch. Plus, they love dog sitting. Of course, Mrs. Lee on the second floor frequently scolds us. (Apologies, but some of us receive packages too large for our small mailboxes. We sometimes forget about them, and they end up sitting in the lobby for a while.) Still, even she can't resist Bobo's charm.

Luckily, as an almost professional dancer, I'm in excellent shape. Bobo sure doesn't mind. Perhaps it calls back to some instinctual desire to climb the Alps.

"Anthony?"

I close the front door and release Bobo from his leash. He bounds off for his water dish.

"We brought you a gift."

I hold out the bag of buns, hoping the scent attracts my hot boyfriend.

"We took the long route through the park because I wanted to visit Ronaldo. He still refuses to run away with me." I ate a soft pretzel from Ronaldo's cart before picking up more carbs. They're as big as my head, and Ronaldo's accent makes me think impure thoughts. Though he's a happily married father of four, I think he enjoys my playful, no-stakes flirting.

I walk into the kitchen.

"Anthony?"

I set his mid-morning snack down on the small table wedged against the wall—my best effort to create a dining nook in our cozy, one-bedroom apartment. Cooking isn't really our jam. We'd rather just keep the takeout menus on speed dial. We have a microwave for reheating leftovers and an electric kettle for coffee and tea. It's more than enough—we're not trying to be Julia Child up here.

"Optimus Prime, have you seen my boyfriend?"

I convinced Anthony to unplug the stove and let me repurpose it for storage for my growing collection of vintage Transformers. He built a cute little display case right over the part on top where you're supposed to cook.

"You're probably in the bedroom." Anthony loves his disco naps. "And my incessant chatter probably isn't helping, is it?"

I leave the kitchen and do a little twirl on the area rug in the living room. "There's an open casting call for chorus members for the new Lin-Manuel Miranda musical. Have you heard anything about it? You think any of the casting directors who have not-so-secret crushes on you could squeeze me in for an audition?" Anthony is the first boyfriend I've had who's a fellow thespian. Typically, I try to avoid it since it can easily devolve into a competition. But fortunately, Anthony doesn't like musicals. His skills are dramatic acting and TV work.

I pick up the mail he left on the coffee table and sift through it. Junk and bills. "I was so close to this latest gig. So close. I'll get them next time."

The exciting and exhausting part about being a Broadway performer is that it's like playing the lottery. Most times you lose, but the next audition could be the jackpot.

"Okay, sleepyhead. I'm getting tired of talking to myself." I push open the bedroom door. "Surprise!"

But the surprise is on me—the room lies in utter silence, devoid of life. Bobo trots past me and hops onto the bed as if nothing is wrong. I pop my head into the bathroom. Empty.

"Anthony?" My voice comes out softer than usual as concern bubbles up in my chest. "Did you go out?"

I run back to the hallway. I check the kitchen again. I check the bathroom. I even check the linen closet. I mean, Anthony is svelte so he could totally fit in there.

My heart picks up, thumping against my ribcage.

"Anthony?" I check under the sofa. Maybe he ran out to grab some coffee. Could he have been hungry? He tends to wake up pretty ravenous.

I pull out my phone to check for messages. Nothing.

New York may be a dangerous city, but would someone climb six flights of stairs to kidnap an actor? Is Anthony secretly working for the mob?

My finger hovers over the number nine on my phone. My throat goes dry. How much trouble is he in? I hear Bobo lurch himself off the bed and saunter into the hall, his leisurely gait showing no signs of worry. Dogs can smell danger, right? Or is it fear?

He grabs something from the coffee table, turns around, and stands before me with an envelope dangling from his mouth. Not exactly surprising—Bobo, like most gay men in the city, has a habit of shoving things into his mouth first and asking questions later.

"Bobo Baggins, what do you have?"

Yes, I know it's Bilbo, not Bobo, but Anthony adorably dubbed him that after we slept through *The Fellowship of the Ring*, and it stuck.

He drops the envelope at my feet. My name is written in Anthony's penmanship, which is as slender and neat as him.

Dear Bryce,

This isn't a fun letter to write, but here goes.

At the wrap party last weekend, this casting director showed up. I thought he was someone I'd had sex with, but I couldn't remember, and it felt rude to ask. So I stood there and nodded along as he said he's casting this indie film—*Boys Only Cry When They Dance*—and thought I'd be perfect for it. Julian St. Laurent is directing it—*the* Julian St. Laurent. Maybe this film will go to Cannes. Is it pronounced Can or Cahn?

Anyway, the actor originally cast dropped out to take a role in the Mr. Potato Head movie. And now they want me. The thing is, they've already started filming, so they need someone to start ASAP. I'm going to the outback! Not the steakhouse. Gosh, I wish. They have the best baked potatoes. The actual outback—the one in Australia. I might finally fulfill my lifelong dream of high-fiving a kangaroo.

I didn't say anything sooner because I knew you'd try to stop me. Which is also why I left while you were out— better to avoid a tearful goodbye. We had a good run, but I think this relationship has run its course. It feels like we're on different trajectories and mine is headed down undah.

You're a trooper, Bryce. You'll be fine. You always are. Bobo will take care of you. And you'll get your big break anytime now. Definitely. Probably. Maybe. Give Bobo a kiss from me.

Later,

Anthony

TWO

BRYCE

PRESSURE BUILDS in my chest as my limbs go weak. I clutch the letter to my chest, trying to numb the pain pounding inside. Tears press at the corners of my eyes, but they don't flow. I'm unable to move or breathe. I just stand frozen, like a tourist on the subway trying to figure out how to use the damn turnstile.

Bobo creeps his front paws onto my feet and stares at me with his giant brown eyes.

"He's gone."

Bobo cocks his head.

I read the ending aloud again for him, hoping he grasps its severity.

"We had a good run."

The tears fall.

"Two years and now ..." I hold the paper up, the writing already smudged by my crying. "... this?"

The numbness in my chest expands to the rest of my torso, quickly fanning out over my entire body.

"I mean, two years for gays is like twenty for the straights."

I sit on the sofa, and Bobo immediately attempts to crawl into my lap. He can only get about a third of his legs on me, but damn, he's trying. I lean over and kiss his head, recalling Anthony's request. And then it hits me—he might walk out on me, but he'd never abandon Bobo.

A jolt of hope rushes through my body. "He couldn't."

Clutching the note, I rush into the bedroom and check Anthony's side of the closet. Empty. With a yank, I open the drawer on his bedside table—bare as a drag queen's bank account after a Sephora shopping spree. His mega pack of Costco condoms is all that remains. How fucking thoughtful. That's when I know it's real. Anthony's gone.

A sound escapes me—something between a cry and a whimper —and I throw myself onto the bed, face down.

How could this happen? Again. After Logan. Bruce. Derek. Fernando. I mean, none of them lasted as long as Anthony. I thought this time would be different—he was different. Why does it always end the same? Why do men always have no problem leaving me? Am I too much? Too little? What about Bryce Derrickson makes it so easy for them to just walk away? It's like I'm some temporary fix, something to pass the time until someone better comes along.

The room spins around me, the weight of my emotions crashing down as hot tears spill onto the plush West Elm comforter. Washing it is going to be a bitch—it barely fits in the machine in the basement, and frankly, I'm not sure what's more exhausting: dragging that thing down six flights of stairs or dealing with the emotional wreckage of my life. Either way, I'm going to need a Xanax with a bottle of wine chaser after this.

I'm alone. Again.

The clack of Bobo's nails on the hardwood floor as he crosses the nine feet from the living room rug to the bedroom alerts me to his presence. I lift my teary gaze. His enormous head rests on the edge of the bed.

"I know, buddy. It's just us now."

I pat the blanket, and he jumps up and lies next to me. I wrap my arm around Bobo's body, holding him close as more tears fall. A soreness in my throat takes over as I attempt to swallow, and he bumps his cool nose against mine.

"Oh, Bobo."

He licks my face, and honestly, between the tears and dog slobber, I've got a full-on skincare routine happening.

"We'll be okay. We have the apartment. I can try to pick up another shift at the Met. Maybe Anthony's right, and my big break is around the corner. Don't worry." I run my hand over his face, his deep eyes reassuring me. "The sun will come out tomorrow. Don't stop believing. What doesn't kill us makes us stronger."

After washing my face, I head back to the living room to console myself with the buns. I pinch off two pieces and toss them Bobo's way then gobble the rest down myself.

"Yeah, doesn't feel like enough, boy."

I hop over to the refrigerator and open the tiny freezer on top.

"Now, a bun followed by a pint of Procrastination Swirl might do the trick."

Back on the sofa, with ice cream and pretzels piled into a giant bowl that was probably meant for salad (but since we never actually eat salad, it has become our ice cream and mix-ins bowl), I grab my phone. Right now, only one person can offer me any solace.

I fire up my playlist, and synths dot the room before a beautiful, soft alto joins the music. The beat kicks in, and I take a perfect bite—equal parts salty pretzel and sweet swirl—then thrust my shoulders back, ready to get my groove on to "Party for One" by my queen. Carly Rae Jepsen.

When she commands me to dance, I place the bowl on the table, stand up, and without missing a beat, step into the rhythm. My body flows effortlessly as I glide across the cramped living room, every move smooth and precise. You might think I've studied the choreo from the video—and you might be right. The ice cream and buns fade from my mind as I immerse myself in the music, spinning and twirling with confidence, the driving beat fueling my adrenaline.

I truly don't know how I survived the horrors of the world before Carly Rae Jepsen came into my life. Sure, there was Kelly and Gaga and Madonna. But none had the right kind of unabashed JOY. Carly's music is pure sunshine, lifting me up, whether I lose out on another audition, or another boyfriend.

Bobo watches, wide-eyed, and I can't help but smirk.

"Fuck that asshole!"

Hearing this, Bobo huffs, takes his usual spot on the sofa, and lowers his head, a sure sign he agrees.

As Carly breaks into the last chorus, I scream the words, stamping my feet when the music drops out and only leaves her voice and the pounding bass drum. This is my party for one. Well, two, if you count Bobo. Which I do.

When the song ends, I collapse on the couch next to Bobo, my breath coming in short, shallow bursts. The high from dancing fades quickly, replaced by a creeping sense of doubt. Before the next song begins, I press stop on my phone, the sudden silence like a siren in my ears. One song is all I've got in me.

Bobo looks up at me, his eyes big brown pools, as if asking why I stopped. I don't have an answer. The music always makes it easier to pretend, but when it's over, it's just me—and even with my canine bestie here, I'm feeling more lonely than ever.

AS A GORGEOUS DAY turns to rainy night, I try to block out thoughts of Anthony and crushing loneliness with food, wine, and bad television. Marsh and Data are away at their cabin this week, so they can't come over to cheer me up. I text my bestie Portia, but she messages back *Stuck on a yacht* 🙄 and she's not even being sarcastic.

My thoughts wander back to the last time I was single—the two months between Derek and Anthony when I experienced a similar loneliness. Feeling the need for some connection, and exhausting all other possibilities, I return to my old foe.

Grindr.

Like all gay men, I detest it yet can't permanently remove it from my life. When Jake Gyllenhaal proclaimed, "I wish I knew how to quit you," he wasn't talking about hottie Heath Ledger. He was talking about modern dating apps.

On the home screen, I'm instantly met with a grid of blurry torso shots and vague taglines. Despite the bevy of potential paramours, once I block all the guys who proudly proclaim they're not into femmes or fatties, I'm left with a scant few choices.

I manage to find a guy with a passable ability to string together a sentence. After some requisite flirting, I tell him to come over and down another glass of wine.

I know I'll hate myself in the morning, but whatever.

At my core, I'm not a random-hookup kind of guy. But apparently, all guys like to do is say goodbye to me. I'm the person you leave. For hotter guys. For richer boyfriends. For kangaroos in the outback.

The giddy ding of the notification alerts me.

On my way. See you in 15.

Not tonight.

Tonight, I will have meaningless sex and kindly ask the guy to leave when it's over. I will be the one who says goodbye.

THREE

EMERSON

I ARRIVE in the Big Apple on a stormy night, and the precipitation only picks up the closer I get to my new, temporary home. Sheets of rain slash against the car, giving the windshield wipers a workout.

A low rumble comes from the front seat. Probably because I'm wearing a hat, my Uber driver doesn't notice my hearing aid. The rain and the club music make it hard to make out what he's saying. I've gotten through our awkward small talk with a coordinated attack of uh-huhs, yeahs, and oh wows.

Perhaps he's onto me because he turns down the music before he speaks again.

"Where you coming in from?"

"Indiana."

He nods, a bit flummoxed how to follow up. "Huh. Indiana, yeah? Oh wow."

That sums up most people's reactions to the Hoosier state. If I wasn't born and raised there, I'd have the same reaction. Whenever I see an Indiana tourism television ad, I think *Why?*

"You can't beat the cost of living," I tell him, my standard defense of my home state. Living here, he gets it immediately.

"You here for business or pleasure?"

"I'm hoping both." There is no greater pleasure than loving your job. I say a silent prayer that the next few months work out.

The driver pulls up to a tall, narrow apartment building with a classic New York stoop. He offers to help me with my suitcase, but I tell him to stay dry in the car.

The stoop may appear romantic, but trudging a suitcase up its steep incline as the rain batters my glasses is hell. I punch the code into the keypad and open the building's entry door. When I realize that apartment 6A means six flights of stairs, I release a mammoth sigh. I've taken two planes and a long car ride to get here. There is a bone-deep exhaustion that comes with traveling. The only thing pulling me up each step is the thought of a big, warm bed awaiting me upstairs.

Shockingly, my ears don't pop when I reach my floor. I rest my head against the door and take a breath. Before I can put the key in, the door opens, sending me tumbling into a barrel-chested man clothed in a black T-shirt and very tight boxer briefs.

"Sorry about that," I say to the man, who I'm assuming is the super. He's unfazed by my appearance. I follow him as he strolls into the living room and plunks on the couch. The scent of an opened red wine bottle on the fireplace mantel fills the room.

He teepees his eyebrows at me. "You don't look like the torso from your profile." He laughs, shrugs, and takes a sip of his wine. "But you'll do."

"Oh." Perhaps there was an added background check I had to pass. While I don't like that he's drinking on the job, nor that he's pantless, I do appreciate his professionalism. "I'm excited to be here."

"Don't cream your pants just yet. We haven't even gotten started," the super says.

I chuckle. My friend Annemarie warned me New Yorkers have a blunt way of speaking.

I hold out my hand for a shake, and he has the horrified expression of someone offered a live snake. "I'm Emerson."

"No. Don't do that. We're not doing names tonight."

"Ooookay. So what should I call you?"

"Anything you want. Just not slut or whore. Some guys like that, but I don't."

"Noted," I say with a nervous laugh, quickly realizing that our senses of humor are, shall we say, different. "Is everything in order?"

"Yeah. Get in here." He nods and pats the seat next to him on the couch.

I stifle a yawn, the exhaustion stretching across my chest. "Actually, I just want to go to the bedroom."

"Cutting to the chase, I see. Okay, then. Why don't we have some fun out here first?"

"I'm a bit tired for fun."

"Don't worry. I'll wake you up." The man hops up from the couch and circles me, scanning me with a critical eye. "You know, you're pretty cute. Beards are hot. And the whole slutty little glasses thing really makes those brown eyes pop."

"Um, I wear glasses to see. I'm near-sighted."

"We don't need to get into life stories." The super has no shyness about checking me out, as if we're at some seedy gay bar.

"Hmm. You've got a nice chest. Good arms, too. I like the whole nerd on the outside, jock on the inside thing you've got going on."

"I wasn't a jock. I grew up on a farm. We grew corn and soybeans."

"Long days in the field ... hot. Did you wear overalls, too?"

This is the weirdest interview I've ever been through. "Can we just get this over with as fast as possible?"

"Typical man." He shakes his head and glances behind me. "Nice ass, too. Really nice."

"Thank you?" My midwestern politeness makes me stay in place and show gratitude for compliments, no matter how out of place they might be.

I can't help but look him over, too. I have a thing for sandy brown hair. Like me, he's a bigger guy, but whereas I'm tall and stocky, he's shorter and thicker. Yet there's a definition in his arms and chest that tells me he's strong underneath it all. Some kind of athlete.

I find myself puffing out my chest and sucking in my stomach as he rakes his eyes over my frame.

"Is that a hearing aid?"

"Yeah. I'm hard of hearing."

He blatantly rakes his eyes up and down my frame. "Well, your hearing isn't the only thing hard right now."

"What? Look, I've had a long day of traveling. Can we finish whatever this is in the morning? I'd really like to go to bed now."

"Who says you're sleeping over?"

I take a step back. The quick thrill of being checked out is replaced with utter confusion. "What is going on here? This is all extremely unprofessional, and I'm two seconds away from calling the management office. What's your name?"

"I told you. No names. We're not walking down the aisle. Excuse me for wanting to check out the goods before making a purchase." He struts back to his wine glass and takes another sip. "Look, before we get to it, I want to lay down some ground rules."

I think he's going to go over how to use the trash chute, but instead he whips off his T-shirt and tosses it on the floor.

"Number one: don't call me baby. This isn't *Dirty Dancing*. Number two: no bite marks on my ass. For some reason, guys love biting my ass. Does it remind them of a Big Mac? I have no idea."

He turns around and wiggles his ... rear. "Yeah, I guess it's juicy. Anyway, it might turn you on, but it hurts like hell."

He closes the gap between us, which I open by stepping the hell back.

"Number three: don't come on my face. It may look hot on your computer screen, but it's a gross mess for me, and most guys don't have good aim, so it'll get on my area rug, and getting an area rug cleaned in the city is a pain in the ass."

The super, or whoever the hell he is, snaps the waistband of his boxers. I head for the door but keep a polite smile on my face. Midwestern-ness is hard to shake.

"And number four, and most important: I'm not here for any emotional attachment, okay? Don't gaze into my eyes. Don't ask me if they're green. They're not. They're hazel." He opens his eyes wide and points to them. "*Hazel.* Don't tell me I'm beautiful or say, 'Bryce, I've never known anyone like you,' or what have you. And if we cuddle post-sex, and that's a big *if,* don't you dare tell me that you want to see me again. If you do, I will search every Equinox Gym on this island, find you, and castrate you. Because I know it's a lie. It's always a lie." He takes a calming breath. "This is just about having a good time. Now take your clothes off. I want to get this over with so I can go back to bingeing *The Traitors.*"

"What the hell is going on?" I yell. "You're definitely not the super."

"What? No. I don't feel like role-playing tonight." Bryce reaches for my jacket, but I smack his hand away.

"This isn't role-playing. You're in my apartment, and you need to leave now before I call the police."

He looks at me, confused. "Are we fucking or not?"

I take a confident step forward, taking back what's mine. "We are doing no such thing."

"Handies then?"

I open the front door. "Get out. Now!"

He drops his look of casual disinterest, now joining me in confusion.

"I don't know who you are or why you are here, but this is my apartment. I'm moving in." I barge past him, throw open the door to the bedroom, and collapse on the bed. In a moment, I'll call the cops to remove this madman. But I need to lie down.

My beat of relaxation is interrupted by a giant tongue licking my face as if I'm a human-sized ice cream cone. I spring off the bed and turn on the lamp on the nightstand.

An enormous dog, one that rivals a small pony back on the farm and has no business being in a one-bedroom walk-up, cocks his head at me.

"Who the heck are you?"

"That's Bobo. Touch him and die." The man who called himself Bryce stands at the bedroom entrance, his shirt back on. "He's sleeping."

"On my bed!"

"*My* bed!"

I storm past him. "This is not your apartment."

Bobo lets out a single, booming bark and follows me into the living room. I wipe the residual moistness off my cheek. "Buy a guy dinner before you do that, huh?"

I hunch over my backpack and rummage around while Bryce and Bobo hover behind me.

"This is insane," Bryce says. "You stumble in here and expect me to up and leave my home just like that? Just because you say this is your place? How do I know you're not the squatter, huh? If this were really your apartment, you'd have some kind of proof."

I spin around and hold up the key the super—the *real* super—left for me in the lockbox downstairs. It's on a keychain with an ANTHONY license plate. Bryce's face flinches with shock. For the first time tonight, he's speechless.

"That's Anthony's key."

"He sublet the apartment to me."

"I bought him that keychain." It almost looks like he's going to cry, but he sweeps past me to the door. "You need to leave."

"No, you need to leave."

Bryce gestures for me to exit. I go to the opposite side and gesture for *him* to leave.

"Excuse me," he says. "Don't gesture to me. I'm gesturing to you. You need to go."

He pulls open the door. A guy in a hoodie who looks like he drinks three protein shakes a day stands in the entrance. He looks up from his phone.

"I was just about to message," he says. He turns to Bryce, then me. "Which one of you am I hooking up with tonight?"

"Me," Bryce says. "Once I get this squatter out of my apartment."

"*You* are the squatter," I fire back. "You have zero claim to the premises."

"No claim? This is my place. I pay rent. I have renter's rights."

"Is your name on the lease?" Protein-shake-guy asks.

"Well ... no. My boyfriend—ex-boyfriend—rents it, but I contribute to the monthly rent. Sure, last month it was only sixty-seven dollars and a killer blow job, but still."

"I'm a real estate attorney," he says. "I deal with these cases all the time."

"You're just here to look pretty." Bryce narrows his eyes at the hottie. "Nobody said you could speak."

"Well, unless your name is on the lease, it doesn't matter how much you paid toward rent. Sorry." The guy shrugs as if it's another day at the office, or another hookup, for him.

"See?" I smile victoriously, but a twinge of guilt digs into my side.

Bryce opens his mouth to speak. Nothing comes out. His face remains bright red.

"You should probably go," Bryce says to the guy, who's tapping away on his phone.

"All good," he replies. "There's a dude down the street who just sent me a pic of his hole, so I'm gonna, like, hang with him. Later. Sorry about being evicted." The guy shrugs, gives us a friendly wave, and retreats down the stairs.

I slam the door shut and rub my temples. "This is my apartment now. I'm tired, and I want to go to sleep. I have an important day tomorrow. You need to go."

"I'm not going anywhere." Bryce barricades himself in front of the door. "I've lived in this apartment for two years. I have rights. And I have a dog to think about."

There's a desperation in his eyes as he speaks, one that seems to go beyond eviction.

I pull out my phone and show him the confirmation email from Anthony and the signed sublet agreement. "It's official. If you have a problem, you can reach out to him."

Bryce's face sinks, all of his sassy energy seeping out like air from a popped balloon. He stumbles into the living room and gazes out the window into the rainy abyss. Bobo trots up to him, and Bryce joins him on the floor.

"Didn't he tell you he was subletting?" I ask.

Bobo licks his hand, but Bryce doesn't react.

"Do you have anywhere to go tonight?" I ask softly. "A friend to stay with?"

"I need a place for both of us." He leans his head on the dog's, and damn if it isn't sweet. "Whatever. Not your problem. We'll survive."

"Look," I say, after a long pause, "You can stay on the couch tonight. Tomorrow, you can figure out where to go."

Bryce gives me the slightest nod of gratitude. "We dated for two years, and he didn't even tell me he was leaving. He wrote me a letter." There's an enormous sigh from the dog, like he's fully aware of his owner's situation. "I always thought I'd have a home here with him, but now ... now I've lost everything."

"You'll get through this. It will be okay." The dog's big brown eyes stare at me, an added gut punch. "Why don't you and Bobo sleep in your bedroom? I'll take the couch. I don't want him barking all night long."

"Thanks." Bryce gets up and walks past me. "And Emerson. Just so you know, tomorrow I'm finding a lawyer. One I haven't almost slept with, and we're going to figure out how to get this apartment back. So don't get too comfortable." He and Bobo enter the bedroom. He shuts the door but opens it back up a second later. "Oh, and your ass isn't *that* nice."

FOUR

BRYCE

WELL, I definitely got fucked. Just not in the way I hoped.

Instead of a quick encounter with a sexy stranger, I ended up with a stranger taking possession of my apartment. A tall stranger. Well over six feet. I'm a respectably average five feet eleven inches tall, and he dwarfed me. He had shoulders you could anchor a cruise ship to. And he's sleeping on my sofa.

He thinks the apartment is his. It is not. Anthony's name may be on the lease, but I've lived here for almost two years. I'm the one who picked out the rug in the living room, the one with the bold geometric pattern I thought would tie the space together. I've spent hours choosing the right throw pillows, rearranging the furniture to make the most of the small space. I feng-shuied my ass off, creating a home in a way Anthony never bothered to. It's my apartment.

Bobo, happier than a twink in a bathhouse to be cuddling with me on the bed, yawns and lays his head on my forearm.

"We're not going anywhere." I rub his ears, running my fingers through his hair. "This is our home. He can't make us leave."

Bobo licks my arm, his giant tongue tickling my skin, and then he lies back down.

"I'm sorry, boy."

It's still dark out, so it must be early. As gently as possible, I move his head off me, sit up, and grab my phone—5:12 a.m. Not only have I been dumped via letter, but the stranger who's moved into my apartment has totally fucked with my sleep cycle. Maybe if he poisons my Corn Flakes, I'll hit the shitty news trifecta.

Well, if I'm up, I might as well get the day started. Bobo and I can take a nice long walk before my audition later this morning for this new show, *The Sound of Muscles*. As if a nun twirling on a hill wasn't gay *enough*. It's for the chorus, but beggars can't be choosers.

Bobo shakes his head, clearly wanting to get up.

"You hungry?" My stomach growls, and he tilts his head, staring at my midsection. "Yeah, me too."

I look at the bedroom door. It's rarely closed, as there's no need. We're either together in here or moving around. But there's no "we" anymore—at least not Anthony and me. Bobo hops down, saunters over, and stares at the barrier between us and Mr. Stealing My Peace. It makes the small space even more confined.

"Okay, we'll have to be quiet, buddy. We have a … guest."

Before my hand touches the doorknob, a loud noise blasts from outside, making Bobo and me jump. Strings. Horns. It sounds like a marching band decided to move into my tiny living room with the stranger who most definitely isn't going to split me in half.

I open the door, and roaring classical music slaps me in the face.

Mr. Carnival Cruise Shoulders stands at the table—*my* table that I picked out and schlepped up six flights of stairs—fully dressed, eyes closed like the world's loudest orchestra isn't attempting to wake the entire building before the sun rises. On the table sits a small portable speaker responsible for the racket, and I'm amazed by the volume it produces despite its size.

"Excuse me," I shout over the cacophony, but he doesn't flinch. I take a step closer. "Emerson?"

Nothing.

Sensing my frustration and possibly wanting the blaring music to stop, Bobo trots up and gives his khakis a little nudge, and finally, he opens his eyes.

"Do you need something?" Emerson shouts, attempting to have a conversation over the noise.

"Do I need something?"

He reaches up to his ear, touches a small plastic piece that sits behind it and takes an audible breath.

"What is that?" I nod toward the speaker.

He says something, but I can't make him out over the blaring orchestra.

"Can you turn it off?" I cover my ears with my hands. "Or at least down?" I'm all but screaming to compete with the classical nonsense.

"Excuse me?"

"Music." I point to the speaker. "Off." I gesture across my neck. "Please." I flash him my best smile.

His mouth opens wide like he finally gets it. He quickly hits pause on his phone, and just like that, the music cuts off, leaving the room blissfully silent.

"Why are you blasting this ... *stuff* before sunrise?"

"This stuff is *Die Walküre* by Wagner. It's a brilliant rumination on love and loss."

"Personally, I prefer something with a little more ... pizzazz." I give my best jazz hands. "The divas are where my heart lies. Specifically, one Ms. Carly Rae Jepsen."

"Carly Rae from the Jetsons?" He fusses behind his ear again.

"I vaguely remember Judy and Rosie the Robot. Which one was Carly Rae?"

My chin dips, almost hitting my sternum.

"You can't be serious. 'Call Me Maybe'?"

"Call you? Why would I do that? You're literally in front of me."

I shake my head in disbelief. This guy can't be serious. No one is this oblivious. But as I search his face, his eyebrows squishing together, I realize he genuinely knows neither Ms. Carly Rae or her signature bop.

"Oh, Emerson," I say, touching his forearm. It's dusted with light brown hair that compliments his short, well-kept cut.

"What?" He pulls back, shaking his broad shoulders slightly. "Unfortunately, the musicology department of the University of New York doesn't have a concentration in disposable Top 40."

"I'm going to blame that bitchy comment on your jetlag, but don't make me have to wash your mouth out with Bath and Body Works soap." I have to roll my eyes at how dismissive people can be toward pop music. Writing a catchy, sticky four-minute song is tougher than it looks. I've suffered through enough bad musicals to know this firsthand.

I glance at a University of New York folder next to his phone. "So you're a teacher?"

"Professor."

"Hot. I mean, cool." Why is it that, for me, the word *professor* conjures the image of someone getting bent over a mahogany desk? "I thought you were a farmer. You said you grew corn—"

"And soybeans. In between tending to the land, I had time to go to school." He arches an eyebrow at me. "I'm here to guest lecture for the semester. Beats and Requiems: A History of Western Music."

"Wow," I utter with absolutely zero enthusiasm.

He checks his watch, the hands ticking away. It's silver and well-crafted, with no digital display in sight. "I have no idea how long the train will take. I need to eat and get my butt out the door."

He turns toward the kitchen, which unfortunately accentuates the butt he's trying to get out the door. He really fills those pants out, which, contrary to what I told him, I absolutely admired last night. Maybe they were a different pair? Crème vs. taupe? It's not that spectacular. And I have no time for plump asses in tight khakis.

I lift my chin and puff my chest out.

"Well, you woke me up. And Bobo. We were trying to sleep."

"He looks pretty awake to me." Emerson nods at Bobo, who's in the kitchen, next to his empty bowl, staring at this new human and me.

Emerson picks the speaker up and plops it into a worn leather bag on one of the two chairs flanking the table.

"Well, you woke him." I open the bottom cupboard and pour dry kibble into his bowl. "He likes to eat as soon as he wakes up. And then later. And usually a few more times. He's kind of like a hobbit. Right, Bobo Baggins?"

"Actually, it's Bilbo." Emerson walks to the fridge, opens it, and scans the contents. "Bilbo Baggins."

"I know it's Bilbo. But calling him Bobo Baggins is cute. Right, Bobo?"

Instead of rushing to my defense, he's buried his face in his bowl. If he had opposable thumbs, he'd be shoveling kibble into his mouth.

"Where's the stove?" Emerson gawks at my Transformers collection. "You removed your stove to store action figures?"

"Don't judge lest ye be judged, okay?" I block his scornful view. "It's still here. Simply unplugged." I offer a wide grin, and he goes for the fridge and pulls out a tiramisu yogurt with such casual ease I have to do a double take.

"What are you doing? You've quote-unquote 'lived here' less

than twelve hours, and already you're like lord of the fridge. That's my yogurt."

"Anthony said anything in the fridge was fair game. He said he paid for groceries."

"I ... we bought them together. Or rather, I hovered over his shoulder as he added them to his Instacart." After two years of dating, I'm finally realizing that Anthony was a petty piece of shit.

"We can share, right?"

"That's the last one. If you eat that, I'll starve."

"I saw a bodega across the street. They sell yogurt, right?" Emerson pulls the lid off. "Now, where are the spoons?"

He moves to open one of the three drawers in the kitchen, and I jut my hand in front of it, stopping him.

"I don't have any."

"No spoons? How do you eat ice cream? Take cough syrup? Oh my goodness. Do you not eat soup?"

"I meant no spoons for you. You're not supposed to be here. This is my apartment."

"That I sublet. From what I'm ascertaining is your ex-boyfriend."

"I'm a starving artist. Literally, since you pillaged my last yogurt. You have your *Die Walkie-Talkie* and your fancy professor job. I have no yogurt and a dog to think about."

Bobo rushes over, plops down at my feet, and pushes the back of his head against my waist. That's my bestest boy.

"It's *Die Walküre*. And I'm only a guest lecturer. I don't have the job yet." His expression shifts, allowing nerves to spill onto his face for a second.

"Oh."

A tiny lump forms in my throat, like a rogue maraschino cherry, unable to go down.

"And anyway ..." Emerson sets the yogurt down on the table

and retrieves the document from last night. The one that shows the apartment is rightfully his. "There's this."

A knot tightens in my stomach, but I close my eyes and ground myself.

"I will not let a stranger in my apartment cloud my sunshine. I will not let a stranger in my apartment cloud my sunshine. I will not let a stranger in my apartment cloud my sunshine."

I ingrain it in my mind as fast as I can.

"Excuse me?"

He adjusts behind his ear again, and a high-pitched sound echoes through the room. My hands rush over my ears, and Bobo takes a break from rubbing his skull against my crotch to tilt his head from side to side. After some more fiddling, the noise finally ceases. Oh, right—his hearing aid.

"Never mind. Here. I'll get you a spoon."

I take a step forward, and he moves, allowing me to open the silverware drawer. I catch a whiff of his natural, manly scent.

"There you go," I say, and he takes the spoon from me.

"Thank you."

He takes a bite of my yogurt. With my spoon. In my apartment.

"So, you said you knew an attorney who might be able to figure this all out?"

There's a tinge of sarcasm in his voice, and I don't like it. Especially not after I gave him a spoon to eat my last yogurt.

But I also don't know anyone.

"Yeah, well, about that ..."

"You don't actually know an attorney."

I grin, and the minute it appears on my face, I realize—this is my persuasion smile. The one I used on Anthony. It's subtle but effective, and I've honed it over time, perfected it for moments just like this. The corners of my mouth lift just enough to convey warmth, approachability, but not too much to give away my intentions. I learned this smile from years of navigating tricky conversations, especially with people like Anthony, who always needed a nudge in the right direction, even if he didn't realize it. It worked on him every time—made him feel like the decision was his, when really, I was the one pulling the strings. It's a smile that says "I'm not asking, just suggesting ... but you're definitely going to agree."

Except this isn't Anthony. This is Emerson.

I move to the sofa, sit down, and bury my face in my hands as the weight of it all crashes down on me. This is it. I'm going to be homeless. Bobo and I will have to find a cardboard box big enough for both of us—maybe one of those giant refrigerator boxes, if we're lucky. I can already picture it: Bobo curled up next to me, his tail twitching in his sleep, while I try to make myself comfortable on a lumpy mattress of discarded newspapers. Not exactly the dream life I had in mind when I moved to the city to become the world's foremost Big Boy Dancer. But hey, at least we'd have each other, right?

Bobo sits beside me on the floor. I lift my head from my hands, and he gazes at me with those eyes that make my heart melt.

"My Bobo. You really are the bestest boy."

"Best." Emerson swallows another bite of my tiramisu yogurt. "Best boy would be the correct version. Bestest isn't a word."

"Thank you, Merriam Webster." I pet Bobo's muzzle, his sweet dog-food breath on my face. "Clearly, you've never had a dog. I make up all kinds of names and terms of endearment for him. Bobo Baggins. The Bobinator. Bobosaurus Rex. And he is my *bestest* boy. Aren't you, Bobolicious?"

Hearing so many pet names, Bobo rolls his head in my lap, his tongue hanging out, as I rub right behind his ears.

Emerson can't help but smile at seeing Bobo all silly. I guess he isn't completely made of stone. "When do you think you'll be able to ... find a new place? ... I don't mean to be a jerk, but ..."

"This is your apartment." I sigh. He has the key, the paperwork, and the control of the communal food. He's trying to nicely ask me to get the fuck out. I guess I can't blame him. If I moved to an apartment and someone wouldn't leave, I wouldn't be this patient. I should show a modicum of gratitude.

I stare at the floor, wishing I could disappear into it. "I'm still figuring it out."

"Um, what? Can you please look at me when you're speaking? It helps if I can see your lips."

"Oh. Sorry." I lift my gaze to meet his. Those warm eyes stare back at me, and I forget my train of thought. "I just said I'm still figuring things out."

"Do you think you could figure things out this week?"

I have no money to move, and even if I did, where would I go? I love this apartment. The neighbors. The location. For fuck's sake, no other rental in Manhattan would allow a miniature horse-sized dog. Even if I could find a place, I have precisely thirty-two dollars and fifty-seven cents in my checking account. There's no way I can leave.

"Bobo and I will be gone by the time you're back."

I head to the front door, and Bobo follows. Grabbing his leash, I click it on to his harness and smile at Emerson. "Have a wonderful first day at school!"

It takes all my willpower not to slam the door, but I don't. With my head held high, Bobo and I head outside to figure out what comes next.

FIVE

EMERSON

PEOPLE OFTEN ASK me if it's difficult navigating the world with my hearing loss, and I always have to tell them, "I don't know." The truth is, I have nothing to compare it to. Thanks to a car accident, I lost a significant chunk of my hearing in my right ear when I was twelve, and I don't really remember what it was like before then. I wasn't navigating cities or getting around on my own at that age, so it's not like I can look back and say, "Oh, it was easier then."

I have to ask people to face me when they're talking, or I'll need to lean in awkwardly with my left ear at times. I've found ways to deal.

Is it harder for me out there? I can't say. Isn't it harder for everyone?

I try not to think about it, but being in New York City I've realized that, yeah, maybe it *is* more difficult. There's just something about all the chaos—the hustle and bustle—that makes it harder to keep up sometimes. I walk through crowds of people to catch the train, elbowing my way past them to find a seat. Once

I'm on the subway, I have to watch the stations closely because the announcements are so garbled that it's nearly impossible to understand them.

But somehow, I always manage to make it to where I'm going.

New Yorkers have a reputation for being rude, but I'm finding they can be surprisingly friendly when you least expect it. This morning, a woman notices me looking confused on the platform and helps me figure out which stop is mine. Small kindnesses go a long way.

Eventually, I make my way to the University of New York campus, an ivy-encrusted intellectual oasis in the middle of the city. I walk through an arch into a quad surrounded by grand old buildings with columns named after very wealthy people, coming to Beresford Hall, a red brick building that houses the music theory and history departments.

The trickiest part of my journey, though, isn't the crowded subway or noise. It's the intercom system at the entrance of this academic building. The voice on the other end comes out so jumbled I can't make out a single word. It takes a bit of back and forth before the security guard figures out I'm allowed inside.

Once I finally make it to the department, I smile at the secretary. "You must be Professor Grant. Or rather, Dr. Grant," she says, eyeing me curiously.

"Yes, but please call me Emerson."

Before I can even look for my office, Sheena comes galloping down the hall and throws her arms around me. The sight of her, familiar and smiling, fills my chest with warmth. Even though I'm nearly twice her size, the force of her hug rocks me back a step. Sheena has always given the best hugs—tight, genuine, like she means it—and today is no different. I linger in her arms for a moment longer than usual, overwhelmed with gratitude that she's here.

"You made it!" She brushes her bangs out of her eyes. It may be August, but Sheena's reliably wrapped herself in a shawl. A baggie of nuts and dried fruit hang from her fist, and an assortment of bracelets spelling out different causes line her right wrist. She grew up outside of San Francisco but got her doctorate with me at the University of Illinois. A time she fondly refers to as her "Crash Course in Winter" because after a few years, she learned that "cold" in the Midwest means something entirely different than it does in California.

"I did. I'm finally here. With you. No parallel fifths ..."

"In Prague!" She finishes our inside joke from grad school and plants a kiss on my cheek. "How was your trip in?"

"It was fine," I say, grasping her elbows. "How are Cindy and the kids?"

"Oh, the same. The boys are in high school now. Aiden's a sophomore and Lucas a senior. We'll be touring college campuses soon. And they're eating us out of house and home."

Before I can ask about their latest escapades, she cuts me off with a grin. "And the place you sublet worked out okay?"

"Well, about that. I've stumbled upon a bit of apartment drama."

She laughs. "Welcome to New York," she says.

I chuckle and decide not to bore her with the details right now.

She leads me into her small, cozy space, nestled in a row of faculty offices. I survey the organized mess, wondering how I'll fit in here for the semester. Her hanging plant is longer than Rapunzel's braid.

"Nice," I say.

"Don't worry. Your office is much neater. Hugo cleaned everything out before he took off for his sabbatical."

We both take a seat.

"Don't be nervous." She leans over, extending her hand, and I take it. "Besides packing up his belongings, Hugo left a syllabus.

Of course, modify it as you see fit." She dips her chin. "You're going to fit in wonderfully, Emerson. I promise."

Sheena scoped me out during our graduate program's orientation, homing in on me like a mama bear. I didn't realize how much I needed taking care of until she helped me navigate the interpersonal intricacies of academia.

"Nervous is a perfectly normal feeling. It's a natural physiological response to a new environment." I keep my leg from shaking. It's one thing to admit nerves, but you don't want to show it. Just because I got a chance to teach at one of the most prestigious colleges in the country doesn't mean I'm immediately crapping my pants. Yet.

"You're an amazing professor." She squeezes my hand then sits back, adjusting her wrap. "Try to relax. These are mostly eager twentysomethings. Take deep breaths. Try to relate, and remember they're here to learn from the best." She winks. "That's you."

Sheena stands and moves toward the door. The windowsill in her office is lined with plants—so many plants, it's like a mini-jungle oasis. I've always been slightly envious of her green thumb. And the way her warmth and ease at connecting with people has helped her teaching career take off.

"You'll do great. The students are going to love you. I've garnered a wonderful music department here. Everyone will step up to help you." Sheena peeks out the door. "Unfortunately, my colleagues aren't in today, but Will is here."

She drags us into the hall, and we walk to another office, this one stuffed with multiple desks. "This is the office for all the department TAs," she says.

She gestures to a young Asian guy with floppy hair and thick glasses. A Mostly Mozart T-shirt hangs on his lanky body. He's two parts academic, one part college bro. He gets up from his desk and shakes my hand.

"Hi, Dr. Grant. Nice to meet you," he yells.

"You don't have to yell," I say.

"I'm sorry! I thought ... never mind."

"I can hear you just fine," I reassure him, trying to brush it off. Most people are cool with it once they realize. My goal is to just act like whatever's assisting my ear isn't there at all.

Brahms softly plays from Will's computer. "Is that Brahms?" I ask.

"It is," he responds, clearly pleased.

"You can turn it up."

I lean against the towering floor-to-ceiling bookshelf crammed with books. The kind of bookcase I love, overstuffed and charming. I breathe in the scent of paper and ink, listening to the music, and in that moment, I've never felt more at home.

"I loved your paper on the development of symphonic form," Will says. "Especially when you go into Beethoven's role in transforming the symphony from classical restraint to emotional expression." His statement is two parts flattering bullshit and one part genuine. "I'd love to discuss it with you more."

"Sounds good. We can do that," I say.

"Will, you take good care of this guy." Sheena reaches up to wrap her arm around my shoulder. She's practically on her tiptoes. "We go way back."

"Grad school wasn't that long ago," I say.

"Professor Grant." She cocks her head. "It's been almost fifteen years."

Sometimes I forget how long we've known each other, how much her career has flourished, and how stuck mine still feels. This really is a big break for me.

"Oh. Yeah. I guess we are ..."

"Old?" Will says.

"Watch it," Sheena snaps, though a smile tugs at her lips. "Dr.

Grant is your new advising professor, and I'm still the head of this department."

"Only teasing." Will's eyes glance down. "Nothing but respect for you both."

"Now, most of the students in your class are great, but there are a few … shitheads," Sheena warns, with a smirk that Will matches.

I laugh. "I'm sure I can handle them." But my stomach churns as the words leave my mouth.

The truth is, I'm not so sure. I've always struggled to connect with people, including my students. It's like there's this invisible wall between me and everyone else, something I can't seem to break through no matter how hard I try. I'm not good at small talk or at making others comfortable around me. I'm better with ideas than with faces, better in front of a lecture hall than one-on-one. The thought of being the approachable, relatable professor they all expect me to be feels like a role I'm never quite able to play convincingly. But I can't let Sheena—or myself—down.

Sheena gives me a quick tour of the office, introduces me to a few other people, and then, most importantly, shows me the break room and the bathroom. Nerves creep in. My first class is tomorrow. I hope I get a good night's sleep tonight—there's been so much drama in my new apartment, and I really don't need any more distractions. Hopefully, the situation is rectified today.

"Thank you again for getting me in here," I say.

"We look out for each other." She pats my back, and my nerves settle a little.

We return to her office, and she checks the hallway and shuts the door. "I have to tell you something."

I raise an eyebrow as she continues. "The university just got a really nice donation to endow a new music professor position. They'll be interviewing in a few weeks."

My eyebrows shoot up. "Really?"

"Yes! And everyone loved your paper on—" She pauses to remember the title. "'The Transformation of Public Music in Early 18th-Century Europe.' It was a huge success. So, you're getting some buzz around here in the department."

"Good buzz?" I ask, trying to suppress a grin.

She grins back. "Good buzz."

I nod, finally feeling a sense of pride. For once, maybe things are going my way. I took a risk leaving my small college in Indiana to come here for a semester, but it's starting to feel like it was worth it. I'm in a robust, well-funded music department headed by my dear friend in the greatest city in the world—home to Carnegie Hall and many other iconic venues. A guy could get used to living here.

"If you do well," Sheena adds, "I think you can nail this interview. I've put in a good word for you, and everyone's excited to meet you."

"Everyone?"

She nods. "I've been talking you up. Laying it on thick. They're expecting good things."

I swallow hard, doing my best to smile.

"Emerson"—she pats my arm—"with all the hard work you've been doing, this is your time to shine." She kisses me on the cheek. "Kick some butt this semester. Your students are going to love you. And if you need anything, Will is here. He's also superb at computers. He minored in Computer Science."

Sheena walks us to the stairs. "There are lots of social events here, too. And, unlike Indiana, there are actual gay people in New York."

I grumble. "There are gay people in Indiana, too ... besides Pete Buttigieg."

"Doesn't he live in Michigan now?"

"We still claim him."

Sheena laughs. "I'm just saying, there's a lot more action here.

A guy like you could have some fun. Just remember," she says, hands on my shoulders, "you're here to kick butt and teach classes, but don't forget to have a social life, too."

I nod, though I'm already mentally bracing myself for the reality of what's to come. "Noted."

She's staring at me intently. "I can tell when you're blowing me off."

"I'm not blowing you off," I blurt. "You've got a department to run."

She grins. "Yeah, but you're part of it now. And Emerson, you never know when someone might wander into your life."

My mind flashes to my accidental roommate. I can only hope that by the time I get home, Bryce and his dog have wandered out of my apartment. And my life.

I TAKE the train home but get off halfway. The ability to walk in New York, block by block, feels like a privilege. Back in Indiana, you need a car to get anywhere. But here, I can wander. People-watch. Breathe in the air of Central Park.

It's all wonderful. I don't want to get my hopes up too much, but I can't help it. If I can get a permanent job here and teach, it would be incredible.

When I finally get back to my apartment, I trudge up the six flights of stairs. It's warm outside but not too humid. Inside, though, the staircase is stuffy and claustrophobic. By the time I reach the top, I'm a sweaty mess. When I open the door, Bryce isn't there, but Bobo is.

He's sprawled across my suitcase, which is buckling under his weight.

"Off!" I yell.

Bobo sits up, creating more strain on my suitcase.

"Off!" I motion for him to move, but he only stares, his tongue sticking out. He knows that's his cute side. It makes it hard to stay mad at him. There's something silly about a big dog sitting on a small suitcase.

I think about pushing him off, but he's way too massive. It would be a losing battle.

"You have a whole couch. It's much more comfortable." I point to the couch like I'm displaying a prize on a game show. "Look at these cushions. Much more comfortable than a suitcase."

Bobo cocks his head, enjoying the show.

"You can't actually like sitting on there." I put my hands on my hips.

Bobo seems to dig in his heels. The suitcase creaks under him, but he doesn't budge. I think back to experiences with my family dog growing up. I'm using human psychology when I need to be using dog psychology.

"That's fine." A smile inevitably curls on my lips. "You enjoy your cramped suitcase. I'm going to sit down on this comfy, plush couch." Dogs are like babies in that they compel you to use a loud, exaggerated voice. I faint onto the sofa. "Ahhhhhh. That's nice. This is a good couch. You're missing out, Bobo. Oh, well." I wiggle myself into the cushions. "More for me."

Within two seconds, Bobo jumps up. Success! But I don't plan for him to rest on my legs. I try to pull myself away from the plushness, but I can't. His legs are too strong, too heavy. They pin mine down.

"Bobo, can you move for a second? I just need to ..."

He turns his head to me, confusion spelled out on his face.

"I know. I just asked you to move off the suitcase. I just need you to move a little bit, but stay on the couch."

My words only confuse him more. He blinks at me, then turns his attention to the front door, a loyal and waiting dog.

"My legs are stuck. And I need to free them. But you stay." I pet his back, sifting my fingers through his hair. He pays me no mind, his attention on the door. I keep doing it because petting a cute dog is kind of addictive.

I try to maneuver out my legs, but it's no use.

"You really find my legs more comfortable than a couch cushion?"

He ignores me. I'm going to be buried on this couch, aren't I? A laugh unexpectedly bursts out of me. It helps break my stress about class tomorrow.

"Okay, you got me," I say, chuckling some more. I give him a good scratch under the chin.

When he hears the key in the lock, Bobo leaps onto the floor, digging into my legs as he goes. Bryce screams his name, squats down, and hugs him tight. They've only been separated for the day, but Bryce acts like it's been a week. His entire face lights up.

"Hi. Has Bobo given you any trouble today?"

"Nope." I eye the dog hair on my suitcase but ignore it.

"Good. He's a great dog. He really knows how to respect people's stuff." Bryce kneels on the floor. "I have something to ask. But before I do, I have to say, apropos of nothing, that your hair has never looked better."

I touch my hair self-consciously. Then I realize where this is going.

"I'm still working on finding a new place. It's hard when most buildings don't allow pets. Let alone a dog his size. I think it's discriminatory, and I'm totally going to file a lawsuit. But in the meantime, I need just a few more days. A week tops. And then I should be able to find something."

Bobo trots behind Bryce and hops back onto the suitcase. He rests his head on the handle.

"Bobo! Off!" Bryce yells.

Bobo's big eyes flick to me, almost as if he's waiting for me to say something.

"I'm sorry," Bryce says.

"It's fine."

"What's fine?" he asks. "Bobo on your suitcase or us in your apartment?"

And maybe I'm too tired to argue, or maybe I'm too amused by a big dog on my small suitcase, but I find a smile tickling my face. "Both."

SIX

BRYCE

I DIDN'T KNOW that Gucci made leotards until I met Portia Black, my best friend and partner in the trenches of the Broadway audition scene.

"I want to get your opinion on something," Portia says in her delightful British accent. She sits across from me in the aforementioned designer leotard, our legs spread and feet touching as we prepare in the waiting area. She pulls my arms to stretch my back, and in ten seconds, I'll return the favor.

"Don't get veneers," I tell her. Half her charm is in her perfectly imperfect smile.

"No, it's not that ... this time. But I might have us circle back. I'm thinking of quitting the crushing world of dancing and starting my own makeup line." She lets go of my hands and rubs hers together. "I'm going to call my line of cosmetics Black Face." She gestures to an imaginary sign in the air. "What do you think?"

I can hear the think pieces being written. "Um ... maybe not?"

"No?" She pouts her bottom lip. "My cosmetics could bring a positive connotation to the term, dontcha think?"

"I really, really don't." I pull her toward me.

"It's okay. I'm not that into starting a makeup line. Father says I need to find a more successful career path. He's threatening to stop paying my rent."

Portia's father has made this threat several times before, and it never sticks. It's practically a punchline at this point. "Would he really kick you out on the street?"

"Worse. A studio in *Jersey City*. I didn't think that was even a real place until he showed me on a map." She sits up and pulls my arms toward me, giving me a much-needed stretch in my back. "I told him I can't give up my dream. We're artists! The struggle is what gives us strength!"

She cups my hands in hers to form an oversized solidarity fist.

"That's us. Struggling artists," I say flatly. I love Portia. She's merely afflicted with the same obliviousness that rich kids and nepo babies have, the kind that assures them they've hustled for everything they have and that the world runs on meritocracy.

Portia's bazillionare parents own a slew of upscale boutique laundromats all over the city. They've been able to buy her everything except a career on Broadway. We bonded on the audition circuit because we're both outsiders used to eyerolls from casting directors. And despite being a quasi-socialite, Portia doesn't have a cruel bone in her body.

The casting director enters the room and calls out numbers corresponding to auditioners. She leads them into a separate space where they'll have a few minutes to prove themselves to the director. My heart thumps as each number is called.

I'm determined to get a paying gig. Be a real dancer in a real show. My time will come—I know it. I've been putting in the hours, the sweat, the pain, and even the doubts, but I can feel it building inside me, like I'm just one step away from that breakthrough. I can't let myself give up now—not when I've come this far.

A familiar foe named Whitney with a tight bun and the inability to form a genuine smile sashays by us.

"Portia, still at it? Haven't enough casting directors told you no yet? You know, you need actual talent to dance." Whitney checks out her flamingo-like body in the mirror. "Remember during the school talent show when you fell off the stage? I hope that doesn't happen here."

"Thanks for the tip, Whitney," Portia says coolly, her cheeks burning red.

"Speaking of tips, you might want to schedule a manicure soon, sweetheart." Whitney shoots a venomous wink Portia's way and flutters off.

Yes, even in a fancy boarding school with the spawn of the insanely wealthy, kids can be bullied. Money can't heal all wounds. I think that's also why Portia and I bonded. Income levels aside, our childhoods weren't so dissimilar.

I lodge double middle fingers at her back which gets a laugh from Portia.

"One day, I'm going to get cast in a show over her, and the victory will be oh so sweet," Portia says, glaring at her nemesis. She shakes her head, refusing to let Whitney take up room. "One more good stretch."

She pulls my arms, and I wince. A stubborn muscle in my lower back remains stiff.

"You okay, love?"

"Yeah. My back is tight from sleeping on the couch."

"Why are you sleeping on the sofa? Did you and Anthony get in a fight?"

The only thing more painful than a horrific breakup is having to retell the story of said horrific breakup to your friends and family. I'd been avoiding sharing the news with Portia, but perhaps focusing on emotional pain can loosen up the physical aches.

I unload about the last few days, and the stress lifts off my shoulders a tad. Portia's big warm eyes radiate kindness and understanding as she takes it all in.

"Wait, you have a hot professor staying with you?"

"Hot? Who said he was hot?" I repeat, raising an eyebrow as I twist my body to stretch deeper, feeling the familiar ache in my legs. Portia gives me her I-know-something-you-don't smirk. She's always one step ahead.

"Don't play coy. I saw your face when you mentioned his name." My quads ache as she leans back, her leggings stretched just a little too tight—of course she pulls it off effortlessly. "Emerson. You were practically drooling."

I snort. "First of all, I was not drooling. Second, he's not staying with me. He literally stormed into my life, taking over my apartment and making an already difficult situation harder."

"Right, dumped by the actor. Anthony was really hot. Couldn't solve two plus two with a calculator, but with that face and body, who needs mathematical ability?"

"Not helping." I pull a little harder, hoping she really feels it. "It's not like I asked to be dumped and have my apartment sublet from under me."

"Anthony's apartment." She smiles. "According to you."

"Whose side are you on, anyway?"

"Yours, sweetie. Always, yours," she purrs in that way people with money and no true troubles do. "No luck finding anything?"

I shake my head, grimacing. "Yeah. I've been going nuts searching for a place. Apparently, a one-hundred-and-twenty-pound dog is a deal breaker for most landlords in the city."

"I could ask my father? He may know of a vacancy in one of the laundry parlor buildings."

"Really?" My heart skips a beat at the thought of living in one of the Black Inc. luxury properties.

"I can ask. Oh wait, Velvet Spin properties are smoke, child, and pet free," she says, flipping her hair over her shoulder. "No offense to your mutt. Or tiny humans." She shrugs. "Plus, there's that pesky income requirement. You make over two hundred thousand a year, right?"

My head drops, shaking at her. "Portia, you go to every failed audition with me. Earn the same as I do at the Met. You know I hardly have fifty bucks in my checking account."

"That's checking. What other assets do you have? Savings account? IRA? After-tax brokerage?"

"Those are all different things? I have some loose change in a Carly Rae Jepsen shot glass?"

Portia may be clueless about certain areas of life but definitely not money. She learned the basics of wealth creation alongside her ABCs.

"I'll figure something out," I say, but even I don't believe myself.

"I know you will. But more importantly, is Emerson *hot* hot or just tall, dark, and mysterious hot? Because you know, I could totally help you with that."

I sigh and finally release the stretch, sitting up. "Emerson's just ... Emerson. He's not dark at all. Quite tall, though. Big. Like one of those football players who throw people around. Not that I follow sportsball."

"Honey, you follow anything with balls."

We share a quick glance, and then a sharp laugh escapes our lips. Even in my darkest hour, Portia's humor, as bright and unexpected as a sudden burst of sunlight, manages to bring a smile to my face. The sound of her delusional laughter comforts me.

"Anyway, he's not my type."

"A tall, hunky football player who could throw you around isn't your type?" She raises an eyebrow. "Sure, Jan."

The truth is, there's something about Emerson that keeps messing with my head. He's brooding and intense, and I get the sense he's hiding something. But right now, he wants me out of his apartment.

The casting director comes out again and calls a new set of numbers. More dancers who aren't us stand and then enter the other room, including Whitney. She gives Portia a diabolical wave.

"One day, your victory will come." I lean in and put a hand on Portia's shoulder. "And I once danced in a chorus with her, and she was ripping ass the entire time. It was noxious. Like, girl, lay off the Luna bars."

Portia throws her head back and unleashes a pure, cackling laugh so infectious I find myself joining in. Other dancers around us glare, like we're two kids in the back of class causing a ruckus.

She makes a sudden gasping noise. "Wait a second, I've got it."

"Got what?" I raise my head, hoping for a crumb of hope.

"A solution to your sudden, unwanted, forced proximity living situation."

My eyes widen, and I dip my chin slightly, waiting for my friend with the three-hundred-dollar tights to fix my life.

"The two of you—Emerson and you—share your little bachelor pad. Think of the drama! The tension! It's like a reality show waiting to happen." Her face lights up like a Christmas tree, never a good sign. "Wait, we could hire a film crew. Capture every conversation and quarrel. This could be a real moneymaker. Bravo would eat this up. I see a multi-season arc. Maybe I should be a reality show producer. I think I'd have a knack for it."

I frown. "How generous of you. But I'm not searching for any more drama. I have enough of it just dealing with my life. My heart was broken two days ago. And now I've got a mysterious hot guy squatting in my apartment."

"So you *do* think he's hot?"

I cock my head and sigh.

Portia shrugs, glancing down at her perfect nails. "I'm just saying ... sometimes, bad situations lead to the best endings.

Maybe you're just one bad decision away from a whole new chapter of your life. I mean, look at us. We've made a career out of poor choices, and here we are." She gestures dramatically to the bleak waiting room. "Maybe living with a mysterious, six-packed, nerdy professor is exactly what you need right now."

"Who said anything about a six-pack?"

"This is my fantasy. Work with me."

I laugh, but it's more out of nervous energy than anything else. "You know what, Portia? You're ridiculous. But right now, I have no other choice. Nobody will even consider me with Bobo. I'm going to have to make this ... situation work."

"Exactly." She leans back, resting her arms behind her head. "I mean, if the man's living in your apartment, you might as well get something out of it. You'll have to shag each other to keep warm at night."

"It's August."

She wiggles her eyebrows like a dirty old man, unaffected by facts. "Darling, if you can't have a little fun with a hunky professor, what's the point of life?"

I groan, throwing my head back. "It's never not a circus with you, huh?"

"Never." She winks. "Give me three rings, the lion tamer, and a bearded lady."

The door opens, and the casting director call out the final set of numbers, which include ours.

"Let's do this," Portia says. "Like Lin-Manuel Miranda sang to me during karaoke at my twenty-first birthday afterparty, 'We are not throwing away our shot.'"

She stands, never letting go of my hand until I'm up, and we head into the studio together, determined to nail this audition.

I'M PRACTICALLY FLOATING on air when I step through the apartment door. Frank, the dance assistant, was totally into the vibe I brought to the audition. He smiled, winked. Hell, he practically rammed his tongue down my throat when he informed me I was on his list for callbacks. Not to yuck anyone's yum, but daddies aren't really my thing. I mean, maybe, but Frank was more of a granddaddy.

Emerson's presence on the couch, a reminder of my current predicament, immediately punctures my cheerful demeanor. He's scrolling on his phone, but his face is scrunched up like he's just smelled the subway platform after a hungover bachelorette party has been through. No matter what he says or does, I won't let him bring me down from my callback high.

"Any luck finding a place?" he asks, glancing up from his phone with a hint of skepticism.

Guess he's not one for beating around the bush.

"Yeah, still working on it." I shrug off my bag and toss it over the back of a chair. "It's hard with Bobo, you know?" Hearing his name, my bestest boy trots over from the corner, where he wisely has been avoiding Emerson, and sits right on my foot. "It's not like I have many options for a roommate situation right now. I asked Data and Marsh about crashing on their sofa, but three grown men and an enormous dog in their apartment wouldn't be fair to the people beneath them. Or the wood flooring."

I can see him trying to hold back a smirk. "So Bobo gets the couch?"

"I get the couch. Bobo can sleep on the floor. I'll make a bed for him with the back cushions. We'll make it work, right, boy? We always make it work."

Bobo's staring up at me, head back, tongue out, while I scratch behind his ears. Ah, to be blissfully ignorant to the struggles of your current tragic life situation. Remembering Portia's words, I figure it's time to take a cue from Bobo and use my cuteness to my advantage.

"And it's only temporary, Emerson. I'll find something. Eventually."

My eyes widen, maybe a little too much, doing my best to pull off a sad puppy look. I glance down at Bobo, hoping he'll catch my hint and join me, but nope—he still looks happy as a clam at our potential homelessness.

Emerson's brow furrows, and I can almost hear the gears turning in his head. "Uh-huh. Just keep looking, eh?"

"Yeah, yeah. I got it. I'm not staying forever." My words probably sound a little too defensive, but there's no way I'm going to admit I plan to stay. That I don't have anywhere else to go and no money to pay for anywhere even if I did. That I don't know how else to make this work because I don't know how to make anything work—which is how I ended up in this position.

But then that warm feeling returns to my chest as I remember the one piece of positivity in my life today.

"Hey, guess what?"

Emerson's head snaps up, his eyebrows lifting in a show of interest. "What?"

"I got a callback."

The words tumble out of me like a tiny lifeline before I can stop them. It's the first bit of good news in what feels like forever. Emerson's expression shifts from annoyance to something softer. He sits up a little straighter, nodding in approval. "Really?" He adjusts the hearing aid behind his right ear and leans forward. "That's great. For a play?"

"Yeah," I say, trying to sound casual. "Technically, it's a musical—*The Sound of Muscles*. And it's not like it's the lead part or anything. They're looking for a name to play Maria von Clapback. This is for the chorus. Ensemble. That sort of thing."

"Wonderful." Emerson lays his phone in his lap.

"But it's something. It could be my big break. The callback itself feels like a win."

"Good work," he says, with actual sincerity.

I smile, but it feels odd, as if I shouldn't be celebrating any successes, given my current ambiguous situation. But maybe, just maybe, I can convince him to let me stay. At least for the time being.

Being cautious to maintain my distance, I sit beside him, trying to keep as much space as possible between us. Bobo rests by my feet, his head on my lap, but he's staring at Emerson.

"Thanks. I need to rehearse the choreo until it feels instinctive, like it's in my blood. Fortunately, I have a few days to perfect it."

Bobo shifts his enormous skull between us, and Emerson reaches for him, hesitating when his fingers approach mine. I move my hand away, and then he takes over. Bobo's tongue falls out and his eyes roll back, clearly loving the attention from this new man. Traitor.

"And thanks again for understanding about the apartment," I say. "I promise we'll be no trouble. We'll be quiet as two church mice. Right, Bobo?"

He's too busy enjoying the attention from Emerson to acknowledge me, but I know he agrees with me. He always does.

"No worries." He smiles and returns to scrolling on his phone.

But one hand remains on Bobo—right behind his ears. I gently rest my palm on the top of Bobo's head, and, with mindful precision, Emerson and I avoid making contact while Bobo relishes a two-handed head massage from his dad and the new man who's waltzed into our lives.

SEVEN

EMERSON

I WAKE up scrunched to one side of the bed as sunshine blares through the windows. Half—no, three-quarters—of the bed is taken up with a big, enormous, giant dog. He's sprawled out, looking like a deflated balloon, his belly up and legs stretched wide in an awkward but somehow endearing way. His fur is all mussed, with one ear flopped over and the other sticking up like a lopsided antenna.

I pat him on the belly. "Hey, Bobo, you have to get off." A low hum of a snore comes from the pile of dog. "Off," I say louder.

Bobo doesn't move. I shake him some more. He's trying to get back to sleep, but I won't let him.

"Bobo. Off."

I keep pointing off the bed, and finally, he seems to understand. He gives me a massive sigh, as if I'm a parent telling a teenager to get up for school. He tumbles to the floor and shuffles into the main room.

I put my hand where he slept, and it's nice and toasty—so warm and cozy I could fall back asleep. But no, I must get ready for my lecture. My first lecture as a New York City professor. My first chance to get in the good graces with the top tier of academia. While the school I teach at in Indiana is fine, it's definitely not anywhere near the same caliber. There isn't enough funding for research, and most of the students take my classes to fulfill a distribution requirement.

The University of New York is highly esteemed, boasting exceptional students and faculty. Sheena's been trying to get me in for years, and I finally have my chance. It's really about who we surround ourselves with that makes the impact, right?

I get ready, trying to be as quiet as possible so as not to wake my forced roommate. Bryce is passed out on the couch, arms and legs akimbo, barely surviving on that thing. It's like seeing a hamburger trying to fit into a hotdog bun. For a moment, I think about saying he can sleep in the bed, but then that feels weird—because then I also think about Bryce in my bed, and I should not be thinking about Bryce anywhere except outside this apartment. Because he needs his own place.

I take the subway, remembering the route and minimizing any conflicts. I no longer have the lost look of an out-of-towner. I get to the music building on campus and pour myself a cup of coffee in the communal kitchen. Not like I need it since I'm jittery with nerves. Finally, Will comes up to me.

"Ready?"

"Yes," I say.

"We're all really excited," Will says. "We've read your papers, and we're eager to learn from you."

I wonder if he's just saying that because he's the TA, and TAs are always about kissing up to their professors. But still, I take the compliment.

"Thank you, Will."

He opens the door to my classroom for me, and when I step inside, my stomach plummets like a faulty elevator. This isn't a classroom. It's a lecture hall. A big lecture hall. Bigger than any room I've ever taught in. It's built like an arena, a tiered amphitheater—the desks go up a few levels with the teacher at the center. Tall windows stretch to the ceiling, pouring in sunlight.

Once I get over the scope of the space, I begin to process the number of students in the room. More than I realized. On paper, fifty students doesn't sound like much, but when you see them all together, you realize—wow, there's a lot of people.

My lungs constrict. My chest tightens. I shake out my hands behind the podium so they don't see. Am I sweating? I can't tell. I turn around to adjust my hearing aid, the high-pitched noise making me, and most likely everyone in the hall, cringe as I pretend to prepare my notes. I take a deep breath and the nerves overtake me like a wildfire.

I try to compose myself, reminding myself I'm a professor with a Ph.D. I've chosen to be here, and I can do this. I turn around and flash a big smile.

"Hello! I'm Professor Grant. Welcome to Beats and Requiems: A History of Western Music."

And then I completely lose my train of thought. The train careens off the track over a cliff leaving a giant plume of smoke in my head.

"I'm Professor Grant." I let out a nervous laugh. "I know I already said that, but sometimes people have a hard time remembering my name. It's Grant. Just like Cary Grant or Ulysses S. Grant. No relation to either of them. Okay, moving on."

I walk around the perimeter of my teaching cage. Students look down at me from their desks, making me feel tiny.

"So, today in class, we're going to talk about—" I trail off and rustle my notes.

The thing that people don't seem to realize is that it's hard to lecture. You're basically speaking extemporaneously for sixty minutes, and you can't have it all memorized. You have to follow your train of thought, which, as you may recall, is on fire at the bottom of an imaginary cliff.

"Right, so we'll be talking about Beethoven and his impact on music history. The composer. Not the dog from the movies." Another nervous laugh escapes my lips. "Does anyone have any questions?"

Students trade looks. A guy in a tracksuit three tiers up says something I can't quite make out.

"Excuse me?"

He's turned to someone behind him, clearly trying to make a joke.

I raise my voice enough to grab his attention. "I ask that you please look at me when you're speaking—"

Tracksuit guy turns toward me and says, "About what?"

"What about what?" I ask.

"You asked if anyone had any questions." He speaks very slowly, like I don't understand English. "About what?"

"Oh. About the class."

A young lady in the front row says something, but a guy in a fedora next to her speaks at the same time.

I shake my head and take a deep breath. "And only one at a time please. I can't understand you when you talk over each other."

"Well, we haven't gone over anything yet," says fedora guy.

A girl three rows up raises her hand.

I point to her. "Yes? And please, speak up."

"Hi! I was wondering on the syllabus ..." She holds up the syllabus over her mouth as she talks. The rustling of the papers turns her words to static.

She puts the paper down then takes a sip from a comically large coffee tumbler, all without stopping talking. I stare at her, unsure if she's done.

"Does that make sense?" she asks.

"Why don't we discuss syllabus questions after class, shall we?" I want to wipe away a trickle of sweat from my brow, but I don't want to call attention to it either. "Did everyone do the pre-reading?"

"There was pre-reading?" another student asks in a yell.

"Oh. I guess not. I didn't assign it. Sorry, I'm still jet-lagged."

"Didn't you come from Indiana?" front-row girl asks. "Isn't that only like an hour-and-a-half plane ride?"

"Yes, but it was a very fast plane. Hence the jet lag."

If I had just been able to move into my apartment and have some peace and quiet for a few days, I would have been able to mentally prepare for this. But no. I had to have Mr. Jazz Hands and Clifford the Big Red Dog as my unintentional roommates.

A guy in the back raises his hand. I'm relieved he gives me something to focus on.

"Yes, you in the back!"

He hesitates for a second before speaking up. "So, uh … you're from Indiana?" His voice is loud and clear, but thankfully, he's not shouting. "Is that, like, where you … started your music career?"

I smile, the question pulling me back to my roots. "Well, sort of," I say. "Indiana is where I first learned what it means to truly listen to the subtleties of classical music. The state might be known for cornfields, but it's got a rich musical history too. I spent years studying under some of the best professors there—working with orchestras, honing my craft. That's where I realized classical music isn't just something to play—it's a language. A conversation with the past, the present, and the future all at once."

I let the words linger for a moment before continuing. "So yes, Indiana was my starting point. But this"—I gesture to the classroom—"this is where I take it further. To understand it deeper. To pass it on."

"But like …" The loud and clear guy interrupts me. "No offense. How are you able to, like, listen to music?" His hand moves up to point to his ear, to where my hearing aid sits, but he thinks better of it at the last minute. "No offense."

The class stares back at me, and now I truly feel the spotlight of this arena layout. I am in a gladiatorial battle, waiting to get mauled by a tiger.

"I am hard of hearing in my right ear, but I assure you, I am more than qualified to teach this class."

I roll right into my lecture and don't take any more questions.

AFTER CLASS, I try to work on my paper but don't get far. Instead, I spend my afternoon walking around New York, taking in the city. I watch a basketball pickup game, listen to buskers in the park, and eat the most delicious slice of one-dollar pizza in history. It helps to lift my spirits.

When I return to the apartment, I can hear Bryce from the stairwell. Well, not Bryce—his music. It is pumped up to full volume. It sounds like a club in there. I wonder why they stopped calling clubs discos. Disco is a fun name.

When I go inside, Bryce is full-on dancing like he is at a disco, but he doesn't have the face of someone who's having fun. He's very serious about his dancing, even moving the coffee table out of the way. And then I get it. He's going over choreography with the diligence of an athlete. He doesn't even notice when I enter. It isn't until I go to the fireplace mantel and turn off his music that he looks up, snapping out of his zone.

I do remember that zone—when I'm fully into my research or when I'm engrossed in a musical piece.

"Hey, why did you do that?" Bryce asks.

"It's too loud. It's like a disco in here."

"A disco? What is this, 1978?" Bryce uses a small towel to wipe sweat from his red face. "Can't you adjust your headset?"

"My hearing aid? I could, but my other ear still works just fine. And it's only partial hearing loss in this one." I tug at my right earlobe. "I don't know why you're blaring music at full volume."

"I'm practicing my steps," Bryce says. "I have another round of auditions coming up this week."

Watching him move, I'm surprised how limber and flexible he is. He kicks his leg up high. He twists around. Even though he's a larger man like myself, he moves like he's light as a feather. It's quite astounding to behold.

"Well, I need you to practice with headphones on. I have to work on my next lecture."

And I have to make sure that I don't face-plant again.

God, I keep going over the class today. Not my finest hour. I really can't be this nervous. I've given lots of lectures before. I have to show that I can handle this. That assistant professor position is in reach. I can't mess this up.

I go to my bedroom, and of course, Bobo is sitting on my bed licking himself. Down there.

"Excuse me, didn't we go over this?" I say to him. "Off."

Bobo ignores me and really goes to town on his doggie business.

"Now I know why you don't date," I snark. I pat his butt and gently push him, but he doesn't budge. "No bed."

Bobo gives a heavy sigh and gives me the biggest look of sorrow as he hops onto the floor.

"It's where he used to sleep before we were kicked out of our place," Bryce yells from the main room.

"I wasn't the one who kicked you out," I say to Bobo as he leaves. He doesn't look back at me, the ultimate power move.

I sit on the bed and lie back. It's dark and cool in here. I close my eyes and start to drift off to sleep as the adrenaline finally leaves my body. But I bolt awake when Bryce's music starts up again.

I march into the main room, and there he is, dancing again.

"Sorry, I thought you were sleeping," Bryce says.

"So you turn the music up?"

"Now we both know what it's like to be woken up with blaring music." Bryce sips from a water bottle. Sweat makes his black T-shirt cling to his torso. "Look, I'm not good at practicing with head-phones on. I do my best work when the music is loud and ambient, and I can just kind of get lost in it, versus when it's just stuck in my head."

"And your ex-boyfriend let you do this?"

"All the time."

"And he didn't go insane?"

"No, because I thanked him with the best sex of his life."

I gulp a lump back in my throat imagining what, exactly, that might mean.

"Could you wait until morning? I'd like to relax in peace tonight. I don't feel like listening to this music."

"What do you mean by *this music?* You had a tone in your voice."

"I'm not really a fan of silly pop music."

"Excuse me? It's not silly pop music. This is 'Emotion' by one Miss Carly Rae Jepsen." Bryce blanches.

I go to the kitchen and pour myself a glass of wine.

"You're a music professor, and you don't enjoy music?" Bryce asks.

"I like quality music. Classical music. Some of the greats, you know—a great opera, or a great orchestra piece. Intricately constructed pieces. It's not some disposable song composed of a mediocre melody and hackneyed lyrics about love."

"Wow, Emerson. Do you ever get tired of being the life of the party?" Bryce chugs from his water bottle. "Carly Rae Jepsen *is* quality music. Have you ever listened to her?"

"I don't know. Didn't you say she did some 'Call Me Right Back' song?"

Bryce breathes fire through his nose. "I'm gonna pretend that was a joke."

"Pop music is a fun trifle, but it's not real music. It's a Ritz cracker, whereas a symphony is beef wellington."

"Did you just compare Carly to a cracker? You would be kicked out of certain gay bars for such slander."

I try to leave the kitchen, but Bryce grabs my arm and leads me to the couch. He sits me down and squats at my eyeline. Bobo lies near the window, staring.

"There's an art to crafting a great pop song. And yes, it is an art. Carly Rae Jepsen is an artist. She encapsulates the roller coaster of the entire human experience in three and a half minutes. The highs. The lows. She's an interpreter who's able to take those feelings that bubble inside your heart, the ones that are so pure and visceral that they can't be described with words, and she sets them to music. She may not have a full orchestra behind her, but her songs burrow into your marrow and change your DNA. They make you believe that loneliness is temporary, that love is forever, that we are worthy of real, actual, ineffable joy in our lives."

Bryce stares so intently at me, it's like he's reaching into places inside me where nobody is allowed.

I stand up. "I'll take your word for it."

"Look, I'm gonna play a Carly Rae song for you. You seem uptight. More uptight than usual."

"I just—I had a rough day," I say.

"When I have a rough day, I dance it out," Bryce says. "You can dance it out to Carly Rae. You can't dance it out to Mozart."

Bryce's eyes widen with passion and fire—for Carly Rae Jepsen, of all people. But I can't help but get sucked in.

"One song, Emerson. We can dance to one song. And if you

don't feel better after that, I will put in my earbuds, dance in my head, and keep things quiet."

"Fine. One song," I say.

Bryce puts on a song. The blips and bloops fill the room, and his eyes light up. He's excited, like it's Christmas morning. He shimmies to the center of the room.

"Okay, well, you gotta stand up, Emerson."

I do a double take. He was actually serious about dancing it out. "I'm not a dancer."

"Obviously," Bryce says, "but everyone can dance. It's what separates us from the monkeys." He turns the volume up. The singer's voice is bright and luminous. "And it's been proven that dancing is like exercise, and exercise will make you happy. And happy people don't kill their roommates. That was from *Legally Blonde*, which I'm assuming you haven't seen, because it's not about Tchaikovsky."

"Fair," I say with a chuckle.

It's hard to resist Bryce's sunniness. It's like standing by the edge of the pool. Eventually you're just going to want to jump in.

So I stand up.

"Do I need to adjust the music because of your ..." Bryce gestures at my hearing aid, then a look of remorse comes over him. "Sorry."

"It's fine. I can adjust it if needed."

"Great. I've never known someone who's hard of hearing. Were you born that way, to quote Lady Gaga, who I'm guessing you also aren't familiar with because she's not Mozart."

I feel myself tense up as dark memories threaten this good time. "Let's get on with it."

Bryce grabs my hips and shimmies them back and forth. "The song is called 'Body Language.' You have hips, Emerson. Use them."

As soon as he moves my hips back and forth, they sink into the rhythm. Oh, this is interesting. Maybe I can dance?

"We're just getting started," Bryce says.

The emotion in Carly Rae's voice builds and builds. Bryce dances faster and faster, almost like he's a windup toy. And finally, the chorus comes on, and Bryce lets go and dances around the room. He dances circles around me, and I do my little—very little —shimmy.

"Okay, we're—we're getting there," says Bryce. "This is good, okay. Well, next, you have to use your arms. Just imagine you're harvesting corn."

If I handled crops the way he's throwing around his arms, we'd have nothing to sell at markets.

"They can't just hang there like wet noodles."

Bryce grabs my arms, and his touch sends electricity through my body. He lifts them up and waves them around. Bobo comes over, trying to join the action.

And that, plus the hips—I think I'm actually dancing. There's a level of abandon. I've never been this silly before, for good reason.

"How do you feel?" Bryce asks.

"Quasi-coordinated!" I exclaim.

"Good."

Bryce spins around and seems to lose himself in the music. He bops his head back and forth as if he has a long mane of hair that's swishing around.

"All the Jepsies know this: Carly Rae is a joy detector."

"The who?" I ask, my shoulders trying to find the rhythm.

"Jepsies. Those are her fans. They all know she finds the joy in our hearts and tells us it's okay to believe in something. It's okay to feel happiness."

"Is she a cult leader?" I ask.

"Better." Bryce moves my arms around with his assured

strength, and the electricity between us continues to build. "Okay, last part of the song. We're at the bridge. Emerson, do they have bridges in symphony pieces?"

"No," I say. "They have movements."

"For this last part, I want you to close your eyes."

Finally, I give in and close my eyes.

"Now dance. Just let the music fill you."

I can hear his voice, but it's distorted. Like someone shouting under water. I open my eyes and look at Bryce's full lips. "The music." I take his chin between my thumb and forefinger and draw his face up. "I need to see your mouth with the music blaring."

The heat of his skin sparks something in me, flaring from my fingertips down to the pit of my stomach. His lips are soft, parted slightly, like he's halfway between laughing and telling me something important.

"Dance, Emerson. Just let the music fill you."

His mouth ... hypnotic, like it's singing even when it's still.

"Pretend like you're possessed by the Canadian spirit of Carly Rae."

And I do. My body goes haywire in all the best ways—arms flailing, hips moving, legs kicking out, and spinning around. A wall knocks me off course, but it only makes me laugh as I keep dancing. Carly Rae commands me not to overthink it, and I must listen. The thought of opening my eyes crosses my mind, but if Bryce has videotaped me, there's no coming back from it. Still, there's a freedom, an abandon that feels too good to stop. All the stress from today melts away for a few glorious seconds, and Bryce's joy overtakes me.

When the song ends, I collapse into him and open my eyes. I'm against his chest. Our gazes lock. There's a charged moment that gives me goosebumps. Perhaps we're both possessed with the spirit of Carly Rae—or something else.

EIGHT

BRYCE

MY BODY STRUGGLES TO get comfortable on the couch. There's only so much space on a sofa that's barely larger than a loveseat for someone my size. Suddenly awake, my eyes snap open to an empty living room. I glance at the vacant back cushions on the floor and my stomach drops. Where's Bobo?

My heart pounds, momentarily frightened. Where is he? He's not at his food bowl awaiting breakfast. Nor at the water bowl attempting to assuage his stomach while he waits for his meal. I throw the sheet off me and swing my feet to the floor. I quickly scan the entire room. The bedroom door is cracked—that bugger.

Padding across the room in my socks, I nudge the creaking door open with my shoulder. In the dim light of the sun filtering through the drawn shades, I see it. Them.

Emerson, sprawled on his side of the bed, looking oddly peaceful for once, his hand loosely wrapped around Bobo—who's not only sound asleep but snoring, his back curled up against Emerson's naked chest. Holy shit.

A dull burning in my chest surprises me. But then Emerson pulls my baby boy toward him, and Bobo emits the cutest little grunting noise. The flame softens to a gentle warmth that spreads throughout my torso. They're so damn sweet together.

Emerson, who seems to always be a bit too tense, is completely still—with the weight of Bobo's enormous body against him. There's a vulnerability, a calmness I've not yet seen. And Bobo ... well, Bobo has a way of bringing out the inner softie in almost anyone. A yearning stirs inside. For a fleeting moment, I wonder what it might be like to join their dog pile. On the other side of Bobo, of course.

My eyes blink, and fuck, I'm staring at a half-naked Emerson. Sure, my dog is there too, but my eyes linger on the man. That chest. Even beneath a button-down shirt and blazer, I could sense it was something spectacular, but now, in the flesh, dusted with just the right amount of hair, my fingers twitch as my eyes focus on each detail.

I shake my head, shooing impure thoughts away. This is all Portia's fault. Why'd she have to go and plant the idea of making nice with Emerson in my head?

Oblivious to the creeper watching him in his sleep, Emerson smacks his lips, and Bobo pops his head up. When he moves back to sniff Emerson's face, he spots me, and upon seeing his daddy, his tail immediately thumps against ... Emerson's leg.

His eyes flutter open just as Bobo scrambles to his feet, the mattress caving under him as he bounds over to me.

"Morning," Emerson mumbles groggily, his voice rough from sleep.

A smirk skates across my face, trying to mask the odd flutter in my chest. "Uh, morning. Didn't mean to interrupt your snuggle-fest."

Emerson wipes his eyes and sits up, and I get another opportunity to take in his bare torso, no longer blanketed by Bobo's fur coat.

Besides the hair that my hands seem to have a magnetic attraction to, I now see just how firm his pecs are. He's a big boy but in a "working on a farm so much has made my body look like I've been working out all the time" way. I'd need to open both hands wide and do my best baseball mitt impression to hold both of his pecs securely. And I've just made a sports reference. Surely, this is the first sign of the Apocalypse.

His lips curl into a lazy half-smile. "Was he on the bed? Guess I was so tired I didn't realize."

"Seems you've been adopted."

Bobo throws his head back, tongue hanging out. I'm pretty sure it's because he feels bad about abandoning me in the night and not because he was just thrust up against Emerson's beefy farm-boy chest.

"Was he in here all night?" he asks, now looking at me, and I make sure to keep my eyes above his neck.

"I'm not sure." To keep my fingers busy, I reach down and scratch Bobo's head. "I went to sleep with him on the floor and woke up to him ... with you."

"Oh. Sorry. I mean, I guess he's my roommate now, too." He sits up, running his fingers through his messy hair and showcasing his flexed bicep and delicious armpit.

"No, it's fine. As long as you don't mind. Anthony didn't like him on the bed. Can you imagine not letting this guy snuggle with you? Right, my bestest boy?"

Bobo knocks his skull against my thigh in agreement. Or to remind me he's overdue for breakfast.

Emerson throws the covers off his lower half, revealing navy sweats, and my eyes zero right in on what must be morning wood. Hello, Dolly!

He adjusts himself, and I can't tell if my eyes are playing tricks, but it appears to have simmered down as he secures his glasses and hearing aid, and stands.

Bobo heads to the kitchen. Emerson gives a big stretch, using both arms. I know he's not trying to put on a show for me, but between his perfect pecs, pits, and stomach—just round enough for both hands to get lost on—yeah, we might need to discuss sleeping attire.

"So, I guess we need to talk about the house rules," he says.

"Huh?" The word fumbles out of me, and shit, is my mouth hanging open?

"Rules. If you're staying, we need to have some boundaries. Understandings."

A sudden lightness washes over me. Staying. At least for now. "Yeah, of course. Absolutely. First, no dog on the bed. Your bed. I'll keep him out with me. We can shut your door when we go to sleep. That will help."

"Bryce." Still shirtless, he takes a step toward me. "I'm not your ex. And Bobo's a dog. He just wants to be comfortable."

Emerson lifts the shade, the sunlight pouring in, giving me an even better view of his physique. He's muscular but not too bulky —and those shoulders—broad like a tank. In the light, I can see his thighs stretching the fabric of his sweats. If I met him in a bar, I'd ask what his momma fed him to make him so thick. Damn you, Portia, for pouring naughty ideas into my head.

"Yeah, sure, um, comfortable. Dog. Bobo. Bed."

My brain seems to have short-circuited.

"But yeah, probably not a good idea for him to get used to bunking with me."

"Exactly, um, could you ... uh, put a shirt on?" I ask, turning toward the kitchen. "Please."

Bobo sits next to his vacant bowl, gazing at it as if food might magically appear if he stares long enough.

"Hungry, boy?" Emerson asks.

YES, I say to myself before realizing he's talking to Bobo.

I take the bag of food from the lower cabinet and fill his bowl to the brim, as relief pours over my entire body. Sure, the couch isn't ideal. Yeah, this apartment isn't meant for a co-living situation like this, but one of my coworkers at the Met shares a tiny studio with another guy. Two twin beds stacked on top of each other, a tiny chair and table, and they make it work. This will be a breeze.

Emerson emerges from the bedroom, tugging a Hoosiers T-shirt over his torso.

"Better?" he asks.

"What?"

He points to the word Hoosiers sprawled over an orange ball on his shirt.

"Emerson, I don't do sports."

A small laugh escapes his lips. "No, the shirt. I put one on."

"Yeah, much better. I think Rule Number One should be—fully clothed in front of each other at all times."

"To be fair, you entered the bedroom while I was sleeping. I can't sleep with a shirt on. Too confining. And I thrash in my sleep. I'd get all tangled."

I dip my head, peering over the imaginary glasses I really should buy, if only for moments like this.

"Fully clothed in front of each other." He gives a firm nod, pushing his very real glasses up. "Got it."

"Rule Number Two," I say, but Emerson interrupts me.

"Maybe try to not let him live on the bed."

"I'll work on keeping him on the cushions next to the sofa. Right, Bobo?"

He's too busy inhaling his kibble to pay attention to the two grown men negotiating their forced living situation.

"He'll be fine out here with me," I say. "Right, boy? No more spooning with the hot professor."

"Pardon?" Emerson takes a bowl from the cupboard.

He reaches up and adjusts his hearing aid, a sharp noise zipping through the room. When it's quiet, he looks at me. Waiting.

"Spooning. Spoons. Right here." I pull open the drawer, revealing the few silverware items.

"Rule Number Three," Emerson says.

"Wait, who said you get to make all the rules?"

"My name's on the sublet. I'm paying the rent. I get to make the rules."

I nod, unable to argue with his point. "Rule Number Three?"

"We share the food. I'm not overly picky, but I prefer organic produce. Peanut butter. Honestly, everything should be organic or at least natural. I grew up on a farm, and the pesticides in most of our food would shock you. We shouldn't be ingesting that nonsense. So if you buy things, I'd appreciate keeping that in mind."

"Oh, I don't cook." I tap the display case over the stove, and Megatron shakes his little gun at Emerson.

"And that's another thing. I enjoy cooking, so please move your ... toys." He picks up Bumblebee, in his original yellow VW Beetle form, and places him on the counter. "Thanks."

I take a deep breath and use the bottom of my shirt to collect them all.

"Sure, I can just put them ..." I carefully release them onto the small coffee table. "Here."

I let out an enormous sigh. I might have been dumped by letter. My apartment may have been rented out from under me. Bobo may have left me last night to spoon with the hot nerdy professor who uprooted my life. But at least we have a roof over our heads. For now.

"And thank you again. For letting us stay. I'm going to buy some groceries. For us. Natural. Organic. No nasty chemicals. Maybe I'll buy some kale. Not exactly sure what it is, but I hear it's healthy. I'm picking up an extra shift at the Met. Gotta make some extra cash if I ever want to get out of your hair."

This grabs Emerson's attention. "The Met? You work at the Metropolitan Opera?"

"Yeah, it's not as impressive as it sounds. I sell subscriptions and ask for donations. Basically, I sit in a giant room in the basement and beg rich people for money. No glitz, no performers. It's like ... the opposite of what you probably imagine."

"Huh. That's ... interesting. I mean, still, it's the Met. You're there."

His tone suggests that he's piecing something together in his mind. I'm not sure what it means, but I'll file that curiosity away. It might come in handy later.

"In the dungeon. Yeah." I shrug. "Anyway, Rule Four: I'll keep Bobo out of your hair. He's my responsibility. You have enough on your plate with a new job and us squatting in your apartment."

I shake my shoulders and present my best smile. The one Portia says could melt the polar ice caps.

Emerson glances at Bobo, who's now lying between us on the floor, sprawled out ready for an after-breakfast nap.

"Anyway, thanks again for being so understanding about ..." I motion to Bobo. The apartment. All of it. "I appreciate it." I flash my winning grin, feeling a rush of relief. "You're a lifesaver, Em. Seriously."

"Yeah, sure. I'm not about to kick you out on the street."

"You okay if I get in the bathroom first?" I ask.

Emerson nods, shoveling his breakfast into his mouth.

"Amazing. I'll be quick." I shoot him a wink, and he nods, swallowing and pointing at his breakfast. "Gotta finish up."

He pats his stomach and scoops up another spoonful of cereal and flashes me a huge grin. I chuckle, even though I'm pretty sure he's not trying to be funny, but with that big, full-mouthed grin on his face, I can't deny how ridiculously cute he is. I can't help but smile back.

NINE

EMERSON

WHEN IT COMES time for my second lecture, I'm feeling much more confident. Or so I think. As soon as I walk into the classroom, the nerves hit me.

The first thing I notice is more empty desks than last time. Is there a bug going around? Or have they dropped? How many are missing? How closely is the administration watching my enrollment numbers?

I take a deep breath. I can't let it get to me. I have to deliver another solid lecture so I can keep all the students I still have.

"Hello. Welcome to Beats and Requiems: A History of Western Music. I'm Professor Emerson Grant. Just wanted to repeat that in case there's anyone new here."

"There's less students." The young lady in the front row gestures to the empty seats on either side of her.

"Lucky us. That means we can have a more intimate discussion," I say, trying to believe it myself. "Okay, well, let's jump right into the lecture. We're going to analyze Brahms. How's that?"

I hate that every sentence that comes out of my mouth has an uptone to it like I'm serving frozen yogurt at a mall food court.

I go to the podium, open my computer, and connect it to the screen. I spent several hours putting together my PowerPoint slides last night, staying up probably later than I should have. To keep up my energy, I admittedly opened a Spotify playlist of Carly Rae Jepsen. Her music is aural sugar: providing an energy boost with no discernible nutritional value.

I open the presentation, but it won't connect to the big overhead screen. I unplug the cord, then plug it back in. No change. The screen flickers but nothing shows up. The dead air in the classroom makes my skin crawl.

"Huh. Technical difficulties," I say. "Please stand by." I can feel my face turning beet red.

Will races up to the podium. "Let's see what's going on."

"One moment, everyone," I say to my students.

A few laugh. Others pull up their phones and start scrolling, and who knows what they're saying about me.

"Okay, maybe we close this and open that," Will says. "I think we can open this up on your browser. The screen might recognize that." He starts clicking around on my computer, eventually clicking to the Spotify tab, still open from last night.

"Oh, no, no," I say. "That's—you can ignore that."

But when I go to move his hand away, I accidentally hit the play button.

Carly Rae Jepsen's most perfect pop hit blasts through the speakers. The screen may be busted but not the speakers. They work perfectly.

Loudly.

The strings pipe through the room's premier sound system, and when the bass drum kicks in and her sweet voice joins, complete horror overtakes my face just as the driving pulse of the chorus kicks in.

Call Me Maybe? Call me a disaster.

ON THIS WARM AFTERNOON, I take the long walk back to the apartment to clear my head, but it doesn't help. I can't stop thinking about the lecture today. Even after I fixed the technical equipment, I couldn't recover from the Carly Rae mishap. And my lecture felt ... dull. The students were even more disengaged than last time. Nobody asked questions.

When I get to my street, I look up and see a body gyrating wildly in the top window.

Bryce.

He's dancing his heart out, radiating pure joy. I watch him for a few moments, enjoying the show, wishing I could be as happy and carefree as that. How does he do it? How does he let go so completely? Does he realize how lucky he is to be able to let go like that? Does he ever question himself? Does he ever wonder if he's good enough? Or is he just ... free? I wish I could feel that ease. My mind wanders back to the lecture hall and a soft ache settles in my chest. Maybe, just maybe, one day I'll find a way to release my fears and dance freely. There's something magical about witnessing Bryce this way. It's a sweet moment when you see someone in their element.

"Hello," I say to him a few minutes later after I walk up the six flights of stairs.

"Hi." Bryce immediately shuffles to the fireplace mantel and turns off his music. "No more music tonight. I did all my practicing, so this apartment is a quiet zone for you for the rest of the evening, Emerson," he says.

"Thank you," I reply. "But I'm taking the night off."

I beeline to the fridge, pull out a beer, and chug half of it. I even let the bottle cap fall to the floor.

"Rough day?" Bryce asks.

"Not my best." I take another sip, running my thumb over the condensation on the bottle.

"Seems like you've had a lot of rough days since you've been here," Bryce notices. "The city can do that to you."

"I don't know if it's the city."

Bryce pulls a wine cooler from the fridge, clinks the bottle against mine, opens it, and takes a drink. "What's up?"

"It's nothing."

"Is the teaching thing not working out that well?" he asks as he cuddles up to Bobo on the couch.

"You could say that." The disaster from a few hours earlier flashes in my head and a rush of disappointment falls over me.

Bryce and Bobo stare at me from the sofa as I walk around the living room, pacing, just replaying the day over and over in my head. When I was back at my home university, I struggled to connect with my students but nothing like this. I was a small fish in a small pond. Even though swimming was hard for me, there was less real estate to take up. Here, I fear I'm drowning.

I let out a big breath. "I'm just flopping all over the place."

"I'm sure it's not that bad," Bryce says.

Bobo hops off the sofa and lies at Bryce's feet, allowing me to sink into the couch next to him.

"Maybe it's just first-day jitters," he says. "First-week jitters."

"I don't know if my jitters are going away." I rub my forehead. Something about Bryce's open face makes it easy to unload to him. "It's not just the lecture. If I do a really good job teaching this class, there's a tenure-track position opening up that I could go for. So I really can't mess this up. And yet, that's exactly what I seem to be doing." I sputter out a sigh.

Bryce scratches at his smooth chin, more intrigued than supportive.

"What?" I ask.

"I know what this is." He nods as a small smile appears on his lips. "You're auditioning. This temporary gig is just one extended showcase. You're being tested. It's like callback after callback." He sits up a little taller. "This is perfect. You're auditioning, and I am great at auditions."

"But don't you have trouble landing roles?"

"Auditioning and getting the role are two different things. The best person isn't always the one picked. Theater can be very political."

It has nothing on academia, I think.

"I may not land the parts I want, but I'm good in a room. I've been on many, many, many, many—" Bryce takes a big swig of his tropical twister. "Many, many—" He takes another gulp. "Many auditions. I know how they work."

He stifles a burp. I chuckle because, somehow, it still comes off as endearing.

"Emerson, you might want to believe that you are in a highfalutin palace of academic study where it's all about merit and intellect. But honey, you're auditioning. So you gotta learn how to dance."

"Not dancing again."

"Not literally." He sits up. "Figuratively."

To my utter surprise, what Bryce says makes sense. This is an audition, plain and simple. If I do well here, and students speak highly of me, then it could go a long way toward securing a full-time position. So maybe there's some truth to his adorable madness.

"So what do I do?" I ask. "How can I improve my ... audition?"

He jumps up from the couch and practically dances in front of me.

"There are four main tips on how to ace an audition. Tip number one ..." He holds out his finger dangerously close to my face. "You have to enter confidently and unforgettably. The casting agents start judging you the second you walk in the door—

not when you start your performance, not when you introduce yourself. The second you're in the door, they're already judging you, and they're already deciding if they want to move you forward or not. Right now, how do you enter your class?"

"I enter rooms exactly as human beings have done for centuries. I walk through the door."

"Well, I'm already bored." Bryce rolls his eyes. "You need to enter with pizzazz. Make a statement. Toss your nonexistent hair over your shoulder and sashay in there. Hmm, let's see. Are there stripper poles in these classrooms?"

I throw my head in my hands. Why did I think it would be a good idea to listen to him?

"I'm kidding," Bryce says with a smirk. "Mostly."

I shouldn't find him cute when he smiles, but I do. Objectively, he's adorable.

"The point is to show these students that you didn't come to play. A big thing about entering confidently is displaying a positive attitude too, because people don't want to work with someone who is a sourpuss. Not that I'm saying you are." He smiles, showing a few teeth. "Even when I walk into an audition that I know I probably won't get, I walk in like I am having the time of my life, and I'm so excited to see everyone, and I'm just having a blast. Because when you're having fun, other people have fun—even if you have to fake it."

I lean back on the couch, wondering if there is some method in the midst of all this madness. I'm also angry on Bryce's behalf that he isn't getting cast left and right. The guy is completely magnetic.

"Okay!" Bryce does a little shimmy. "Tip number two: you need to start strong and end strong. People never remember the middle, but they remember beginnings and endings. So, how do you start your lectures?"

"I say, 'Welcome to class. I'm Professor Emerson Grant—'"

"Stop." Bryce puts a hand up. "I've already fallen asleep."

"I just said my name," I say.

"Grant Emerson has a better ring to it."

I cock my head at him. "Bryce, I appreciate your help, but I think this is just not the right milieu for you to advise upon."

"Emerson, I know my milieus. Do you?" He arches an eyebrow my way, thinking he made a point when his sentence doesn't make any sense at all. "You have to start strong. I don't care if you're talking about Mozart or vibrators. It starts with that entrance. You have to say who you are, what you want, and why you're there. Like, 'Hi, I'm Bryce. I'm auditioning for the role of Fieryo. Super excited to be here and jump in.' And when I do my audition—those first steps? I am *perfect*. I'm amazing. And even if the middle gets a little wonky, I *always* end strong."

"The start of my lecture has to be the most compelling part," I say, nodding along, letting the wheels turn.

"Find a way to connect it to the present day. These kids might all be smarties, but they're also into dumb shit, like all college kids are. So, I don't know, show them a TikTok video. Show them a picture of Billie Eilish. Teach them a viral dance. Make it engaging. And then you go into your boring music stuff."

"Thank you," I say, cocking an eyebrow. I happen to find the history of Western music highly stimulating, but admitting that will only elicit a sassy retort from my roommate.

"As I was saying, you go into your boring music stuff—blah, blah, blah—and then you end with bringing it back to that first part. Or another fun connection to the present day. Or maybe showing how Chopin connects to a present-day artist who may or may not be Miss Carly Rae Jepsen."

"No more Carly Rae Jepsen." My face flashes red at the embarrassing part of class today. I don't tell Bryce what happened because I don't want to give him the satisfaction of knowing I listened to her music of my own volition.

"You need to catch people in the first few seconds, or else

you're done. I remember there was one time I auditioned, and it took me a while to get into the steps. But, man, by the end, I really got into it. Still didn't get it—because my beginning was lackluster. Beginnings and endings. They don't remember middles."

"Fair." I brace myself with another gulp of beer. "Okay. What's tip number three?"

"Know what questions they're going to ask in advance and have answers prepared."

"Easier said than done."

"Not necessarily," Bryce says. "People aren't as smart as we think. Most questions you can probably anticipate, especially since you've been doing this for a while. I know for me, when I go into an audition, there's always gonna be questions about my 'size.'" He makes air quotes and sighs. "But we all really know what that means. They want to know if I'm physically able to do this." He understandably rolls his eyes. "There's gonna be questions about what resonated with the material. There's gonna be questions about my availability. So rather than stammering and stuttering through those answers, I can fire off quick responses that keep the momentum from my hot entrance going. It makes me look like I know what the F I'm doing."

"Huh." I didn't expect such insight from Bryce, but as I focus on his plump lips, I find I could listen to him all night long.

"What will people remember? They'll remember an answer you give to their question versus you yammering on from a lecture. Does that make sense?"

Sheena has always tried to help me, but I think she's too close to the situation. Nobody's ever explained it to me like Bryce. He's blinking at me, waiting for me to answer, and I realize I'm staring.

"It does, actually. Total sense." I laugh to myself. "These are actually really good tips. I was not expecting this at all. The wheels are turning. I'm coming up with new ideas. All right." I take a drink of my beer. "So, what's the fourth and final tip?"

"Dress slutty," Bryce says.

I almost spit out my beer. "Funny. Okay, no, what is it? For real."

"I'm dead serious. Dress slutty. Not *slutty* slutty. Just *slutty*, you know."

"No. I don't know. Grammatically, that sentence makes no sense at all."

"We are visual creatures. And the fact of the matter is, people pay more attention if you dress hot. They'll be more engaged in class. They'll write nicer reviews for you if they want to fuck you."

"That is so reductive, Bryce." I stand and place a hand on my hip. "These people are some of the sharpest minds in our education system. I doubt they care what I wear to class."

"They care," Bryce says. "Even at the best universities in the world, there are people hooking up and having crazy sex. Trust me. Now, I'm not saying you have to wear a tube top and a mini skirt—although that'd be really funny to see—but your outfit right now? It's giving professor, but it's not giving *professor*."

"Again, these sentences don't make sense, Bryce."

"I think your clothes can be a little more tailored." He reaches for my glasses, adjusting them on my face. "The glasses are hella sexy. And you have a good body."

He walks around me, checking me out, and I flash back to our first meeting. I know exactly how he feels about my body, and it gets me a little warm inside remembering all the things he said.

"You know, if we get your jacket a little tailored, get the pants a little tailored, tuck in your shirt, trim your beard and fix those eyebrows—you will be a very sexy professor. People always show up for sexy professors."

I look at myself in the mirror on the far wall.

I think I look perfectly fine. I'm not here to be in a fashion show. But perhaps Bryce has a point, and now I can't stop looking at my beard. And eyebrows. Are they really that bad? Are my clothes really that baggy?

Bryce claps his hands. "Oh, this is gonna be great. You're gonna get your tenure position. We're gonna have a makeover montage. These students aren't going to know what hit them."

"I hope so," I say, feeling more positive than I have since I started. "Thank you, Bryce."

I turn around from the mirror to give him a hug. He puts a piece of tape between my eyebrows and yanks it back before I have a chance to react.

Two hairs flail on the piece of tape.

"Oh, I've been wanting to do that for the longest time," Bryce says.

Standing here, with a sudden sharp pain right between my eyes and Bryce holding the remnants of what was between my eyes moments ago, a warmth stirs in me. It's strange, uncertain, yet ... good. I smile, and he returns the gesture. Something feels different—maybe it's hope ... something to hold on to for now.

TEN

BRYCE

PORTIA ACCOMPANIES me on my walk home from jazz class. Neither of us got cast in *The Sound of Muscles*. (Whitney did. Ughhh.) We danced out our feelings vigorously.

"I reckon the original *Sound of Music* isn't even that good. I tried watching it for research and fell asleep. I prefer Julie Andrews in *The Princess Diaries*," she says, her arm linked in mine as we stroll down the sidewalk. Our size difference makes me look like her bodyguard. Her eyes are hidden behind large round sunglasses that likely cost more than my rent. Anthony's rent. Emerson's rent. Whatever.

"I can't believe Whitney got cast in the chorus. May she perpetually be one second off her moves." Portia lets out a sigh.

"Yeah," I say, trying to maintain conversation though my mind is elsewhere.

"What is going on with you? I've been monologuing for our entire walk. When you have a chat with friends, it's typical for one person to say something, and then the other."

I stare ahead and let out a sigh of my own. "I'm not in a chatty mood."

"That is highly unlike you, Bryce Derrickson. Did you pull a muscle in class?"

Thoughts bounce around in my head, daring me to say them out loud. "Do you ever feel yourself ... getting tired? Like, with the whole grind?"

As a performer, I've just vocalized something we're never supposed to say out loud. Pessimism spreads like wildfire. We have to project optimism. We're supposed to love the hustle and believe that our big break is just around the corner. "I worked my ass off to prepare for that audition, just like I worked my ass off to prepare for all the auditions before it. And yeah, once in a while I'll hear a maybe, but those sporadic maybes aren't adding up to a yes." I stare down at my feet walking over the cracked pavement. I've always prided myself on being positive, but I'm starting to wonder if hopefulness is a non-renewable resource.

"We're always one audition away from everything changing," Portia says.

"Well, I'd like to know when that life-changing audition will happen. I've got bills to pay and a dog to support."

Portia flushes slightly. I don't talk about my economic struggles with her because it can make things weird between us, upset our delicate friendship balance.

"Sorry," I say after a quiet beat.

"Don't be sorry. This is tough. Really tough. But we're daring to do great things."

"Dancing?" I ask skeptically.

"We are artists, and our bodies are the brushes!"

Portia's enthusiasm gives me a boost. I remember that I came to New York because I wanted to be on Broadway. If I wanted a safe life, I could've stayed in Pennsylvania.

"Portia, when you're right, you're right." I squeeze our linked arms, and we continue down the street. There's still a niggling frustration and wondering if my time dancing is coming to a close, but I block it out with laughter and Carly Rae in my head.

We stroll a few more blocks until we reach my building.

"You didn't have to walk me home," I tell her.

"I wanted to get a glimpse of your hot professor roommate." Portia rubs her hands together. She may be younger than Emerson, but she is in full cougar mode.

"He's at class," I tell her.

"Disciplining a student," she says with a sly smile.

"I doubt that."

"Don't interrupt my fantasy." She kisses me goodbye, and I head up the front steps.

Data and Marsh are by the mailboxes. We don't actually have a mail room. It's more of a small corner where the boxes are crammed in like sardines. It's nothing fancy, but we get our mail. Most of the time. There's a long, low table in front where the usual mix of junk—ads, flyers, and menus—collect until Carl, the super, recycles them.

"Hey, Bryce!" Data says with his usual grin. He's holding a bunch of kale in one hand and a bag of potatoes in the other. They always look like they just stepped out of a magazine about gay city living—hashtag couple goals.

"Hey!" I nod, offering a smile, but it's the kind of smile that's still more about the mail than anything else. I grab mine and shuffle through the envelopes, trying to hide that I don't even know where to start with the bills. Water. Electricity. Internet. They all still have Anthony's name on them.

"Anything good?" Marsh asks, his voice warm. He's wearing an oversized hoodie, the one that looks like it's a size too big but suits him. He's got a carton of eggs tucked under one arm.

"Same old," I mutter, shaking my head as I flick through the stack. "Mostly junk."

"No million-dollar checks?" Marsh raises an eyebrow. "How's Anthony?"

I freeze for just a second, and my heart skips a beat—damn, I haven't seen them since he left. They were away, and then I was too embarrassed to reach out. "He's ... gone," I say, trying really hard to sound like I'm okay. "He got a movie."

"A movie?" Marsh perks up. "That's amazing."

"Yeah, except it's in the outback. The one in Australia, not the steakhouse."

"But he's coming back?" Data steps forward, placing his hand on my forearm.

I shake my head and bite my lower lip. "No. We're over."

"I never liked Anthony," Marsh says. "Great cheekbones but no soul."

"You can do better." Data rubs my shoulder. "Maybe I'm crazy, but I thought I saw a cute guy move in the other day. Like a nerdy linebacker."

"That's my new roommate." Data opens his mouth, but I continue before he or Marsh can say anything. "Anthony sublet the apartment to some ... guy. A professor of music history or theory or something like that."

"So that's who I saw leaving the building the other day," Marsh says. "He's cute. You guys should hook up."

Heat flashes on my face. "What? No. Just because we're two guys living together, it's assumed that we should have hot, sweaty sex?"

"I only said hooking up. You were the one who made it hot and sweaty." Marsh holds up his hands in defense, and I turn even redder.

As we talk, I hear the familiar creak of Horton's door opening. I glance over just in time to see him—tall, slightly hunched—reach down and grab a large box from his doormat. Camilla, his little gray parrot, wobbles out from between his legs, her tiny feet dragging as she totters down the hallway, chirping loudly.

Horton looks down at her, his face lighting up with his soft, almost fond smile. "Camilla, get back here," he mutters under his breath, but before he can corral the bird, she squawks, "Cracker! Cracker!" in her raspy, almost comically human voice.

"Oh, sweetie, I wish I had a cracker for you," I say. "You don't happen to like organic beer?"

Camilla stares at me with her little bird eyes and squawks. "Fuck you!" She juts her head out like the miniature raptor she is as Horton carefully picks her up.

"Camilla!" Horton admonishes her.

"Camilla, I don't understand why you don't like me," I say, staring into the bird's overly alert eyes.

"Fuck you!" she squawks back.

"I am a person! With feelings!"

Data puts a hand on my shoulder. "You're yelling at a bird, Bryce."

"She started it."

I'M ACTUALLY GETTING USED to sleeping on the sofa. Sure, it's a little like cramming a foot-long hotdog into one of those mini pastries for pigs in blankets, but hey, beggars can't be choosers. There's a roof over our heads, and Bobo and I are safe.

Which is a good thing, because tonight there's a storm raging. There's something peaceful about heavy rain in Manhattan. It serves as a reminder that, regardless of how busy and developed the small island may be, Mother Nature remains firmly in control. The thunder wakes me, and I stare out the window, waiting for the lightning to light up the sky as the rain pounds against the glass. I reach down to comfort Bobo, but the bed I made for him from the back couch cushions is empty.

And then I hear it.

Scratching. Claws on wood. He's at the bedroom door, clawing with his massive paws. That's going to leave a nasty mark. And wake Emerson up.

I roll over, pushing the blanket aside, and squint at my phone. 3:17 a.m. Jesus. I sit up slowly, rubbing my eyes. Bobo is relentless, desperate. I try calling to him, my voice still thick with sleep.

"Bobo, it's okay. C'mon, buddy." I pat the sofa, hoping to lure him over. I'll sleep sitting up and let him lay his head on me. But he doesn't stop. He keeps clawing at the door, the sound sharp and annoying. I groan, throw my feet over the edge of the couch, turn on the lamp, and shuffle to the door.

I kneel next to him, and he pauses to stare at me. With his enormous eyes wide and tail tucked between his legs, the poor thing looks like he's about to crawl out of his fur. I reach to pet him, but he squirms away and goes back to trying to force his way into the bedroom.

"Bobo, I know, the storm is scary, but we don't sleep in there anymore."

I grab his collar, hoping to gently pull him over to the sofa so he can settle down with me. When I apply light pressure, Bobo does something he rarely does—he barks.

Now, besides the storm raging, my one-hundred-twenty-pound dog, who has only barked thrice in his two years on earth (twice times when workers on the roof banged against the window as they did some repairs and once the night Emerson arrived), stands at the door, growling low, his body tense. The storm outside is nothing compared to the unease in his eyes. He's never been afraid of thunder, but tonight ... something is different. Something has him on edge, as if the winds have carried a warning, and he knows something I don't.

"It's just a storm, Bobo," I murmur, tugging a little more.

He lets me pull him over to the sofa while I grab my phone and quickly cue up "All That." The slow synths and dreamy melody mix with rain tapping against the window. When Carly's voice joins the music, Bobo jumps up and tries to crawl into my lap, but even though my thighs might resemble tree trunks, there's just not enough room for him.

When I release him to turn up the music a bit more, he rushes to the door like the world is about to end and resumes scratching.

I sigh, and before I can think of what song to try next, the door opens and Emerson stumbles out, half-awake, shirtless and in those damn navy sweatpants.

A huff escapes me as I raise an eyebrow. "Emerson ... Rule Number One. You know, the one about being fully dressed in front of each other?"

He looks at me, blinking, and yawns as he puts his glasses on. "Excuse me, I was sleeping. It's the middle of the night."

"Yeah, sorry about that. Bobo's usually fine with storms, but for some reason he's terrified of this one."

Emerson sits next to me on the couch and pats the space next to him. Bobo, as if on cue, scrambles up, immediately laying his head in Emerson's lap. I watch the big guy sigh in contentment, like the world just shifted into a much softer place. The storm doesn't seem so bad anymore.

"All That" plays on repeat, soft and gentle, and Emerson pets Bobo, his fingers moving slowly through his thick fur. I sit back, watch for a moment, and then the power flickers off. The lamp cuts out, leaving the room in darkness as Carly sings about keeping her lights on.

As Emerson reaches up to adjust his hearing aid, he mumbles under his breath. "Do you have a flashlight?"

"No, but I have something better."

A moment later, the room is bathed in the warm glow of my

Tutti-Frutti Fresh and Fruity candle. The living room transforms under the soft light and sweet aroma. It's peaceful, almost making the storm outside seem miles away.

"Bobo should sleep in the bed with me," Emerson says, glancing over at me. "Just for tonight. Only because of the storm, though."

I smirk at him. "You're letting him break the 'no dogs in the bed' rule?"

He shrugs. "He's scared."

I look down at Bobo, who has practically melted into Emerson's lap, and I can't say no to that teddy bear face. "I'll help him get settled, then. Come on, boy."

I stand and head into the bedroom, and when Emerson follows, so does Bobo. I don't think either of them needs my help, but it feels right.

Emerson slides under the covers, and just as he settles, Bobo leaps in, eager to be right there beside him. I can't say I blame him.

"Now," Emerson says, "let's all try to get some sleep."

He removes his glasses and pulls Bobo close.

"Thanks, Em." I step back, watching my dog snuggle with the professor.

Who am I kidding? The hot professor.

As I move to return to the couch, a flash of lightning illuminates the room, and I notice a framed picture on the nightstand. I haven't really been in here since Emerson arrived, and this is the first time I'm seeing it. A young woman, smiling and perhaps in her late teens, stands in a field. It's one of those photos where the carefree energy of the subject shines through space and time.

"Is that your girlfriend?" I ask, even though I already know it's not.

But I want to be sure.

Emerson wraps his arm around Bobo then glances over, his eyes softening as he looks at the picture.

"That's Melanie. My sister," he says with a soft smile. "She's the reason I got into classical music. I was about ten years old. Stubborn and only interested in video games."

"You? Stubborn?"

He smiles, not taking the bait.

"Melanie was always patient and calm. She was seven years older than me, but always took time for her little brother. One afternoon, I was helping her sort through some old records, and she pulled out an album of Beethoven's symphonies. 'You should give this a listen,' she said. 'I bet you'd love it.' I rolled my eyes, but, not wanting to disappoint her, I reluctantly put the record on. The moment the first notes filled the room, something shifted. The music was powerful, sweeping, and full of energy in a way I hadn't expected. I was hooked—each crescendo and delicate piano passage drew me in deeper. Melanie sat next to me, smiling knowingly as we listened together."

Emerson pauses. Bobo's burrowed into his chest, and his faint snores join the rain.

"From that moment forward, classical music became the soundtrack of my life—a gift from my sister. Whenever I seek comfort or clarity, I turn to those symphonies, recalling how Melanie opened my ears—and my heart—to a whole new world of sound."

I listen carefully, processing his words. "Your sister sounds amazing. When is she coming to visit?"

He looks down at Bobo, whose snoring has transformed into a low rumble. Emerson's fingers gently brush through the dog's fur again.

"She ... she died when I was twelve."

I blink, processing the weight of what he just said. The silence between us feels heavier than the storm outside.

I look at Emerson for a moment, unsure of what to say. The

lights flicker again, and I find myself just standing there, unsure of how to fill the space between us.

I want to do something to console him. A hug. Wrap him in my arms and tell him how proud Melanie would be of him. But that wouldn't be wise. So, instead, I simply say, "I'm sorry."

He looks up at me, his eyes tired, but there's a small, quiet smile on his face. "It was a long time ago. I'm fine. Really."

But I can tell he's not as he removes his hearing aid and pulls Bobo close. I don't know what else to say, so I let Carly Rae's soft voice, drifting from the sofa, fill the quiet space between us as it joins the raging storm outside.

ELEVEN

EMERSON

IT MAY BE a gorgeous summer day outside with the birds chirping and the sun shining, but for the sake of my career, I'm inside. I spend the day hunched over my computer at the tiny table in my tiny apartment, working on my next article. Connecting the dots between baroque and modern pop music could be the catalyst for my temporary colleagues at the University of New York to bestow a coveted tenure position.

Maybe renting an apartment on the sixth floor without central air was not my best decision. I toil through the sweatiness. I have the fan going at full blast, and I'm working my way through. I'm also compiling notes for my next class. Oddly enough, I'm eager for it. Bryce's tips were a little ridiculous, but maybe there's a kernel of truth in them.

I'm comparing harmonic structures, melodies, and themes across baroque music, pulling at sources, using every inch of brain power to figure out how it influences modern pop music. There's a reason why so many people are moved by the music Bryce adores, and this paper will lay it all out. If I can wow Sheena and the department, this could be my chance.

I shouldn't be so nervous, but I am.

Of course, it doesn't help that Bobo keeps staring at me.

"Buddy." I turn to him. "Bryce will be home very soon, and then he can take you out."

Bobo raises his head as if he thinks I'm saying something worthwhile. But then, once he realizes I'm not budging from my seat, he shrugs and plants his head back on the sofa.

I keep typing away notes for my next class, but I have to stand up and stretch. I'm filled with nervous energy, and I don't know why. I walk to the front door. Bobo jumps off the couch and walks up right next to me, hopeful.

My phone lights up with a text from Bryce: *Running a little late. This audition is taking forever. The director is talking to everyone who comes in. Be home soon!*

"Bryce will be home soon," I tell Bobo. I hold up the text message, and he stares at the phone confused. "Sorry, buddy. We're not going outside. We can walk inside the apartment."

That does not satisfy him. He's a big dog, and even he can clearly see it's a beautiful day outside the giant window. I don't blame him.

As I walk back to my computer, I imagine that I'm in my classroom, and I'm, dare I say, sashaying down the rows to my podium. I'm waving to my students as if I'm Oprah making an entrance onto my talk show.

"Hi, I'm Dr. Emerson Grant, and welcome to class. Are you ready to learn?" I say. "Did you know Handel composed the entire 'Messiah' in only twenty-four days? That's just over three weeks. *Hallelujah* indeed!"

A wave of confidence and joy overtakes me. Here comes my groove. Maybe I needed someone to simply show me the way. Explain things in a new way. Among his other positive qualities, turns out Bryce is also a fantastic teacher.

I turn to Bobo. "We won't tell Bryce about this. He already has a big enough head."

Bobo sighs.

"That was a joke. His head is perfectly proportioned. I just mean he'll never let me live it down, knowing that I used his tips." I catch myself in the moment. "You're a dog. Why am I explaining this to you?"

I push my glasses up, sit back in my chair, and try to do some more work, but the words start fading together. The sunshine is so strong it even blasts through the curtains, forming a glare on my screen. Bobo gets up and starts doing a trot toward the front door. He jogs forward and backward, forward and backward. It reminds me of the pee-pee dances I used to do when I was small and I've seen little kids do.

"Bobo, do you have to pee?" He does a little hop. I don't know if he understands me, or maybe he's just so hopeful that he can get outside.

"Your dad will be home soon." I point at my computer. "I'm still just working through this research paper. I really have got to focus on it, but he'll be home soon."

Bobo's pee-pee dance picks up the tempo, his nails click-clacking on the floor near the front door. I look at my screen. I'm so close to almost being done with this paper. I'm so close to a break-through, but the trotting of his feet is inescapable.

I shut my laptop.

"Okay, buddy, time for a walk."

Bobo literally leaps in the air. He's so excited I think he's going to jump on top of me and start licking my face, but instead, he races past me and grabs the leash from a crevice in the couch. He brings it up to me in his teeth.

Smart dog.

I click the leash to his harness, and as soon as I open the door, we barrel down the steps.

I'm on a roller coaster, going down, down, down the steps toward the street. I hold on to the banister, digging in my fingers and nails, and try to go at a steady pace. But Bobo is a dog with a full bladder and no patience. We race on the steps, passing an older lady with one of those fold-up shopping carts.

"Sorry," I say.

"Hi, Bobo." She smiles at the dog. There's nothing but glee and desperation on Bobo's face.

I try to pull back, but he keeps leaping forward pulling me down, down, down the stairs.

"Bobo, we can't break through the door. Gotta stop."

Don't be so sure, his confident galloping tells me.

Just when I think we're going to crash through the wall of glass that makes up the Bigby's front entrance, the postman opens the door to deliver the mail. Bobo soars past him, yanking me along. We leap over the threshold and over the stoop, smashing through the air. My feet leave the ground, and for a brief, exhilarating moment, I believe dog and man were born to fly.

We land on the sidewalk. I bend over to catch my breath, opting not to dwell on how close to death I came while barreling down the steep staircase.

It really is a beautiful afternoon, one of those days where the sky is a perfect shade of blue. There's not a cloud in the sky and almost no humidity. It's like one of those dreamy days that you get at the start of spring, and you think it's gonna be like that for the next six months, and then you realize, oh, wait, summer's usually hellacious.

Bobo darts to the first tree he can find and lifts his leg. I don't even know if this is legal, if dogs are allowed to go here, but there's no way I'm stopping him. His tongue hangs out in pure bliss, and his eyes roll back with relief as he empties his bladder.

And damn, that is a lot of urine. We could solve California's prolonged drought with what's hitting the tree.

Bobo soaks the mound of dirt and starts going on the sidewalk. I avoid eye contact with passersby. This is New York, though. People are used to public urination, right?

"Okay, you've relieved yourself. You must feel much better," I tell Bobo. "Let's get back inside."

Bobo ignores me, pulling me down the street.

"Fine. We can go a few blocks so you can stretch your legs," I say, yearning to feel somewhat in charge of this situation. "My legs could use some movement, too."

Bobo walks fast then abruptly stops to sniff every other tree and trashcan. He makes a sharp right, and suddenly he is a man on a mission. He walks with determined steps, taking us somewhere only he knows about. He pulls against his leash, and I struggle to keep up.

Tons of people are out. We weave through them. There are shop owners out with displays. It's a bustling city day. I wish my hometown had more outdoor walkability besides shopping malls.

Bobo stops at a small restaurant, and I glance up at the bright red and white canopy—*That's a Spicy Meatball.* The aroma of savory meat is incredible. My stomach immediately rumbles.

"Bobo, we're not eating."

He ignores me completely. Is he more a cute kid or bratty teenager?

A man with a very big mustache and even bigger cheeks bounds from the store. If Chef Boyardee were a real person, I imagine he'd share a striking resemblance to this guy.

"Bobo!" he exclaims. He squats down and rubs Bobo's face. Bobo immediately melts into his touch, his tail wagging wildly.

"Who are you? You are not Mr. Bryce," the man says in a thick Italian accent.

"I'm Emerson. I'm his ... I'm Bryce's ... I'm walking Bobo for him."

"Ah, I see. Well, we have a wonderful meatball for Bobo today."

The man goes back into the store and comes back out a minute later with two small meatballs on a little paper plate. He puts them down on the ground. They smell like absolute heaven. Bobo immediately gobbles them up. The sounds of his loud chewing resonate along the sidewalk. My stomach growls. I have never been so jealous of a dog.

"Bobo loves my meatballs," the man says.

"I can see that."

"Would you like to try one? Best meatballs in Manhattan."

"Sure." I resist the urge to stick my tongue out and bob my head up and down like Bobo.

The man brings one to me on a toothpick. I eat it, and it is more delicious than I dreamed. I don't think I've ever had a meatball this delicious. I can feel the craft and the quality of ingredients, the tanginess of the tomato sauce.

"We love Bobo here. And Mr. Bryce," the man says. "He helped us out so much. Business was rough a while back. We thought we were going to close. Bryce got the Metropolitan Opera to hire us to cater an event. Imagine, little me at the opera! Someone there loved our meatballs so much, they wrote about us in the *New York Sentinel*. Imagine, little me in the newspaper! Business has been wonderful ever since. Without Mr. Bryce, we wouldn't be here."

"Wow," I say, stunned into silence. "That's incredible."

"He's a very good man."

"Yeah. He's ... he's really the best." I think about how he took the time to help me with improving my lectures, something he didn't have to do.

"I tell him free meatballs for life, but he insists on paying. Bobo never has to pay, though." The man rubs Bobo's head again. Bobo's tongue falls out of his mouth in ecstasy.

"Ciao, Bobo!" The man waves us goodbye.

Bobo, sensing that his time of controlling the leash is over, turns and starts walking back to the apartment. With his full belly, he moves slower, letting me lead.

"We had a nice walk. We should get back. I have to finish my paper. Bryce will be home soon." I inhale the balmy breeze. Birds chirp in the tree above us. I can still taste the delectable meatball on my lips.

We come to an intersection. Bobo tries to step into the crosswalk, but I stop him.

"Actually, buddy, I saw a park a few blocks from here." Bobo raises his eyebrows. "Might as well enjoy this gorgeous day."

Bobo glances up at me, and I swear there's a smile on his mouth as the sun hits his face. With a nod, we walk toward the park, the promise of a peaceful afternoon ahead.

TWELVE

BRYCE

"BOBO? WHERE'S MY GOODEST BOY?"

I'm sweating like a whore in church as I walk shirtless into the apartment after my audition. Between the intense choreo, the heat outside, and climbing the stairs, I need a shower, stat. But first, Bobo needs a walk.

"Bobo? Emerson? Are you here?"

I dip into the bathroom quickly, but there's nothing. It's not like Bobo to not run to the door and greet me.

"Where are you guys?"

There are only so many places a man the size of a hunky football player and a dog the size of his mascot can hide in this barely five-hundred-square-foot apartment. It's like playing hide-and-seek in a closet.

They're not here.

As I reach for my phone to text Emerson, the door flies open. Bobo trots to his water dish and laps like he's been stranded on a desert island for days. My eyes move to Emerson, who's leaning against the doorframe, looking too damn handsome for his own good.

He's not wearing the khakis, dress shirt, and blazer combo I'm used to during the day. He's swapped them for a tank top and khaki shorts. My eyes linger, perhaps a little too long, on his exposed perfect armpit as he leans. Bobo walks over to my feet and sits. He melts into me, and I pet him as his panting scores our conversation.

"Hey there," Emerson says with flushed cheeks. "Not sure I'll ever get used to all those stairs."

He looks like he's gotten some sun, and there's a slight sheen on his face that makes him look like an angel—the kind that wears tank tops to show off his massive arms.

"Hey," I say, still half caught up in the fact that Bobo's already had his walk. "You didn't have to take him. Rule ... um, which rule is it again? The one about me taking care of Bobo?"

Emerson raises an eyebrow, his head tilted in that way he does when he's trying to figure me out like I'm a new appliance.

"Rule Four," he replies with a half-smirk. "But his eyeballs were yellow. And I needed some fresh air." He gives me a small shrug, like it's no big deal.

I sigh, running my fingers through my sweaty hair. "Well, thanks. I didn't expect the audition to go so long."

Emerson steps closer to Bobo, who's now flopped down on the cool floor by his water dish, looking entirely too pleased with himself, and gently scratches his head. "Did you get it?"

I wipe a hand down my face. "No, just kept me waiting around forever. I don't think they were expecting so many dancers." I shrug. "But when your show is produced by a certain Latina pop diva with a propensity to get on the floor, everyone shows up. And most people don't mind waiting for tonight."

Emerson's face scrunches but then softens, his eyes glinting with a mix of concern and empathy. "I'm not sure what most of that means, but I'm sorry about the audition."

I let out a small grunt, walking over to the couch and flopping onto it, finally letting myself breathe again. "Meh. I'm used to it."

The room quiets, the weight of the day settling. I've been through this routine too many times to count—getting my hopes up only for them to come crashing down when I don't land the part. It's become almost second nature now, this quiet acceptance of my place in the dance community. I've learned not to take it too personally, because this industry is brutal, and rejection is just part of the game. You don't get the role, but you keep going, because what else can you do?

Emerson stays by Bobo for a moment, watching me like he wants to say something more, but he doesn't.

I toss my shoes aside. "Anyway, where'd you guys go?"

He smiles, his entire face lighting up with an upbeat energy I'm not used to from him. "Oh, we had the loveliest time. We walked down to the park, and I let Bobo run around a bit. Did you know on hot days Central Park is full of shirtless men? A few women, too. So much skin." He shakes his head, but not in a nega- tive way, more like he's trying to shoo salacious images away. And then he looks at me, and his eyes move down to my naked torso.

"Oh, gosh," I say, popping up, riffling though the dresser in the corner where I've shoved my clothes. "Rule Two or Three, I can't remember. Fully clothed."

"It's fine, Bryce." Emerson grabs a glass and runs the cold water. "It's hot. I'm in a tank top. That's practically shirtless."

"No, we have rules, and I'm already breaking them," I say, wishing he'd pop his off and break this one with me.

I grab a green shirt I don't recall at first and slip it over my head. As soon as I pull it down, I realize the issue. It's not mine. I think it's an old shirt Anthony left behind. For a brief moment, I'm reminded of my dumped-and-squatting-on-the-sofa predicament, and then, to add insult to injury, it hits me.

I'm standing in front of Emerson looking like a sausage trying to escape its casing.

The fabric clings to me in all the wrong places, and the sleeves cut off circulation in my arms. My stomach is being squeezed by a vise, and if I breathe too deeply, I'm pretty sure the shirt's going to revolt.

Emerson's smile morphs into this big, boisterous laugh. I've never heard him laugh like this before—my stomach actually drops, but it's definitely not because of the damn shirt. It's his booming, infectious laughter. And the way he's looking at me.

"You okay, there?" he asks, his voice light and teasing.

"Totally fine," I lie, tugging at the fabric again, like that's going to help. "I must've washed it in hot water. It's shrunk." I pull at the front and finally, with a little more room to breathe, I let out a deep breath. "A lot."

I yank again, desperate to get this thing off before I suffocate or pass out. The fabric's way too tight, clinging to my chest like it's been superglued. But as I try to wiggle out of it, the shirt gets stuck over my head, like it's holding me hostage. Great.

"Uh ... hey, could you—" I stop myself, embarrassed that I'm even asking. But I sense him next to me already, the heat of his skin so close to mine, and then his hand lands on my naked back, guiding me to the edge of the sofa.

"Come here," he says, his voice soft and calm.

I freeze momentarily as his fingers brush against my skin when he tries to pull the shirt off. My gut says to bolt. Although I'm not sure where in this tiny apartment. But it doesn't matter because I can't move, not with the shirt ensnaring me, not with him standing so near, his breath just barely grazing my neck.

For a second, everything feels charged, like we're balancing on the edge of a cliff, and I can't tell if it's just the shirt or the heat in the room or something else entirely. His hand is still on me, steady, but then, through the thin fabric of this damned shirt, I'm keenly aware of just how close Emerson's face is to mine.

And just when I think this is it, that we're about to take a leap, or at least cross some line, I pull back quickly, tugging harder at the shirt, suddenly desperate to avoid whatever the hell this moment is about to become.

My heart's pounding like I've danced in one of those twenty-four-hour marathons for charity, but at least the shirt's finally off.

"Thanks," I say.

I'm half-naked, but at least I can breathe. "I'll just grab one that hasn't … shrunk."

"Bryce, it's all good. We're roommates. We can be shirtless around each other. It's like we're at the beach."

I collapse on the couch, exhausted from the audition, the stairs, and the shirt fiasco. "It is so fucking hot. It feels like a beach in here. Without the hot guys in banana hammocks or refreshing ocean breeze." I use the shirt to wipe the sweat from my forehead. "We really should get an air conditioner. Or at least another fan."

Emerson sits next to me. He's not too close, but with this heat and my bare torso and his naked arms, it's suddenly feeling like a sauna in here.

"Thank you again for taking Bobo for a walk."

"Really, we had a lovely time." He shifts so he's facing me, and I do my best to keep my mouth in his line of vision. "Before we hit the park, we were walking down the street, and this Italian guy came running out to give Bobo a meatball. It was like a scene out of a beautiful foreign film. And then he gave me one, and it was the best meatball—no, make that the best food—I've ever eaten."

"Oh my goodness! You met Luigi? He's the best. That's a Spicy Meatball is an institution in the neighborhood. People think it's all about the ambiance with restaurants, but it's actually about the food. The place may be a hole in the wall, but Luigi knows food—especially turning meat into balls." My face flashes hot. "Plus, he has a thing for big boys, right Bobo?"

"Luigi? If you tell me his brother's name is Mario and they have a plumbing business on the side ..."

"No, no," I say with a laugh. "It's just him and the meatballs."

"I swear, this dog is living his best life. You should've seen his face. It was like he'd reached doggy nirvana."

I laugh, the image of Bobo devouring the meatballs so vivid I almost feel like I was there. "He doesn't get many treats and those meatballs are ..."

"Pure bliss," Emerson says. His eyes drift off, and I watch, waiting for him to lick his lips. "Look at him." He nods toward Bobo, who's fallen asleep with his tongue out. "He's still riding that meatball high."

"He's the goodest boy."

"He really is."

Bobo has a way of making everyone smile in a big, heartfelt way. Right now, as Emerson gazes at him, snoozing after his meatball-infused walk, that signature Bobo smile is shining on his face.

"I promise I won't let it happen again."

"Bryce, I told you, shirtless is okay. We're at the beach." His eyes shift from Bobo to me, and the heat of his gaze on my chest makes my blood simmer.

"No, no, I mean, Bobo. I'll make sure I'm home to take him out."

"Oh, that. I mean, honestly, I enjoyed it. He's easy. And who else could get me a free meatball on the streets of New York City?"

"Very true. Okay, well, I should grab a shower. Do you need ..." I nod toward the bathroom.

"Nope, all set."

I stand up, our eyes meet, and an unexpected wave of emotion hits me—somewhere between the need for connection and the weight of everything that's happened. I hesitate, and the urge to do something, anything—a hug, a high-five, a simple gesture to show my gratitude—creeps up.

But I can't mess this up. Bobo and I have nowhere else to go.

So, instead, I lean over and tap his shoulder lightly, my voice quiet but full of sincerity. "Thanks again. For everything."

Emerson's eyes soften, and for a moment neither of us says anything. There's nothing more to say, but in the silence, I realize something's shifted between us.

THIRTEEN

EMERSON

HERE GOES NOTHING.

I burst through the double doors at the back of the classroom, just like Bryce suggested. Except now it feels ... ridiculous. Too loud. Too extra. But I toss my nonexistent hair over my very real shoulder and stride down the steps toward the podium like I belong in one of the overproduced pop videos Bryce watches on his phone.

The students look up, confused but not exactly amused. One student actually snorts. Another mutters something under his breath. My pulse hammers.

"Hey, how's it going? Hey, how are you?" I clap a young man on the shoulder, hold my hand up for a high-five, which another student reluctantly meets. "Glad you all made it."

I can feel the crash coming. Abort mission. Go back to Power-Point. Talk about Mozart's patrons and call it a day.

But then I remember Bryce's words—don't half-ass it—so I swallow the embarrassment and keep marching.

"Beautiful day out, right?"

A few scattered laughs. A woman near the front raises an eyebrow, amused. That's a start.

I reach the podium and plant my feet, even though I want to run.

"I'm Dr. Emerson Grant," I say, voice shaking just a little. "And today's lecture begins with two subjects you probably never expected to hear together."

I pause.

"Carly Rae Jepsen," I say, then raise my hand dramatically. "And syphilis."

Heads shoot up.

Someone in the back actually chokes on a drink.

I take a breath, the smallest bit of adrenaline kicking in. "What do these things have in common with Mozart, you may wonder? Stick with me."

I nod to Will at the soundboard. The opening sax riff of "Run Away With Me" spills into the room. A few kids chuckle. I turn my hearing aid up, and I swear one of them whispers, "No way."

I move away from the podium and start bobbing my head awkwardly, robot-style. "This is Carly Rae Jepsen," I say. "This song is a modern miracle. It's pure joy, bottled. Pop magic. And ... now—"

Will cues the layered track. A classical music piece slips into the beats of the song. "We have Mozart's 'Eine kleine Nachtmusik' layered on top."

Students move slightly in their seats. They can't fight the rhythms.

Some blink. Some of them sit up straighter. One starts unconsciously tapping her pen against her desk in rhythm.

"Many of the themes in Miss Jepsen's song can also be found in this piece by Mozart, which uses repetition to build on the beat. The first movement's string sections and driving rhythm evoke a vibrant atmosphere. It's a stylistic trick formalized in the Viennese Era, which we've been studying."

A few heads nod.

"And the strings in Mozart's piece?" I push my glasses up the bridge of my nose. "As the youth say, they slap."

A student giggles. Another groans. I point to the one who groaned. "That was a fair response."

Now I'm moving more, spinning on my heel—a move I stole from Bryce—and someone claps. I actually hear a clap.

A hand goes up. "Um ... what does any of this have to do with syphilis?"

Bless you, brave student.

"I was hoping someone would ask that. Syphilis was rampant in Mozart's time. Before antibiotics, late-stage infection often led to dementia. And some researchers argue that the neural degeneration might've influenced creative expression in composers like Mozart."

The class listens, astonished, mouths agape, heads bopping. They don't realize that while Mozart's piece is in G Major and Jepsen's is in C Major, both utilize diatonic melodies and a 4/4 time signature, so naturally, they sync up. Bryce was dancing to "Run Away With Me," and the similarities were astounding.

Silence. But then someone near the front speaks.

"No way."

"Way," I reply. "Music history is messier than we pretend. And sometimes, incredibly human."

The music plays on. A few heads start bobbing. Shoulders sway.

"You've been sitting for fifty minutes. Why don't you get up and dance? Seriously. Your blood flow will thank you."

At first, no one moves. Then a woman in a green hoodie shrugs and stands. Two of her friends join her. A guy from the back leaps out of his chair with an exaggerated shimmy.

The room cracks open.

They dance.

And so do I.

Even Will throws up his hands and joins us.

It's not perfect, but it's real. And for the first time since I started teaching here, I'm not the only one sweating.

I PRACTICALLY DANCE through the front door of the apartment later that afternoon. After class, I was so inspired that I went back to my office and worked on my paper some more. It was flowing out of me. Oddly enough, the weird angle I took for class gave me new ideas and concrete examples. My coworkers came by, as word quickly spread about my banger of a lecture. One of them even invited me to attend a picnic in the park this weekend, and I said I'd bring Bobo. With Bobo, it's always love at first sight—for everyone. I immediately texted Bryce to make sure that was okay, and he replied with a heart emoji.

The weather outside might be gray and cloudy, but I'm all sunbeams and rainbows.

"Hello, gorgeous," I burst through the front door with a big whoosh. But I don't find my usual sunshine there.

Bryce sits by the fireplace, throwing pieces of paper into the empty nook.

"You know it's customary to light a fire in one of those things," I tell him.

He turns to me, his usually buoyant face droopy and dismal.

"What's wrong? Is everything okay?" I ask.

Bobo plays with a chew toy in the corner, oblivious to his owner's hurt.

"Oh, don't mind me. My career is just a sad dumpster fire at the moment." He throws another piece of paper in.

"What are those?"

"Old playbills from my productions. Guess I don't need them anymore." He raises one to toss, but I stop his hand.

"This sounds like a fun show. Don't throw this out," I say, reading the front page and taking a seat next to him. "What happened?"

"Another failed audition," he says, hurt filling his voice. "I made it to the last round, too."

"Oh Bryce. I'm sorry. Did they say why?" I asked.

"No. They never do. That's show business—you get crapped on until you're a big celebrity. Then you crap on others. It's the circle of crap." He extends his arms and lifts the playbill above his head. "And it moves us all."

"Man, I'm really sorry. It's their loss."

"I know. But will I get the next one?" Bryce sighs. "There's only so much rejection a person can take—in my career, my love life ..."

"Well, hey. Who's talking about rejection in your love life?" I say. "Anthony didn't sound dependable. Leaving you and Bobo without notice? Not a stand-up guy."

"It's not just Anthony. It's all of them. They say they love me, then they bolt. I think I've hit my rejection threshold. Maybe I should get one of those account manager jobs. What does an account manager do? Manage accounts? I can do that. I can say words like 'Excel' and 'run it up the flagpole' and 'circle back.'"

I take his playbills, wipe them off, and put them in the plastic baggie on the floor. "We're saving these."

Bryce sighs. "What's the point, Emerson?"

"This is just a setback," I say. "Can I tell you about my day?"

Bryce raises an eyebrow. "You sure know how to read a room, but go ahead."

"I promise I'm not being obtuse." I sit back down next to him. "I had the best class of my career. The students were engaged, asking great questions, having fun—and it was all because of you. Your inane tips actually worked."

"You got lucky. You would've figured it out on your own eventually," Bryce mutters.

"No," I insist. "Without your advice, I'd still be struggling. You turned things around for me. And you can turn things around for you too. All it takes is one audition."

Bryce softens. "What's gotten into you? Cheery, positive Emerson. It's weird."

"Well, this sour Bryce thing you have going on is weird too."

We lock eyes. I smooth a loose lock of hair behind his ear, then pull my hand away as if I've touched a hot stove.

"For the first time since I've been here, I feel the power of the city—the excitement that luck can change in a New York minute."

"God, you're corny. But I'm listening," Bryce says.

"There'll be other stuff. You've got a place to stay for as long as I'm here. Don't give up, because I was about to—and you didn't let me. So, I'm not letting you."

"It wasn't even a good show." He laughs. "It's like getting rejected by an ugly guy you sleep with to improve your confidence." He bites his lip. "Not like I know about that from personal experience." A smirk pulls at his lips.

I'm not here to judge. I'm just happy that he's more himself. The world makes more sense when he's smiling.

It's hot in here, and I pass Bryce's bag to open the window. I spot an envelope with the Met logo peeking out from his bag.

"What's that?" I ask.

"Oh, those are from work," Bryce says. "I get comp tickets from time to time." He shrugs. "But I never go. Only stuffy people go to the opera. You have to dress up."

"Bryce," I say. "You're a fan of the arts!"

"I like Broadway," he clarifies. "Opera's different. It's all in German."

"And French. And well …" I grab the envelope and pull the tickets out. "Italian! This is Puccini's *Turandot*. Even the name is beautiful." I run my fingers through my beard. "It's one of the best—gorgeous music. You'll be transformed."

"You really like opera?"

"Of course. And tonight, we're going."

"I don't know." Bryce hesitates. "If I wanted to get sung at by women with garish costumes and obscene cleavage, I'd just go to the drag show around the corner."

Bryce deserves a night on the town. I doubt any boyfriend has taken him anywhere worthwhile, and he deserves better. "You, me. We're going. Find something nice to wear. Or borrow something of mine."

Bryce narrows his eyes. "Are you asking me on a date, Dr. Grant?"

I freeze. Nerves hit. Is this a date?

"It's … friends cheering each other up," I stammer.

Bryce smiles slightly, if a bit defeated. "I guess … you've twisted my arm."

A mix of relief and disappointment swirl inside my chest, unsure if I've just dodged a bullet or missed a golden opportunity. Either way, I'm determined to make tonight special for Bryce.

FOURTEEN

BRYCE

I STARE at myself in the mirror, adjusting my collar. This is ridiculous. I don't belong at the opera. Not in this get up. Not in that world. I've only ever worn this monkey suit to weddings and funerals. But Emerson insisted. Well, more like asked politely. How could I say no?

Bobo is lying on the floor, staring up at me like he knows I'm about to do something dumb. "What do you think?" I ask, smoothing out the wrinkles in the shirt that's choking me. "Do I look handsome?"

He yawns, his eyes half-closed, and one of his cute little yelps comes out before he rolls over.

I sigh. "Yeah, I don't enjoy dressing up either."

The butterflies in my stomach are doing a full-on chorus line. It's just the opera, right? A fancy show where people spend a lot to dress up and watch people sing in German. Or Italian. French? I need my cheat sheet from selling subscriptions in the basement.

I was planning on giving the tickets to Emerson, anyway. A little thank you for helping with Bobo the other day. I figured he would take a friend. Maybe someone from work. Or a guy if he's seeing someone. The last thing I expected was for him to ask me. But here I am, in a suit, without a bride or dead person in sight.

Then the bathroom door opens, and Emerson steps out.

My breath catches.

Holy shit.

He's wearing a suit I've yet to see him in, dark with a bowtie. He's like something straight out of a black-and-white movie. Almost like a tuxedo, but not quite. Nothing like the khakis and blazer he wears to teach. It's cut perfectly, and the way it fits him, with his biceps stretching the sleeves, makes it clear that all that farm work in his youth continues to yield rewards. Knots tie in my stomach as he walks toward me.

"You look ..."

He grins, his eyes bright. "Is this okay?"

"Okay?" I laugh, though it comes out a little strained. "You look like you're about to break some hearts."

He just shrugs. He clearly doesn't realize how effortlessly handsome he is. "You don't look so bad yourself," he says, giving me a once-over. He smiles, and there goes my stomach doing somersaults again. "Are you ready?"

I look down at myself again, at the stuffy suit that seems more like a costume than anything. "I guess so," I mutter.

I walk to the door, trying to shake off the awkwardness that's been hanging over me like a cloud. Bobo opens an eye as I pass, his eyes full of adoration even when he's half asleep.

"We'll be back soon," I tell him, giving him a pat on the head. "Be a good boy."

THE LOBBY of the Met is even more ostentatious than I imagined. A far cry from the basement, that's for sure. It's so goddamn glamorous it feels like I'm stepping into a movie. Marble floors gleam under the soft golden light of the chandeliers, and everything seems so polished, so perfect. So expensive. I guess this is why they need us to beg for all those donations. There's a huge grand staircase spiraling upward, and walls lined with beautiful paintings I've never seen. People are mingling in tuxedos and gowns, and here I am, just hoping I don't accidentally step on someone's heel or spill anything on my suit.

As long as I've worked here, I've never been in this part of the building. They don't let us peasants out of the dungeon, and even with the offer of free tickets, I've never thought about actually attending. Not until now. This is the world of the rich, of people who have more than thirty-three dollars and forty-two cents in their checking account. Nobody here is sleeping on the sofa of the apartment that their ex sublet from under them. These people know how to move, how to talk. They belong here. I'm an outsider. A fraud. They all probably can tell I don't fit in.

"You okay?" Emerson asks, noticing how I'm staring around at everything, wide-eyed, like a fish out of water.

"Yeah, yeah. Just ..." I shrug. "This place is ... a lot."

He gives me a calm smile. "It's impressive, huh?"

"Yeah," I say, but it comes out more like a question than a statement.

We stand there for a second, taking it all in. I'm clearly out of my depth, but I'm here now, with Emerson, in this ridiculously expensive place, and part of me is excited about what we're about to experience.

The lights in the opera house flicker. Emerson nudges me gently, his voice low, and a little amused. "We should probably take our seats."

After a kind usher helps us, I glance around at the not-so-great view we've got. It's not like we're front and center or anything, but at least we're not in the nosebleeds. The seats were free, and as Emerson's fond of reminding me, free is good. I sink into the plush fabric, trying to acclimate myself to the theater and people surrounding us. I feel underdressed, but Emerson doesn't seem to care. He's clearly in his element here, which is both comforting and a little intimidating.

As the lights finally go down and the orchestra begins tuning, Emerson leans over and whispers, "*Turandot* is one of Puccini's most famous operas."

I turn to him, still trying to adjust to the dimness, and he's watching the stage intently. There's something about his excitement that's contagious, like he's inviting me into this world with him.

"It's Italian. They have these translation screens ..." He points to the small screens in the seats in front of us. "But we don't need them." He presses a button, and the screen fades to black. "It's way more immersive without staring at a screen all night, and you can follow the story without really understanding what they're saying." His eyes twinkle as he speaks. "So, the story ... It revolves around a princess named Turandot. She's impossible to get close to."

"Sounds like most of my boyfriends."

Emerson grips his program, rolling it and tapping the tube with his thumb as he speaks. "Well, she initiates this deadly challenge where suitors must answer three riddles or die."

"Okay, maybe not so much. Although, that could be useful."

"And the main guy, Calaf, comes in and falls for her. He wants to win her heart."

I nod, trying to catch a spark of his enthusiasm. He makes me want to understand, to get it, be a part of this world with him.

He reaches up and adjusts his hearing aid. "There's a setting that pipes the sound right to my hearing aid. Pretty cool, right?"

"Really? That's handy."

"Yeah, one of the few benefits."

The curtain rises, and he shifts his attention to the stage. He's so damn excited, like a kid in a candy store. I try to tap into his passion as I settle in for the performance. The stage is massive. It's way bigger than any Broadway stage I've seen. They could hold the Super Bowl halftime show on this thing. Music fills the air, rich and sweeping, and I find myself leaning forward, caught up in the drama of it all. My eyes stay fixed on the stage as the performers belt out their lines, their voices so powerful and the acoustics so perfect that the sound envelops the entire space. And Emerson was right. Even without understanding Italian, I can sense their emotions and the tension building between the characters. And somehow, sitting here beside him, watching his infectious enjoyment, transforms something I never considered doing into an astounding experience.

By the time the curtain falls for intermission, I'm a little dazed at how much I'm enjoying myself. Am I into opera now? With all the plot twists in my life lately, that was one I didn't see coming. Emerson clicks something on his hearing aid and then nudges me as people start shuffling out of their seats.

"Let's get a drink," he says.

"Oh, I'm not thirsty."

"You got the tickets." He puts a hand on my leg, and a current of electricity shoots up through it and into my spine. "My treat."

"Yeah, sure. Okay."

I stand near the banister, staring out the massive windows. It's like the churning chaos of the city outside doesn't dare pierce these hallowed halls. In here, bathed in culture, the gaudy rich folks are immune to it. I take out my phone and snap a quick selfie for Portia.

Emerson appears, holding two flutes of champagne. When he hands me one, his fingers brush mine, but I try not to read too much into it. Maybe it's the fancy clothes, or the opera, or being on what appears to be a date, but the air between us seems thicker.

As we descend the stairs and approach the glass, the fountain outside serves as a stunning backdrop while Emerson, brimming with excitement, recounts the first act.

"It's just ... incredible, right?" he says, practically glowing with enthusiasm. "Puccini's music is so rich—every note resonates. The emotions are right there in the strings. You can feel everything he intended. It's ... It's ..."

"Magic."

"Exactly. That ..." He motions to the theater. "That's magic."

When the lights flash, we finish our drinks and return to our seats. As the lights dim again and the final act begins, I brace myself for the finale. When the tenor steps forward, and the music swells, my eyes widen. "Nessun Dorma." I've heard this song before.

Before each shift down in the basement, Courtney, our manager, shares little facts and snippets about opera. It's meant to help us sell tickets and secure donations from people, but mostly, we just zone out on our phones. Yet, there was this one time she played an old video from the Grammys. Pavarotti was scheduled to perform but got sick and had to cancel at the last minute. Instead of scrapping the song, the ultimate soul diva icon herself, Aretha Franklin, stepped in. There, in front of all those famous singers, Aretha belted out this operatic piece in Italian. There's a part at the end where the music and her voice soar, and it's fucking transformative. Just like Ms. Celine Dion, who was in the audience, we were all in shock. She received a coveted standing ovation —at the Grammys and in our dingy basement workspace. I may have watched that video a few times at home.

As the tenor's voice rises, something twists inside me. His raw emotion hits me like a train. Everything I've been feeling—being dumped, almost homeless, the opera, the connection with Emerson, the strange vulnerability I'm not used to showing—comes to the surface. My breath catches, and before I know it, I'm crying. Not a few tears, but waterworks. I don't even realize it until Emerson's hand gently wraps around mine, squeezing it in a quiet, understanding way that makes the tears flow even harder.

Grounded by his touch, I grip back. When I glance at him, and his gaze meets mine, we share a silent understanding about the power of what we're experiencing. Thanks, Mr. Puccini.

When the last notes of "Nessun Dorma" fill the space, the entire audience seems to hold its breath, and my chest tightens until the thunderous applause erupts. I clap along with them, taking it all in, unsure how to process what *Turandot* has done to me. I know I'm not the same Bryce Derrickson who walked into the Met a few hours ago. It's like the opera cracked me wide open, and I don't know if I'll be able to put myself back together the same way.

And maybe that's a good thing. Again, grazie, Mr. Puccini.

As the applause simmers down, I turn to Emerson, my heart still racing. I open my mouth to say something intelligent or profound, but nothing comes out. Maybe I can ask him what he thought. But before words leave my lips, he's leaning toward me, his eyes shining with something new. Something I can't quite place.

And then, without warning, he kisses me.

The audience's focus returns to the action on stage while my pulse revs up to a manic pace. Emerson's lips are on mine. And not in a "you're dying so here's mouth-to-mouth" way. This is most definitely a kiss. He's a gentleman; there's no tongue, but he's wrapped his fingers around the back of my head, holding me in place, and I'm more than happy to stay right here in these less-than-perfect seats and let this perfect moment last forever.

I lean into him, letting the kiss deepen, the warmth of it spreading from my mouth through my entire body. Feeling brazen, I slip him my tongue, and he releases the faintest moan. Yeah, kissing Emerson in the Met might be my new favorite thing to do. It's like we've been transported into our own little world where everything falls away, and it's just the two of us—and the three thousand eight hundred patrons in the packed house.

When he finally pulls back, my mind races with what to say, a massive smile plastered on my face.

"I guess opera really is ... magical," I whisper.

Emerson grins, his fingers still laced with mine. "It really is."

FIFTEEN

EMERSON

I STRUM my fingers against the side of my leg the entire cab ride home. Bryce and I make small talk about the show as the sights and sounds of New York whizz by our windows. I love watching the neighborhoods change. From the poshness of the west side to the bustle of midtown to the grittiness south of 30th Street, New York is a city with many different moods.

The same could be said for the energy between Bryce and me. We've crossed into a new neighborhood. One where my tongue enters his mouth.

Usually, I'm good at keeping my feelings in check. As a Midwesterner, my childhood comprised being told to always keep a smile on my face and that boys never cry, which molded me into a tank when it came to emotions. But seeing Bryce break down at the opera, his entire body a shaking pillar of vulnerability ... it drew me toward him. The parts of him that are most dissimilar to me are the qualities I cherish most.

Bryce may just be the Xs to my Os.

Unless he felt forced to kiss me back or risk being thrown out on the street. Crap, I should've asked first. The power of Puccini compelled me. Did I cross a line? He and Bobo have nowhere to go. I'd never want to put him in a precarious position.

I turn to him, an awkward smile stamped on my lips, no idea what to say.

I'm sorry.

But I'm really not.

I want to kiss you again.

Everywhere on his body.

I strum my fingers harder against my leg, out of view from Bryce. I came to New York to rehabilitate my career, and I can't lose focus.

I turn to him again, unsure what to say to his sweet face. I'm seconds away from saying "How 'bout them Yankees?" when the cab mercifully pulls up to our building.

We walk up the stoop. Each step jolts my pulse a little higher.

I try not to stare at Bryce's juicy butt, but like Mona Lisa's smile, it follows me wherever I look.

Bryce checks the mailbox. The vestibule is a tight fit for two grown men. I keep some space between us—afraid of what I'll do if we start touching.

"Great show," I say, officially out of things to talk about that don't include kissing and rubbing up against each other.

"Yeah, it was." Bryce hands me an envelope, some bill or piece of junk mail I quickly cram into my jacket pocket.

"Listen," Bryce says, his adorable forehead crinkling. "I'm sorry about that weird outburst at the opera."

"Don't be sorry."

"I usually don't let music get to me unless it's performed by one Miss Carly Rae. I guess this weaseled its way in somehow. So just ignore it. I didn't mean to make anything weird."

"It wasn't. You didn't." I'm very adamant about this. The more Bryce tries to back away, the more I'm compelled to cross the imaginary line between us. "You didn't make it weird." I think about rubbing his arm but decide against it. "I made it weird by kissing you. That was highly inappropriate."

Our bodies are suddenly very close in the tight vestibule, as if pulled together by a gravitational force. We're practically touching, vibrating.

Bryce studies my face, a knowing smile on his lips. What the hell is he looking for? What the hell does he know?

"You know what else is totally inappropriate?" Bryce says.

"What?"

"That I want to keep doing it."

He licks his lips, and that is all the green light I need. I push him up against the mailboxes and plant a ferocious kiss on him. All the sweetness and emotion from the opera house replaced with lust and wanting. I had an appetizer, and now I want the main course. I'm ready to feast.

Bryce moans against my lips as his tongue presses into mine. Our tongues wrestle in the space between our mouths. His hot breath sets my body ablaze.

He gasps into my ear as my hands traverse his body. Neither one of us is small, but with a good five inches on him, he's like a little teddy bear in my grip. A teddy bear I want to devour.

"We should do this upstairs," I say, pulling away, barely catching my breath, not knowing how much I truly wanted him until now.

"You're right. Our neighbors don't need a free show."

I pull open the door to the stairwell. "After you."

Bryce goes first as my heart rages in my ears. We are six stories away from continuing this, six stories from me getting my hands all over him, from tasting him again.

My desire compounds as Bryce walks up the stairs, his plump ass right in my face, but I hold myself back. I'm throbbing in my pants.

I'm a nice boy, and we're waiting until we get to our apartment. Yes, we are. I'm keeping everything in check.

When we get to the landing of the first floor, we make eye contact like two predators in the wild. That's all we need. Bryce pushes me against the wall next to Mrs. Van Houten's door, and we go at it again, tongues wrestling like our mouths are trying out for WWE. I run my hands through his hair—his beautiful, silky hair—letting them graze down the light, very light, stubble of his cheek.

"Bryce." Someone says behind me. "Fuck you, Bryce!"

"Who was that?" I pull back.

"Bryce," someone squawks again from behind the opposite door.

"Is that a parrot?"

Bryce sighs. "That's just Camilla. Horton's bird." He points to the door behind us. "She can sense when I'm around."

He grabs my hand and pulls me up. "We should keep moving before her owner comes to the door."

We move to the next landing, pausing for another kiss. Bryce smells like pineapple from the lip balm he plastered on in the cab. I never knew making out with a piña colada could be so tasty.

"I could do this all day." Bryce runs his fingers through my beard, scratching under my chin like I'm Bobo. And it feels ... nice. My tail is definitely wagging for him. He nuzzles into my facial hair as his fingers dance on my neck.

"Yes. You feel so good," I whisper.

I let my greedy hands filter over his chest and his stomach. He's thick, but you can't be a dancer and not have muscle. Under his curves, the firmness, the ripples of his biceps and pecs, tantalize my fingertips.

Bryce lifts his leg up to my arm in an impressive show of flexibility.

"Baby, you're gonna be so happy you had sex with a dancer."
He arches an eyebrow.

I hold up his leg, letting my hand graze down his thigh, getting so close to an area I really want to venture to. Once we make it up to the sixth floor.

Bryce pulls back.

"We ... we have four more floors."

"That's right," I say.

"We shouldn't be doing this here."

"Obviously," I say. "Very inappropriate to our neighbors. I haven't met most of them, but this is not the first impression I want to be making."

"Exactly."

"Well, let's keep walking. Actually, I'm walking first," I tell him. I can't be distracted by his ass again. God knows what I'll do.

This time, I go first up the next flight of stairs. My dick pokes against my suit pants, making it hard to balance. I can barely walk. All my blood is rushing to one core area. Just as I feel myself cooling down, two gutsy hands grab my ass cheeks when I approach the third-floor landing.

"What the ...?"

"My hand slipped," Bryce says behind me.

"Both of them?"

"Whoops." He squeezes my ass again. Hard.

I let out a low moan and lose my balance. I don't make it to the third floor. I fall onto the steps. When I spin around, a stair digs into my back, and Bryce is on top of me.

He laughs as he kisses me, his hot breath tingling on my tongue. I laugh back, my heart feeling especially full. I love the way his sturdy frame feels on top of me, and I pull him closer.

We make out like crazy, starting up just where we were. Hands all over each other, hands traveling and exploring each other, tongues zipping in and out.

I unbutton his shirt and reach inside, eagerly feeling his curves and muscles. I rub my beard across the skin peeking out from his dress shirt, and he moans into my ear.

Bryce's fingers fumble down to my belt. My pulse quickens, matching the rhythm of my throbbing cock.

"Wait," I say with a desperate gasp.

"Right," Bryce replies, his hair askew and skin flush. "We can't do this in the stairwell. It's not appropriate. We don't want to destroy our camaraderie with our neighbors."

"No, we ... we only have a few more flights to go."

Damn. Why did I sublet a six-story walk-up? Of course, I did not foresee this issue happening.

"Just so you know, we are totally going to fuck like jackrabbits the second we're inside the apartment." Bryce gives my bottom lip a nibble.

I sit up and kiss his lips, now red from all the attention ... or maybe my beard. He kisses me back, and god, I could keep doing this all night long. But not here.

I manage to stand up, even though I feel like a goddamn tripod right now.

"Do not grab my ass," I tell him with the utmost seriousness.

He holds up one hand and puts the other one over an imaginary bible.

"I won't. I promise."

"So help you, god?"

"So help me, Carly Rae."

I climb the stairs faster. I'm not good with this kind of cardio, but Bryce doesn't huff and puff. I need to reserve my strength for the apartment.

I spin around. Bryce has both his hands up.

"I'm not touching you!" he says.

Damn, how I wish he was.

I make it up to the fourth floor. But god, just the thought of having Bryce in this stairwell gets me so wild, I can barely focus on moving my feet.

Right before the fifth floor, I stop. Bryce bumps into me.

"Why'd you stop?"

I turn around, pull him into a kiss. We fall backward onto the staircase again, another stair hitting me in that exact same part of my back. But it's all worth it. The pain is worth the pleasure.

His shirt still unbuttoned, I smooth my hand inside, over his chest again. I grab at his pec. *Mine.*

"Emerson," he whispers my name, hungry and desperate.

I pull his bare belly against me, needing to feel his weight.

"Don't make too much noise," I say.

Bryce nods, then whispers, "We're near Marsh and Data's apartment. I don't think they'd mind." He continues his fancy work on my belt, undoing it, reaching inside my pants, and grabbing at my aching cock. I arch my back in exuberant relief, wanting more, knowing that this isn't the place to do it. But I can't stop, won't stop.

Bryce stares directly at me as he strokes my cock. I could blow like a volcano right now, but I hold myself back using the small reserves of willpower I have left.

I throw my head back, hitting the flat, hard carpet. I rut my hips in the air, pumping into his fist.

"God. Fuck yes," I practically whine, because I can sense what Bryce is planning. I can see the wheels turning in his head.

He lowers his head to my crotch. I should stop this. This is improper. This is communal space. All sense and sensibility flies out the window as he pulls my raging boner from my boxers, and it disappears into his mouth.

Jesus. We're only three seconds in, but it's already the best blow job of my life. Not that I've had many, but still. Top ranking. Number one. Holy ... crap ... what is he doing with his tongue? My body crackles with life, every pore and every vein blistering with energy. I look down and watch his pretty mouth take my cock, his tongue creating some kind of magic on my engorged head.

I loosen my tie and unbutton my shirt. Fuck it. Let's add to the chaos. Bryce raises a hand to feel my furry stomach. Our neighbors' apartments are footsteps away, but I need this more than I need to be a good neighbor.

God, I feel like I'm gonna blow right now, but I can't. I have to hold it in. The temperature gets hotter and hotter. Heat rises, they say. They've never meant it as much as they meant it now.

Bryce releases my cock from his mouth with a startled pop. Saliva drips from his chin, tethering his lips to my dick before he wipes it away with the back of his palm.

"Come on," he says. "Almost there."

We run up the last flight of stairs laughing like teenagers. Bryce's face is so damn beautiful when he laughs, so full of joy. I'm holding up my pants because I didn't want to waste time buttoning them. My cock throbs with need. My chest is scorched with heat. If the kiss at the opera was an appetizer, then what just happened is like smelling the food from the kitchen and still not getting to dig in.

And Bryce's ass is swishing in front of me on the stairs, only taunting me more. He looks over his shoulder and snorts a laugh.

"You look like such a fucking mess."

I'm sure I do, with my hair sticking up and pants and shirt undone. But I'm *his* mess.

Just before we turn the corner to our floor, I push Bryce against the wall, and I stroke him over his pants.

"I can't wait to fuck you," Bryce says. It's not a question, it's not a demand—it's just a statement of fact.

I agree, even though I'm so close to blowing right now. I have to hold back. I need to feel Bryce around me. His lips. His hole. Both clenched around me, begging, begging for more.

"We're almost there," I say. I trip over my damn pants on the final stairs. Bryce topples with me. He laughs into my mouth as he kisses me.

I don't want to break this up because I don't want this to go away. I just want this. I want to disobey all the laws of physics and transport us to the bedroom right now, together.

Bryce gets back on his knees, takes me in his mouth. This time, he's not trying to be quiet with his sucking sounds. The slurping echoes in the stairwell.

I fist his hair as I pull him down on me. He looks up at me with hungry eyes, a smirk on his lips as they're stretched around me.

"Get up here," I say in a low growl.

Bryce climbs on top of me, and we kiss. My lips are swollen, my mouth is dry, but I don't want to stop. I slip a hand down the backside of his pants and let it trace his crack. I push his pants down so I can grab more of his bare ass. I pull his cheeks apart, wishing my fingers were elastic and could stretch down to his hole.

"What if we have sex right here?" I ask, completely wrapped up in this moment.

"Without lube? Honey, no. But I love the enthusiasm." He nibbles at my ear. "A few more steps. We can do it."

Our door is in sight.

We scramble up the last steps. Bryce's hands shake with the keys, but finally—after the longest few seconds of my life—he manages to unlock the door, and we're inside.

His pants fall to the ground, as do mine, and we shuffle to the bedroom, trousers around our ankles.

"Bobo! Off the bed!" we both scream in unison. Bobo leaps onto the floor, and Bryce lovingly nudges him toward the living room.

"I'm sorry, buddy. I'll give you all the pets and treats in a little bit." He pats him on the head and closes the bedroom door.

As soon as the door clicks shut, we're on each other again. His taste on my tongue sends rocket boosters shooting through me. We collapse on the bed together, making out, pantless, our cocks rubbing against each other, yearning for more friction.

I try to take off my blazer while on top of him, really testing my shoulder flexibility.

"Leave it on," Bryce says. "It's sexy."

My hairy chest mashes against his smooth one as the tip of my cock tingles with the heat of his.

"Did you clear out my nightstand drawer?" Bryce asks.

I shake my head no. I don't use nightstand drawers, so I never thought to clear it out.

Bryce reaches over and pulls out a bottle of lube and a garishly large box of condoms. There's got to be over forty in the box. "Hop fucking to it."

He throws his legs over his head in another impressive display of flexibility. He's half steel and half putty. And he's all mine. At least for tonight. It's not like I'm looking for something serious, and judging by the giant box of rubbers in Bryce's possession, neither is he.

Even without a ton of experience, instinct takes over as I coat his hole with lube, slipping one and then two fingers inside him. His body tenses to my touch until he takes a deep breath, allowing me to slide in and out more easily.

"Fuck, Em," he moans as his cock leaks precum on his stomach. "Let's get that farm-boy cock of yours inside me."

Sometimes, sex requires a lot of foreplay, and other times two guys just want to, well ... hop fucking to it.

"Rail me, Emerson." He holds his cock up. "I need you inside me."

Has anything sexier ever been said? I fucking melt.

I roll on the condom and coat myself generously with lube. I lean over him, balancing on my elbows. Bryce tangles his fingers around my tie and pulls me close. I thrust into his tight hole as we kiss, and it's goddamn everything.

He gasps and pants against my lips as I fuck him, deep, forceful humps into his eager hole. I'm sweating extra hard thanks to the six flights of stairs and my heavy blazer. Our slick chests glide together. He pulls harder on my tie, until my face is within reach, and his fingers tangle in my beard.

I push his legs closer to his face, making him spread wider for me. And then, as one of my derelict former students once said of Berlioz's affair with his mistress Marie Recio, I take him to pound town.

I rest my forehead against his as I fuck him hard and deep. The bed squeaks for dear life under us, creaking like an out of tune piano. The headboard bangs with such force I swear it's going to destroy the drywall. I cradle Bryce's beautiful face, soft and perfect in the midst of all this dirty sexual chaos.

I don't know what I want to say to him. I don't know what we are to each other. I've never felt a connection this strongly to another man. Before the terror of that realization paralyzes me, my orgasm rushes from my balls, and I kiss him while emptying myself inside his clenched hole.

With my cock still hard, I fuck him with my last ounces of strength, and he jerks himself off. When his ass trembles with pleasure, he gasps, whimpering as he shoots his load. I stare down at him in awe as the first blast hits his chin. The next actually goes further, covering his cheek and barely missing his eye. He laughs, and I plunge deeper as the last burst coats his stomach.

A guttural groan flies out of him as his legs fall to the bed. "If I knew professors could fuck like that, I would've gone to college."

I collapse next to him, my body sinking into the softness of the bed, still warm from the heat of what we just did. The room is quiet, save for the faint rustling of the sheets and the soft hum of the city outside. Bryce's heart beats steadily against the side of my body, a comforting rhythm that grounds me in a way I didn't expect.

It's strange, how everything seems clearer now that we've fucked like ...

"What did you say we were going to fuck like?" I whisper into his damp ear.

"Mmmh? Oh. Jackrabbits." He snuggles into me, holding me tight.

"Yeah. Jackrabbits. Did we?"

"Oh, hell yeah. Those jackrabbits have nothing on us." He kisses my shoulder.

I close my eyes, letting myself drift in the softness of the moment, the steady beat of his heart lulling me into a peaceful calm. Whatever comes next, I know we'll face it together. And for the first time in a long while, I'm not worried.

SIXTEEN

BRYCE

I WAKE to the soft hum of the city outside. The blend of traffic, an occasional honk, and a distant siren—sharp and quick—intertwine in a steady, almost comforting rhythm. It's the city's heartbeat, and a smile tugs at my lips. And then my grin widens at the warmth beside me, pulling me back from the edge of sleep. Emerson. His thick bicep draped around me, our limbs tangled under the sheets, his chest pressed against my back along with ... Hello, morning wood! He's grinding softly into me, but his breathing informs me he's still asleep. I ought to stay put and cherish this time with him, yet something feels off.

This moment is perfect. Except ... aren't these moments always perfect? In the early morning light, I start to think back on all the morning-afters I've had in my adult life, all the times the guy held me in his arms and kissed my neck and made me feel safe. And how eventually, they always leave.

It feels different with Emerson, but didn't it feel different with Anthony and all the others? Everything goes fuzzy in my head.

I shift slowly, doing my best not to disturb him. His body relaxes a little more as I ease myself out of his embrace, careful not to jostle him awake. He shifts again and makes the cutest little grunt, yet doesn't wake. I guess all the activities last night really wore him out. Studying his handsome face, his peacefulness tightens my chest. I don't want to go, but I can't stay. I'm on an Emerson tightrope, trying not to fall flat on my face.

Bobo lies curled up in the corner of the room. He must've opened the door in the middle of the night. Or maybe Emerson got up and let him in. It's past his breakfast time, so he's awake. I catch his eye, and he stares at me with a judgmental look. I shrug and mouth, "What?" while I reach for my underwear on the floor next to the bed. His gaze doesn't move, but he releases a giant Bobo sigh.

When I exit the bedroom, he follows, and I quietly shut the door.

"Let's get you some breakfast and go on a nice walk."

While he eats, I use the bathroom and get dressed. As soon as Bobo begins licking his empty bowl, I put on his harness, and we head out.

The Bigby's door clicks shut behind me, and the cool morning air hits my face. The streets of New York City are already buzzing, people rushing to places. But not me. I'm ... avoiding. Again.

I text Portia from the stoop, and Bobo and I head off, hoping to get lost in the city. The remarkable thing about New York is that you can be surrounded by millions of people yet feel completely alone. On the streets, nobody knows me. If anyone's paying attention, it's only because of my giant adorable dog, and right now, I'm happy for him to steal the spotlight.

Bobo trots beside me as we make our way down the street. He's practically a walking reminder of my poor life choices. In what universe did I think I was ready to own a dog? Let alone one the size of a pony. I can barely take care of myself. He may have been an impulse purchase, but he's the best one I've ever made.

Bobo is the only thing that calms me down when the world spins too fast.

When we approach the French bakery a few blocks away, Portia's already seated outside. She's wearing a large floppy hat and giant sunglasses as she sips her latte. Another coffee sits on the round table across from her, along with a plate of pastries. A smile crosses my lips as I near her, pleased that my friend was willing to get out of bed so early to meet me without any explanation.

She takes one look at me and raises an eyebrow. "You look like you just snuck out of a lover's bed."

"And you look like ... a million bucks." I'm impressed at how glamorous Portia looks at all times. It's a power of the super-rich.

"Thank you." She raises her cup. "Now, why are you slithering away from Emerson?"

I open my mouth to object, but she's already shaking her head. "Don't even try it. I know that look. You hooked up last night, and now you've ditched him."

"What? How do you know that?" I look over my shoulder, then under the table. "Are you a witch? Do you possess some kind of British clairvoyance?"

"The power of Maggie Smith compels you." She cocks an eyebrow at me. "You said you were going to the opera with Hot Prof last night. I had a feeling you two would shag after something as romantic as that. Yet you asked me to meet you for a last-minute brunch, which tells me you've gone and ditched him."

Portia's powers of deduction would leave Sherlock Holmes shaken. I rub my temples. A headache is creeping in. "I didn't ditch him."

"You totally ditched him."

"Did not."

"Ditch, please." She giggles, her tongue peeking out between her teeth. "If you were a character in *Wicked*, you'd be the Wicked Ditch of the West."

Her comment makes me think of how Emerson resembles a stockier Jonathan Bailey, and I get a little funny in the tummy.

"If you were an animated film, you'd be Lilo and Ditch."

"Are you finished?"

"One more." She glances toward the sky for a beat. "If you were a scrappy movie about an all-girls acapella group, you'd be Ditch Perfect." She nods. "Okay, now I'm done. What do you think, Bobo?"

Bobo barks. Tattle tale.

I rest my head on the table and groan. "Can they serve me a bottomless mimosa in a trough?"

Her smirk of victory subsides into one of concern. "What happened, darling? Was he bad in the sack?"

"No. Last night was incredible." I think of being tangled in his arms, and a flood of warmth spreads across my chest.

"Then where is he? Or better yet, why aren't you back in bed canoodling, basking in the afterglow?"

"He's still sleeping. I didn't want to wake him."

Portia draws down her sunglasses and glances at me, her eyes widening as her brows lift. I'm surprised her face remains so agile with all the preventive Botox.

"I'm assuming you left him a note explaining where you are? Or you're planning to go right back and be there when he wakes up?" She lifts the plate of cardamom buns between us. "Maybe he'd enjoy one of these buns ... after feasting on yours last night?"

I pull my lips in as my stomach churns. I'm too upset to even eat a cardamom bun. And that's saying something—because if there's one thing that can heal my soul, it's carbs. "I ... I just—"

"Went full drama mode?"

I shake my head no.

"Did you two discover that you're actually related?"

"I didn't ditch him. I got out of bed early. He was still sleeping. Bobo needed a walk. I decided to meet you for brunch."

"Bryce." She puts her hand over mine, stopping me from fiddling with my fork. "Love, it's too early for brunch." She lowers her sunglasses for a moment. "This is clearly breakfast. Now tell me, what's going on? You have this great guy sleeping in your bed mere hours after having incredible sex, and yet you're here not eating cardamom buns with me. Now, I love hanging out with you, and I'm content to spend breakfast people-watching and talking shit about Whitney as we're wont to do, but surely you'd rather be back in your bed getting spooned by the Hot Prof, who by all accounts is a pretty fantastic guy."

I sigh, then nod, slumping in my chair while Bobo hopes for crumbs. "It's just ... Emerson is ... different. He's not Anthony. Or Logan. Bruce. Derek. Fernando. Something feels ..."

"Special."

"But maybe it isn't. Maybe the pattern will repeat."

"Oh please," Portia interrupts, folding her arms across her chest. "Do you hear yourself? From what you've told me, this guy is sweet, smart, and—most importantly—employed. You're running away from the one person who might actually not break your heart, because you're scared of it happening again. You're like Bridget Jones without the cleavage."

I scowl at her. "Yeah, well, my parents were a walking romance novel cliché. Until they flipped the script to *War of the Roses.*"

Portia's eyes soften for a second before her usual smirk takes over. "Bryce, sweetie. You're an adult. At some point, you have to take responsibility for your life. Stop using your parents' dumpster fire of a relationship as an excuse to screw up your own happiness." She pauses, then adds, "Unless you're really just in it for the drama. In that case, carry on."

I open my mouth, but the words don't come out. Instead, I stare down at Bobo, who's now sitting next to Portia, wagging his tail in her direction as if he's joined her in judging me.

"Don't look at me like that," I mutter at him. "You're not helping."

Portia lets out a sharp laugh. "Look, you need to stop sabotaging yourself before you lose someone worth having. From what you've told me, Emerson's a good guy. And you know it."

I drag a hand through my hair. "I know. But what if he changes his mind? Decides I'm not worth it? Finds someone better. Moves on. Like Anthony. And everyone else."

She gives me a pointed look, but I'm already shaking my head. "I can't do it. I can't walk back into that apartment and face him like nothing happened."

Portia sighs, clearly frustrated. "You need to get over yourself. You're not a lost cause, honey. But you'll become one if you keep sprinting away from anything that makes you feel something real."

I give her a dry smile. "Is that your expert therapy advice? Go back and kiss him?"

She shrugs, not backing down. "Kiss. Puckerball. Donkey Kong. The Flying Dutchman. Whatever you boys do." She waves her hand in the air then wipes a bit of sugar from her lips. "I'm just saying, Bobo looks like he's ready to go home to his new hunky roommate." She leans down to pet his head in her usual cool, mechanical manner. Two pats. No petting. "What does Emerson think about the beast?"

"I think he's falling for him."

"Wait, Emerson for the dog, or the other way around?"

"Both."

"So, the kind, handsome, nerdy professor who's built like a tank—your words, not mine—who didn't kick you out even though he had every right to, also loves your enormous slobbery dog?"

"Yeah. Pretty much."

She throws her hands up. "Well, if you can't figure this out, you clearly don't know your head from your arse." She folds her napkin and places it on the empty plate. "I've got to get to Pilates. This body isn't going to remain banging on its own."

I stand when she does, and she pulls the brim of her hat back and gives my cheek a soft kiss.

"Walk your dog and then go home, Bryce." She pulls her glasses down again. "Take it from me. A hard man is good to find."

"Don't you mean ..."

"You heard me."

Bobo tugs at his leash, eager to get moving. I glance back at Portia, my mind racing. Even with all her absurdity, she's right. I've been avoiding all the hard stuff, and now it's all piling up like a Tetris game on steroids.

"I love you, Portia." I give her another kiss for good measure.

"Of course you do, darling." She adjusts her hat, making sure the angle is just right. "I'm the peaches to your cream."

I snort as she sashays away.

Turning my attention to Bobo, I say, "Okay, boy, let's take a stroll."

Before I turn to head toward the park, without stopping, Portia spins around and gives me a wave. She's so effortlessly glamorous. Tension builds in my shoulders as Bobo and I walk away. Maybe she's right. Maybe I need to stop running.

But for now, I'll let Bobo take the lead—because, honestly, he's way better at this whole "not overthinking everything" thing than I am.

We spend the rest of the morning wandering the city. The streets feel lonelier than usual, but the weight of it all still hangs in the back of my mind.

As a boy, I never witnessed a healthy relationship. Mom worked long shifts at the bakery and dreamed of being a dental hygienist, but her dreams faded along with her energy after they divorced. At seven, I faced instability, bouncing between two homes where my parents struggled to co-parent. My father was never warm or affectionate and seemed to know I was different before I did, yet he never accepted it. I clung to my mother, a woman whose hard work crushed her dreams. Lacking a healthy model of love, I fell for the wrong men over and over. Men who never really valued me beyond what I could offer on the surface.

I never connected my childhood to my poor life choices—how could I without knowing love, care, or acceptance? What is it about Emerson that has me putting the picture together? I'm lost in a concrete jungle, searching for a sanctuary I've never had the chance to call home.

I do that strange thing where I'm moving, paying attention to the traffic, crossing signals, and watching Bobo, but I'm unaware of where we're going. When I spot the Bigby, my stomach does a back handspring. Bobo pulls toward our front door, but I keep walking. "Come on, boy. Let's see if Luigi has made the meatballs yet."

By early afternoon, I'm sitting on a bench in Central Park with Bobo's head on my feet. His belly is full from the two meatballs Luigi brought out to us, and all I have is an ache in my chest—a gnawing feeling I can't shake. I know I'll have to face Emerson sooner or later.

I'm just not ready yet.

"Come on, Bobo." He stares at me with his tongue hanging out. "We deserve a little treat. How about ice cream?"

He tugs on the leash, and I pick up my pace to keep up with him. I may not have the answers to life's most difficult questions, but I can buy us a big scoop of ice cream, which is almost as good.

SEVENTEEN

EMERSON

IT IS A BEAUTIFUL DAY OUTSIDE, yet I am in my apartment. Working. Trying to work.

I stare at my computer screen, trying to make headway on my research paper. It comes in fits and starts. I'll get some work done, and then my mind will inevitably wander to Bryce.

He got out of bed early this morning and took Bobo for a walk, and I thought they'd be back in a little bit, but now it's early afternoon, and he still hasn't returned.

A part of me is worried that something could have happened to him. But in terms of Occam's razor, it's more likely that he's just ... out. It's a beautiful day and maybe he and Bobo are just enjoying the sunshine.

I turn back to my computer screen and keep typing away. I get a few sentences down, and my mind tries to wander, but like Bobo's leash, I yank it back.

Last night was incredible for many reasons. For one, the opera was unparalleled. I've listened to classical music and operas my entire life, but to see a production like that at the Met? I'm not sure anything could top it. Except being there with Bryce. Getting to experience it with him was magical. As was everything that happened on the walk up to our apartment and in bed—where I could still smell him on the sheets when I woke up.

I don't really have much experience with guys. I had a boyfriend for a short time in college, but that was almost twenty years ago. After graduation, he got a job overseas teaching English. I decided to focus on my work and building my career. Romance and relationships are just too murky for me. They're not worth the risk of getting hurt.

But last night, it was like a door opened that had been locked for the longest time. I didn't realize I could feel this way about another person. And that they could feel this way about me.

Or so I thought.

I look to the floor. Only there's no Bobo staring back at me.

I thought we had a good night. I mean, judging by Bryce's moaning, screaming, erection, and subsequent ejaculation, it seemed like he had a good time as well.

Not to mention us falling asleep together, him cuddled in my arms. Nuzzled against my neck.

I realize it's the first time I actually slept with someone—actually slept—in years and years. I woke up this morning filled with hope and excitement, experiencing emotions I hadn't allowed myself to embrace in a long time.

And yet it's early afternoon, and Bryce and Bobo still aren't back. And I have an important paper that I can't focus on.

I take a break to scroll on social media, and what do I find? A pic of him with a lady friend at breakfast.

So he left me in bed to meet up with a friend for coffee? I'm far from an expert on sexual mores, but I thought it was standard to at least acknowledge the person you slept with before leaving the apartment. I've never been snuck out on before, and it's a gut punch.

My heart sinks.

"Why didn't he want to have brunch with me?" I ask the ghost of Bobo at my feet, wishing he was here for a reaction. Or breakfast in bed? Or just spend the whole day in bed with me?

I've never been one of those people who wants to spend the day in bed. Hell, I'd rather get a jump on the day. But Bryce—he could make me switch up that pattern. He's the first person I could actually see myself doing that with and actually enjoying it. Someone to be lazy with.

But he chose brunch instead of me.

I get up from my desk and pace.

"Focus." I eye my computer screen. I've never been someone to talk to myself aloud, but I can't take the quiet and emptiness in the apartment. "You're finally on an upswing with your class. You're going to this picnic today, and you'll continue to wow your colleagues. That tenure-track professorship is within reach. You can finally claim your place in academia. Don't let a cute boy distract you."

I should go outside and get some fresh air. But then I worry—what if I bump into him on the street? What if he's flirting with another guy already? Or still at brunch and talking about that weird hard of hearing guy who's in his apartment?

He wouldn't. Would he? He doesn't seem like a guy who would do that.

But how well do I know him?

When it comes to eighteenth-century composers, I'm an expert. With twenty-first-century gay guys, I'm a total neophyte.

I go to the couch and lie down, close my eyes, and try to calm myself. I turn on the television to a sitcom to ease the noise in my head. The bad punchlines and laugh track help me forget about the outside world until I hear footsteps.

And the shaking of Bobo's collar.

"Hey," Bryce says, charging in with his usual energy. Nothing seems changed in his voice, as if nothing of note happened over the past twenty-four hours. "It's gorgeous out. We really lucked out with this weather."

He gives Bobo some pets, and Bobo comes over to me and immediately starts licking my hand. Then he jumps on the sofa and rests on my legs, essentially holding me in place.

Bryce looks at my computer and the papers scattered about. "Oh, you've been working on your paper? I was never good at papers. Or writing. I think that's why I'm a dancer—I just have to be moving at all times."

No statement has ever sounded truer. He's flitting around right now—buzzing to the kitchen, filling up Bobo's water dish, getting himself a drink, wiping the two feet of counter, and tidying up. I nearly get whiplash watching him.

"It looks beautiful out. I've been plugging away before going to that faculty picnic event in Central Park," I say with forced cheer. It seems we're both dancing right now.

"Oh, did you still want to bring Bobo?"

"That's okay. I don't have to."

Bryce was the one who said that people love dogs, and there's no dog more lovable than Bobo, so it could help score me more points.

"He's already been out today," I say.

"Bobo loves fresh air. He doesn't want to be cooped up in here, do you, boy?"

Bobo lifts his head, perks his ears up, as if just the whisper of going outside again gets him excited.

"Yeah, Bobo is all for it. He's gonna charm the argyle socks off all your coworkers," Bryce says. "They're gonna be like, 'Oh my god, we have to give this guy a tenure-track position. Not only is he a great lecturer and an intriguing mind, but he has a very cute dog.'"

"You're the one with the cute dog," I say.

Bobo isn't mine. This apartment isn't mine. In fact, this life isn't mine. It's all temporary. This morning is a good reminder of that.

Bobo looks at me as if he's sensing the ability to go outside is in my court, and, as we've already established, it's very hard to say no to Bobo. "Okay. He can come."

"It'll be good. Everyone will adore him." Bryce waters plants on the fire escape, something he did yesterday evening. "And don't worry about chasing him around. He's usually very good. He can be kind of shy around new people, so he'll be by your side. He won't run off."

Bryce crams himself into the kitchen and begins emptying the dishwasher. The kitchen is narrow enough that pushing the dishwasher door down essentially bars me from entering. As if his emotional distance wasn't enough.

"I need to get better at unloading the dishwasher!" he says with a laugh that ticks me off.

"Did you have a good walk this morning?" I ask, thinking about how just a few hours ago, we were tangled naked together, and now, besides both being fully clothed, there's even more layers building between us.

"Oh, it was great, yeah. I mean, Bobo—since we didn't get a long walk in last night—was really itching to go, so I wanted to get out there."

"And then you stayed out. I saw that you went to brunch with your friend."

"A gay guy meeting his hag for brunch is par for the course in New York. Are you checking up on me?" Bryce asks with a nervous laugh, meeting my eyes only for a beat.

"No, I was just scrolling through social media, and I saw the post. As one does."

"I forgot you added me on Instagram." Bryce wipes a coffee mug dry. "Yeah, Portia and I have a standing date for brunch, so it was already planned. So, you know, I didn't want to stand her up because she got something waxed and had to tell me all about it. You know how it is, right?"

Last night, we were intimate and kissing and saying all these sweet things to each other, and now we feel more like strangers than we did when we first met. Of course, maybe I'm reading everything wrong. I can do that. But I feel like I'm in one of those dreams where I reach out for someone and no matter how far my arm stretches, they keep fading away.

"Look, I think there's something that we need to address." I stand on the edge of the kitchen. I started off confident with "look," but nerves quickly take over my brain. When you're direct with someone, you risk them being direct right back. "Last night ... things happened. We're roommates, and things happened. And typically, that seems like something that two people would discuss or acknowledge, seeing as it is an extraordinary situation. And so, I'm acknowledging it."

I pause, wondering if anything I'm saying is making sense, but it's one of those things where I've already started talking, and so I can't stop until I reach my point. One of the downsides of being a long-winded professor.

"Seeing as this did happen," I continue, "it seems proper protocol that we acknowledge that it happened and think about the repercussions of our actions."

What I really want to say is: *Did you have a good time last night? Do you want to do it again as badly as I want to do it again?* But judging by the way Bryce has been keeping his distance so far, I think I have my answer.

"I get it. I know this is a common occurrence for you," I say.

Bryce pulls his head back. "A common occurrence?"

"You know, you've had an assortment of men, from what I've gathered. I—"

"Are you calling me what I think you're calling me?"

"No, no. But, you know, if I may state the obvious: when we

first met, you thought I was an anonymous stranger coming over from a hookup app. So, just putting that out as a fact, you know? It seems like you have a lot more experience with this than I do. You've kind of been through this a lot more, so I definitely get that this is just another fun experience you had."

Bryce is a very smiley person. There's always a grin on his face, even when he's mad. It's like he's *playing* mad. But this is the first time when I actually see his face curdle, where there's no trace of joy on it. It all escapes like air from a flat tire.

"Oh," Bryce says, taking a painfully long beat. "Yeah. Right. I've hooked up with plenty of guys before. And that's what we did last night." He closes the dishwasher door with more force than necessary. "We hooked up," he says with a sour tone. "Excuse me."

He scoots past me into the living room, wiping his damp hands on his shirt.

"We don't need to talk about it again," Bryce continues. "We got caught up in the opera and the staircase, and that was that. Obviously, you're only here, what, a few more weeks? And I'm busy with auditions and finding a new apartment. So, I just have a lot going on. You have a lot going on. Together, we have a lot going on. So much going on. So let's not add more goings-on to all the things that we have going on."

I think I follow most of this train of logic. Whatever it is, it seems like we're both going in the same direction—that we want this conversation to end as quickly as possible.

"Good," I say. "Last night was great, and we can be adults about this and still cohabitate in the same apartment in a room-mate capacity."

"Just because I've seen you naked doesn't mean I can't take out the trash."

"Exactly." I adjust my glasses. "And just because I've seen you naked doesn't mean that I can't load the dishwasher."

"Right. We're adults," Bryce says, his face flat. I'm talking with a zombified roommate. His joyous smile shows no signs of returning.

"Adults," I repeat.

And then we stand there in awkward silence.

Even though we've come to a mutual decision, I'm very unhappy about it. But I can't let Bryce know that.

I catch my reflection in the mirror. If he really wanted to be with me, he would have stayed in bed this morning. Right? He would have canceled his brunch date. He would have come back as soon as he walked Bobo, and we could have stayed in bed together all day—if that's what he wanted. And as much as I want to tell him that, as much as I want to just pull him close and kiss him, it's better not to make things more awkward than they already are.

"Okay," Bryce says. "I'm gonna ... I'm gonna shower because I didn't shower last night, and I feel gross. So I'm going to walk past you, go into the bathroom, and use the shower."

"That's perfect," I say. "Because I have showered, so I'm all good. And then I have to leave for my picnic ..." I check my watch, the numbers all mushing together. "Right now, actually, so I can get there in time. And I will take Bobo."

Bobo leaps off the couch, eagerly going to the door, completely oblivious to what happened between the two people trying to act like adults. Or ... does he know more than he's letting on?

"Emerson," Bryce says behind me.

I stop, hand on the door.

"Despite what you think, I haven't been with a lot of guys," he says. "What we did last night isn't a typical thing for me."

"Oh," I stammer out.

"I just ... I'm not the slut you think I am."

"No, I don't think—"

"You do," he says cutting me off, his jaw tight with actual

anger. "You do. Or did. And that's ... I wanted to set the record straight. But anyway, have a great time at your picnic."

Before I can object, before my heart can sink even further, Bryce closes the bathroom door and turns on the shower.

"I wasn't calling him a slut, Bobo," I say as we go down the steps.

But even Bobo has a hard time looking at me.

EIGHTEEN

BRYCE

WE STAND OUTSIDE another run-down apartment building, and I squint at an ad in the paper that's supposed to sell what's inside, but I'm pretty sure it's only mocking me. "Charming One-Bedroom for Rent." Maybe, if you're a rat.

"Bryce, this one's got potential," Marsh says, his eyes wide like he just found a unicorn.

He's wearing a red Fire Island T-shirt that's a little too snug, but it looks cute on him.

I look up at the building like I'm trying to figure out where the monsters emerge from. "Potential for what? A horror movie?"

Marsh and Data had offered to take me apartment hunting after I told them Anthony kicked me out. I'm finally taking them up on their offer now that Emerson and I are on shaky ground. Speaking of shaky ground, was this current offering built atop an ancient gateway to hell?

"Bryce," Data chimes in, pointing at the paper in my hand. "It has granite countertops. That's a win."

"You know I don't cook. Unless you count ramen noodles."

"Well, look here." Data points to another part of the listing. "The building has a gym. We don't have that at the Bigby."

"No, we have six flights of stairs. That's more than enough for me." I cross my arms, cringing from a disturbing rumble in my stomach that I'm pretty sure isn't hunger. "You know, if you two really want me to have a new place to live, I could just move in with you. You both love Bobo, and he adores you. And we're quiet. Clean. Respectful. I'll have no gentleman callers over." I hold my hand up. "Scout's honor."

Marsh stares at me with a raised eyebrow. "You're saying you'd rather cram into our tiny one-bedroom apartment than stay with Emerson?"

Emerson's name slams into my brain like a truck.

"I mean, it's not my apartment anymore. I need to vacate the premises."

Data takes the paper from me, folds it neatly, and tucks it into his back pocket. "Would this have anything to do with the, um ... noises we heard last night?"

Oops. I forgot the bedroom in my ... our ... Emerson's apartment is right above theirs. They've joked about hearing Anthony and me.

"I don't know what you heard," I say, blinking quickly. "Maybe Bobo was running around. He gets antsy sometimes in the middle of the night."

"No, he doesn't." Data cocks an eyebrow. "What we heard was fornication."

"I'm truly impressed your bed didn't break." Marsh wiggles his eyebrows, and my face flashes with heat. I'm fairly certain I resemble a hothouse tomato.

My lips part, and I smile in that way where only my teeth are showing. "Guilty."

"Good for you!" Data slaps my back. "He's tall. Broad. Those blazers. He's ..."

"Hot," Marsh says. "Smoking hot. Nice job, Derrickson."

They both nod their approval, and there goes my stomach churning again.

"The thing is, I woke up and kind of freaked out, so I took Bobo for a walk and didn't come home until the afternoon. I think Emerson and I had a fight. Well, our version of a fight. And now it's super awkward, and I just want to move out. But …"

"You have nowhere to go, no money, and a dog the size of a pony," Data says.

"Exactly."

"Here's how I see it," Marsh says, leaning against the building like he's auditioning for an action movie. "You don't need to leave."

"Yes, I do. After what we did last night and how I left and what he said to me. I can't stay."

Marsh places a hand on my shoulder. "Bryce. You don't have any other options. Just try being friends with him. Rewind to pre-sexytimes. Go back to being roommates."

"How can we be cordial, let alone friends, after hooking up?"

"We're gay men. It's our superpower."

Marsh has a point. When your friend pool is the same as your dating pool, you learn to adapt to awkward situations like these. But this time with Emerson feels different. It was hot, physical sex, but I can't call it a hookup.

"You need to talk to him." Data's next to me now, the two of them huddling around me with support. "Maybe you can apologize for bolting this morning."

"And being a dick by not coming back until the afternoon," Marsh adds.

I toss what they're saying around in my head. Maybe they're right. Maybe we can chat. Rewind before last night. Try to go back to the friendly roommate situation.

"I don't know if I have the emotional bandwidth to be friends with Emerson right now. Not after ... what you heard. It's just easier to pack all my stuff up and move."

"Okay, let's keep looking," Data says. "Something will turn up."

Data continues walking down the street. I'm about to follow when Marsh's big hand pulls me back, and we walk a little slower.

"Look, I say this as someone with direct experience, don't let this distance grow." Marsh peers at me with genuine emotion, something I'm not used to seeing in him. There's no windup, no punchline. "You'd be shocked to see how easily people can grow apart if you let it happen."

"Is that what happened with you and Data?" They may be hashtag couple goals now, but when I first met them, they were separated. Some big fight. Back then, Data lived under his own cloud of sadness, missing Marsh, knowing he needed to move on but not knowing how.

"You and Emerson obviously have some kind of connection. Maybe it's love. Maybe it's lust. Maybe it's somewhere in between. But if you let him drift away, you may not be able to get him back."

"We're not all lucky enough to get snowed in with our ex-boyfriends during an epic blizzard and patch things up with boxes of Mallomars."

"Who knows? With the way climate change is going, maybe you will be. But you can't count on it." He flashes me his comforting smile. "When we were split up, I missed Data like crazy. I wish I hadn't been stupid enough to let him go the first time."

"Emerson and I aren't a couple. We're not in ..." I don't have the guts to admit we're not in love, because I don't know yet if I'd be lying to myself. I don't want to speak that energy into the universe. "I appreciate your concern, Marsh."

Data pivots around. "Come on, slowpokes! What's taking so long?"

"Nothing. I just like walking slowly so I can blatantly check you out is all," Marsh says. "That reminds me, where are we going to eat after this?" He jogs up to his husband and gives him a loud slap on the ass.

After another two blocks, we reach the next apartment. Surprise, surprise: it's too small, smells like onions, and the landlord's idea of "pet-friendly" is only rats and roaches are allowed.

Marsh checks his phone. "Okay, well, at least there's good pizza nearby. I'm texting Preeti. Her apartment is right around the corner." He thumbs out a text while talking. "Let's go there and lick our wounds. You might have seen your roommate naked, but we can drown your sorrows in extra cheese. Maybe that will help you forget about Emerson."

"Emerson's not the problem," I mutter, knowing I'm lying.

"Of course not," Marsh says sarcastically. "It's totally not about the hot professor who makes you act like a teenager who can't stop getting hard in class. That's not the problem at all."

We head to Ferrazoli's, which has the best pizza in New York City. They even have a neon sign in the window letting you know. I've been coming here since I moved to the city, and it's always predictably awesome. If we were searching for the perfect pizza instead of the perfect apartment, we'd have hit the jackpot.

Just as we take our seats at our regular table near the back, Preeti arrives. She's got this aura of perpetual movement—like a tornado in heels.

"Over here," Marsh shouts.

Preeti joins us, smiling and giving hugs all around.

"Did you cut your hair?" I ask. It's at least a few inches shorter.

"I'm in my Velma Kelly era. Glad somebody noticed." She taps the bottom of her bob with her palm and gives Marsh some side-eye.

"What? I totally noticed," Marsh says.

"Marshall Goldberg ..." Preeti sits next to Data. "I love you more than lesbians love a U-Haul after a first date, but no you didn't. I've seen you three times since I got it chopped, and you've yet to say a word." She focuses her attention on me. "But thank you, Bryce, for noticing. It's much easier to manage and has the bonus effect of attracting even more ladies."

"So pretty," I say, winking at her. "It really frames your face."

"You, my friend"—she boops my nose with her index finger—"are a doll. I told this clueless one to text me the next time you were with him."

"You did?" I ask, trying not to look too surprised.

"I did." Preeti winks at me as Data heads over to grab a pizza for us. "I'm working on something super secret. Super exciting. Super gay." She shakes her shoulders, and her chest jiggles like a bowl of jelly. "A new sketch comedy pilot. *Queer in the Headlights*. Think SNL meets Trixie and Katya. But gayer."

"Gayer than two drag queens talking about other drag queens?" Marsh asks.

"Gayer." She raises her eyebrows, and gosh, between her and Marsh, I could be entertained enough to forget about my problems for a few hours.

"Anyway, we want to have some dancers. Mostly for between sketches, but also maybe *in* some of them. There will obviously be musical numbers. Think Fly Girls, but ..."

"Gayer," Marsh and I say together.

"Now you're getting it." She nods, and a massive grin forms on her face. "So what do you think?"

"It sounds amazing," I say. "I can't wait to see it."

"No, silly." Preeti slaps my arm harder than I expected. "About being a part of it. I want you to choreograph and dance in it."

"But don't you want ..." I pause, fumbling for the right words. "Twinks?"

"Baby, baby, baby." She takes my hand gently, and my chest settles at the warmth of her touch. "No," she says simply but with conviction. "We want our troupe to actually mirror the diversity found in the queer community. We want you."

I blink. Once. Twice. The ground shifts slightly under my feet.

"Oh. Wow. Okay." My voice comes out thinner than I expect, like the words haven't quite caught up with the realization.

We want you.

It doesn't sound like charity. It doesn't sound like pity. It sounds like truth. Like someone looking at me and seeing something worthy. My chest swells as my mind races to keep up—what this could mean. A steady job. Real money. The ability to move out. A chance to be part of something, not just orbiting the edges, waiting for someone to notice me.

Marsh is practically vibrating with joy, grinning like this is the greatest idea since sliced bread and crop tops. He definitely knew.

And under all the adrenaline and surprise, there's this quieter thing stirring in my chest—relief. I didn't realize how much I wanted an opportunity like this.

I laugh, but it comes out shaky. I hold up my hands in mock surrender, hoping it covers how much my heart is thudding against my ribs. "Okay," I say, nodding. "I'll do it."

Preeti winks. "Amaze-balls. I'll text you the details. It's going to be fantastic."

She gives me the biggest, warmest bear hug, and I'm momentarily lost in her jasmine perfume. When she pulls back, she says, "Full transparency, there will also be twinks."

"I figured," I say. "And hoped. I have nothing against twinks. Just want them to share the spotlight a little."

"Amen to that," Marsh says.

"Amen to what?" Data returns with a tray of pizza, and we each grab paper plates and napkins from the table.

"Twinks and big boys coexisting peacefully."

"I fully support that message." Data holds his slice up, and we all toast, tapping the tips of our own.

I may not have a new apartment just yet. I might still be squatting on the sofa in a perpetual state of awkwardness around Emerson. But at least I have pizza with extra cheese, and friends to remind me that even amid the stormy chaos, the sun still waits behind the clouds. For now, that keeps my spirit afloat.

NINETEEN

EMERSON

BOBO SEEMS a little tired from his earlier walk with Bryce, so I treat us to a cab ride up to Central Park for the faculty party. I lie and tell the driver he's my service dog, then point to my hearing aid. Not my finest moment, but we can't be saints all the time.

Bobo sticks his head out the window and takes in the rush of wind. I wish I had his unabashed joy rather than the neurotic voice playing on a loop in my head.

Central Park is packed with throngs of people biking, jogging, talking, laughing, being. Everyone seems on some kind of mission. I still can't get over how many people are here; I never realized how quiet Indiana was. The buzz of the city is real. There's always something going on, even just in a park on a patch of land.

Bobo navigates us through the crowd until we have space, then I take the lead. I walk us down a path until we come to a big fountain. On the patch of grass, a tent is set up and my coworkers are mingling.

I march up to my colleagues and adjust my hearing aid to accommodate the number of people and outside space. They greet me, but right away Bobo is the special attraction. A few of the TAs squat down to pet him, rubbing his fur vigorously and talking baby talk to him. For his part, Bobo laps up the attention. He falls to the grass and rolls around on his back, proud to be an attention whore.

"Oh, he is such a cute dog," Will says.

Sheena rubs his belly, her fingernails adding an extra kick. Bobo's tongue sticks out in ecstasy, trying to lick someone's face—anyone's face—as he lolls on the ground.

"Will, he looks like you in that photo you showed us from your visit to San Francisco. He's even wearing a collar, too," Sheena says. Will's cheeks flame red. I give him a quick nod, letting him know his puppy play kink is none of my business. Though this is an unexpected side from my buttoned-up TA.

"You never told us you have a dog," Will says, desperately trying to change the subject.

"He's not mine." I push my glasses up and give a half-smile. "He's my roommate's."

The word *roommate* feels so weird in my mouth, maybe because the taste of Bryce is still on my tongue.

Will rubs behind Bobo's ear, who flops back on the ground. This dog really knows how to put on a show. More people gather around, and Bobo can't get enough. They give him pets and treats. I'm not sure if there's a doggie heaven, but if there is, this has got to be what happens there.

I feel bad for the other dogs that people brought—some small designer dogs in purses that aren't as big of a hit. There's something about a big dog that is just so warm and lovable. They're meant to be hugged because they're almost human-sized.

"I can't believe this big guy lives in a small apartment," Will says.

"Me neither," I laugh. "He barely fits, but we make do."

Again, I think of Bryce.

Someone grabs a tennis ball and throws it across the grass. It snaps Bobo from his attention coma. He jumps over Will's lap to retrieve the ball. Bobo and I wind up doing a few rounds of catch, which helps me stay calm. I'm less nervous about talking to my colleagues. They congratulate me for what they've heard have been some good lectures over the past couple of weeks.

Another reason why I keep thinking about Bryce.

Sheena wraps her arm around my shoulders. "You know," she says, "folks have been watching you, Emerson. And I've heard nothing but fantastic reports."

"Even from my first day?"

"Nobody's watching the first few days. Everyone needs a week or so to find their sea legs." She knocks her hip against my thigh. "You have to apply for the tenured position now. You still want it, right?"

I glance down at my friend and blink.

"Emerson, this is what you've been dreaming about. A full-time tenured position. In New York City. With me. Don't you want to stay?"

Stay. Here.

My fingers get lost in my beard as I glance around at the staff. The park. Bobo drooling as he returns the ball to Will, who's now squatting.

"I do," I say.

"Good. Well, the interview process is going to start soon." She guides me to a long folding table with refreshments and grabs us both a glass of white wine. "Don't be nervous. Just be yourself."

Myself. A few weeks ago, that would've sent me into a spiral. But now, with how Bryce has helped me ...

"I'm excited," I say.

My free hand rubs over my phone in my pocket. I'm itching to text Bryce and tell him the good news. Why is he the first person I think about? I can't help imagining the big smile on his face, some snarky comment coming out of his mouth, a strong desire to celebrate even though nothing's happened yet with the position. His energy is infectious, and I never want antibodies to form.

The afternoon flies by, and I appreciate the fun times because it keeps me from thinking about who's waiting when I get back to the apartment.

Bobo is sad to go, and he whimpers a little as we leave. He's really playing it up, trying to look behind him at the guests with their unlimited pets and treats.

"Oh, come on. You know how to milk it, I'll give you that," I say as we walk away. "You have dinner waiting at home."

We make our way through the park, meandering down the paths until, oddly, we come across a quiet area.

"Bryce is going to get such a kick out of hearing about our day." I laugh to myself as I go through the highlight reel. "He was totally right about you being a draw. I can't wait to tell him how cute you were. How you were playing into everyone's hands and filling up on treats. Ah, that's our Bobo."

I stop walking.

"*His* Bobo. Because you're not my Bobo. We aren't your parents, Bobo. Well, Bryce is, but I'm not." I start walking again, but then stop a few steps later. "Not that I don't want to be your parent. It would be ... nice." Bobo stares up at me, his giant brown saucers trying to make sense of what I'm saying. "The three of us, going for walks together. Bryce and I cuddling in bed talking about your silly antics."

In spite of how bananas that sounds, I smile. Of course, if Bryce heard all that, he'd run away screaming. Metaphorically, since he can't find a place of his own.

"You're dangerous, Bobo. You get me talking."

We stop at a hotdog cart, and I buy myself a pretzel. It's warm and has that crisp, slightly burnt bread smell with a hit of salt. I pick off a corner and throw it to Bobo, then toss a piece into my mouth. There's truly nothing like a New York pretzel.

He gawks at me for another piece.

"You had so many snacks at the picnic! I barely ate anything. I was too busy schmoozing. I'm famished."

He whimpers and stares at me as if he hasn't eaten in a week.

"Fine." I toss him another piece. "But you're not getting the soft center. That's my favorite part."

I sit on a bench and hold onto his leash, yet he nudges me back toward the hotdog cart. He's insistent, and being a big dog, there's only so much I can resist.

"What? You want a Diet Snapple?"

He drags us past the cart, though, to a lamppost. A poster is taped on both sides of it. It's of a male dancer's body in silhouette. Too slim to be who we're thinking of but close enough.

"Look, Bryce and I, we had a great time, and ... that was it. You saw how he was when he came home this afternoon. He could barely look at me. I think he was embarrassed. You know, we both crossed the line. We got wrapped up in something. So I was giving him a way out. I was giving us both a way out."

Bobo looks at me, and I swear he cocks his head as if he thinks I'm spewing BS.

"It's true. And it doesn't matter. I came here to get my career back on track, and I'm doing just that. I'm up for this amazing position. They want me to come in and interview. That's where my attention needs to be."

Bobo looks up at the picture again.

"I know the reason I even have a shot at the job is because of the serious headway in my lectures thanks to Bryce. You don't have to rub it in."

Bryce knew how to help me make my teaching ... better. For as little as we have in common, he seems to really have insight into my life.

I pull us back to the bench. I'm the human here. I should be the one in control. "We are not talking about Bryce anymore."

I take a big bite of my pretzel. I offer a piece to Bobo, but he declines. He keeps staring up at me with those big eyes that are like two gumballs injected with truth serum.

"I know. I screwed things up. God, I ... I wasn't calling him a slut. I know he's not, and that was the wrong word choice. I know that."

I wash down my pretzel with some orange pop.

"Bryce just has experience I don't have, and there's a reason for that."

I look down at my hands, trying to shake this feeling that I really messed up. Bobo rubs his nose against my hand.

I stare at all the lovely people gallivanting past us, all with their full, busy lives to get to. It reminds me of how quiet my world can be, how I can be in the most populated city on Earth, a place with so many people that a park can feel claustrophobic yet still evoke a sense of loneliness.

"I haven't been close to a lot of people in my life. You wouldn't get it, Bobo. You're a dog. You've always been a dog. You fit in that box to a T. Whereas I ... I never fit into any box I was supposed to. I was a kid in a small town who wanted to listen to and talk about classical music instead of the NFL. I wanted to stare at boys, not girls. I was a mystery nobody wanted to acknowledge, let alone solve." I turn the soft center of the pretzel around in my hands, grains of salt sprinkling to the sidewalk. "The last person I was truly close with was my sister, and look how that ended."

Her face lights up my brain. As I've gotten older, I've realized I'm one of those people not meant to have a large social circle. I don't make friends easily. Finding real friends has been a struggle all my life, while others can do it without thinking. The people who I manage to connect with, I want to hold close. They're rare gems. That's what makes my sister's loss feel like a sinkhole inside of me that won't close. I feel myself finding that connection with

Bryce, but my body can't bear another chasm if things didn't work out with us.

"I have to focus." This time, I'm the one staring at Bobo. "The fact is, I'm going to lose him no matter what because this *thing* is temporary. And surely, I can't stay in this apartment, even if I do get the job."

I stare at the soft, warm center of the pretzel. It's a golden brown versus the dark brown of the outside.

"It's time I get Bryce out of my head." If that's even possible.

I offer the rest of the pretzel to Bobo, and he gobbles it up as I stand.

Maybe the city has answers for me.

"You know," I say, "Even if Bryce and I stop talking, I'm still going to find a way to talk to you."

Bobo trots along, finding a pathway to the street.

Maybe, despite everything, I've found myself caring about my loopy, zany, very hyperactive—really, really hyperactive—roommate.

It's strange how someone can drive you up the wall one minute and make you laugh until your cheeks hurt the next, but that's exactly what he's done to me.

Bryce is a rare gem.

He's my rare gem.

And I called him a slut.

I wasn't calling Bryce out. I was pushing him away.

Bobo tugs on the leash, wanting to go home, and yet I can't move. I'm frozen with realization and shame.

"Bobo, I messed up." He turns around and cocks his head. "I messed up bad."

For a second, I think Bobo is going to respond with something profound, but then he trots to a tree and lifts his leg.

This isn't the end for me and Bryce, though. A flicker of hope sparks in my chest. Like a Carly Rae Jepsen song, this is merely the bridge that will lead to an explosive, emotion-packed final chorus.

"I need to show Bryce how I feel. And I think I have the perfect idea. Let's go, Bobo!" We walk briskly through the park, Bobo pulling on his leash.

Bryce isn't the only man in apartment 6A who has a flair for the dramatic.

TWENTY

BRYCE

IT'S BEEN a week since the night at the opera. A week since Emerson and I, well, tore into each other like ravenous wolves. The unspoken weight of it hangs in the apartment, lingering for days like the time Marsh cooked fish at his place. Emerson and I have found this odd rhythm of cohabitating where we don't talk about that night. Actually, we don't talk about much or even look at each other for more than a fleeting moment. Like maybe if we keep pretending it didn't happen, it'll magically resolve itself. So far, it's working. Sort of. Or at least it hasn't combusted into a dramatic scene. Yet.

Sneaking out on Emerson the morning after was not my finest moment. Okay, I was an immature baby. With time to reflect (and lectures from Portia, Data, and Marsh) I'm starting to unpack why I did it. If I could afford therapy, it probably would've happened a lot faster. But on my starving artist's income, the advice of friends will have to suffice.

My self-diagnosis: Every time I let my guard down with a man, he bolts. Starting with my father, who emotionally abandoned me the minute I showed the smallest sign of being a homo. Don't all six-year-olds recreate the entire choreo from Britney's "Stronger" video (including the iconic chair-ography) in their bedrooms and then ask their folks to watch in the living room? Apparently not.

Every boyfriend I've had has up and left. Some, like Anthony, stuck around longer than others, but I'm always the one being bid adieu. "Goodbye, Bryce," has become the ending I expect.

Something about Emerson, that night out, drinking champagne, watching the opera, the kiss, the trip up the stairs, the way we became unhinged with each other, the way his eyes gleamed with excitement the entire night ... it all made the evening electric. But what's truly unique? It's the way he listens, really listens, as if every word I say matters. He makes me feel seen and understood in a way I've never felt before. That night, amid the opera's grandeur, it just felt different. Transcendent even.

And frankly, it scares the shit out of me. Make that *scared*. Past tense. In the last week, with all the quiet around the apartment, I've done a lot of thinking. I've realized relationships are kind of like learning new choreo. It feels scary as fuck at first, every new step, twist, turn, dip. Wondering if my body can keep up with my brain and if my brain can remember the timing and moves. But, with a little hard work and sweat, I always nail it in the end. But that first run through—it's a leap of faith.

Emerson deserves the same chance. And so do I.

I stroll past the bodega on the corner at the end of the block and pause to admire the fresh flowers on display. The vibrant colors seem to brighten up the street, and the sweet fragrance lingers in the air. They're way too expensive, but I can't help stopping to take in their beauty, their delicate petals, and I imagine someone buying them for a loved one. Someday I'll be able to afford little luxuries like flowers—or double-ply toilet paper.

I've spent most of the last week rehearsing for the comedy pilot with Preeti. Honestly, I'm having the best time—dancing with a small troupe of talented, diverse dancers. Preeti was right, all shapes and sizes are represented. And yes, there's a twink. It's in the Queer Manifesto: There must always be at least one twink. And Ricardo is the twinkiest twink to ever twink. But he's a sweetheart, so I forgive him for his god-given supercharged metabolism. But most importantly, we're all getting paid.

Could this be my big shot? To dance out from the background and into the spotlight? To create something? Yeah, I want this. I want it bad.

Kind of like Emerson.

It's been killing me, not talking to him about it. He'd have some pragmatic insight about why this thing with Preeti is a good idea, but mostly he'd be smiling with that big goofy grin, his soft beard adjusting with his face as he cheers me on. Since the moment he barged into my, well, *his* apartment, he's been supportive. Even when he could have forced me out on the street, he didn't. He even let Bobo sleep with him when the thunder scared him. Emerson is a good man.

Hold up. Wait a minute.

And then the final slap of reflection hits me.

Emerson. Is. A. Good. Man.

I'm so accustomed to dealing with awful men that when a good one comes along, I don't even recognize it. My mind has become so wired to expect disappointment, I don't know how to appreciate someone who actually treats me well. Crap, I've royally fucked things up with him. I just hope it's not too late.

The sun sets behind the taller buildings in the distance as I enter the Bigby and climb the stairs. There's definitely a few butterflies in my stomach, knowing I'm about to see Emerson, but the ball is in my court. With a deep breath, I open the apartment's front door, expecting the usual—Emerson, Bobo, and a general sense of avoidance.

But ... no Emerson. No Bobo. The apartment is eerily quiet. Maybe he took Bobo for a walk? That would make sense. He's been taking him more frequently lately. Regardless of the tension between the humans in the apartment, those two have fallen into a total bromance.

I walk back to the front door and scope out the hook where Bobo's leash typically hangs. It's gone, but there's a small piece of folded paper with my name on it in its place. A note.

I pick it up, my brow furrowing. My heart skips a little, but I'm mostly confused.

Wash your face.

Um, rude. But also, after a full day of dance rehearsal, I probably should shower. But the note specifically said only to wash my face. Hmm. I head to the bathroom, splash water on my face, and when I grab the bar of soap on the vanity, I spot another note right next to the soap dish. Is this a game? Those butterflies in my stomach are now dancing. My hands are wet, so I quickly dry them and grab the note.

Put on something nice.

Something nice? A grin appears on my face. What is he up to? It's been a long day, and I'm not sure if Emerson is pulling some weird prank on me, but I'll play along. The only thing I own that would be classified as nice is the suit I wore to the opera. But with the adrenaline flowing through me, and wanting to figure out this mystery, I'm not putting a whole damn ass suit on. The jacket will have to suffice.

I rummage through my closet until I find it near the back. It was stashed there after the opera like evidence I didn't want coming back to haunt me. I put the jacket on over my sweaty shirt and shorts. It's ... a choice, but he's seen me in worse.

As I check myself in the mirror, I notice something poking out of the front pocket. I don't own a pocket square, and it's not fabric ... another note. My lips curl into a massive smile as I pull it out.

Grab the wine coolers in the fridge.

Okay, this is too cute. But where the heck is he? I head to the kitchen, and for all that's good and mighty, I'm skipping. Emerson has literally put a skip in my step. When I open the fridge, right in the front of the top shelf, there's a four-pack of mixed berry wine coolers with ... another note attached. I grab the drinks and read the note.

Your presence is requested at a private party on the roof.

My heartbeat skips in time with my feet as I turn and head for the hallway. The roof access is separate from the main stairs, so I go around the corner to the entry and climb the steep incline. Each step is a little tease about what's waiting for me. The night air grows cooler as I ascend, refreshing against the warmth brewing under this silly suit jacket. The faint sounds of the city below are muffled but alive. With each step, the excitement swells. I haven't been up here since last summer when the building hosted a potluck. I push the door open at the top, and the city unfolds against the backdrop of the setting sun.

It's beautiful. But then my stomach flips, and my mouth drops open.

What has he done?

Fairy lights are strung up around the entire perimeter, soft and twinkling. There's a small table set up with dinner for two. There are plates of pasta with meatballs, and then I spot the bag on the ground—Luigi's. There are flowers on the table. He bought me flowers from the bodega. A small laugh escapes my mouth, and my heart thumps loudly in my chest. And then I catch sight of Bobo. He's sitting next to the table, wearing a bow tie.

Bobo. Wearing a bow tie. My heart melts like butter on warm toast.

This is ... honestly, it's too much.

I stare for a second too long, just trying to take it all in when Emerson steps out from behind a wall, looking like a snack. No, make that a whole buffet, wearing the same fancy suit he wore to the opera.

"Didn't get the memo about dressing up, huh?" Emerson says.

He wiggles his eyebrows, and I chuckle. Between those brown eyes and that beard, he's so next-level handsome, even when he's being goofy.

I glance down at my outfit—a blazer over dance gear—and snort. "Give me a break. I was rushing to find out where the notes led."

"You should know better. This is a date, Bryce Derrickson. A *date* date." A little smug grin appears on his face, and I'm tempted to throw him on the filthy ground and take another ride.

I can't help but smile. "So, this is what? A rooftop rendezvous with Bobo as the third wheel?"

"Well, he's becoming my emotional support dog, so ..." Emerson shrugs, like this whole thing is perfectly typical.

I glance at the table again, the warm glow of the lights, and then back at him. "You really went all out, huh?"

"Yeah, well," he says, his voice quieter now, more serious. "I want to talk. No—we need to talk."

I sense the shift. The air between us changes, and for the first time in days, I'm not just wondering how this situation will play out. I'm ready to explain myself. Apologize. Lay it all on the table. Next to the flowers and Italian food. It's time. The tension that's been looming over us has finally come to a head.

I take a breath, steadying myself. Emerson's right. We need to talk. About everything. What happened ... and what's next. Plus, my dog is wearing a bow tie.

"Where did you get the bow tie?"

"Come, sit. I'll explain everything."

Emerson pulls out a chair, and I walk over and take my seat. Warmth spreads through me as our eyes meet. I'm ready for this. For him. For us.

TWENTY-ONE

EMERSON

"SO TALK." Bryce stares at me from across the table. He's not even touching his meatballs. His arms are crossed. Bobo looks at him, then me, then at the delicious food on the table not being eaten. I don't know who's being tortured more.

In his defense, I've suddenly gone speechless. I've been wanting to talk with him and clear the air all week, and now that it's finally here, I have stage fright. Bryce Derrickson, a professional performer, has little patience for stage fright.

"Come on, Sister Mary Ignatius," he says. "Explain it all for me. We've barely spoken at all this week. You've been like a ghost." Bryce is trying to be stoic, but I can see emotion breaking behind his eyes. He still wants me. Us.

I take a deep breath and stare at my uneaten food.

"I lost someone very close to me when I was younger, and I'm not the type of person who gets close to people. So when I lose someone I care about, it hits hard. Really hard."

"Your sister?" Bryce asks, his voice softer now.

"Yeah." I pause, the weight of the loss pressing down on me like quicksand. "We were driving home from a movie. Melanie had gotten her license a few months prior. She'd promised me a Friday night out—just the two of us. I was itching to see *Armageddon*, and even though she had zero interest, she took me. That's the kind of big sister she was." My head dips, and I stare at the table, fingers lost in my whiskers. "The other car came out of nowhere." I close my eyes and swallow hard. "I lost her and my hearing, too. It's ... hard to explain, but it all happened in the blink of an eye. The doctor said a piece of glass from the windshield punctured my ear drum. We're in the car singing and laughing one second, and the next, my entire world was upended."

Bryce's gaze softens. "Oh, Em. I'm sorry."

"I promised myself I wouldn't get close to anyone again, to avoid feeling that kind of pain. But then ... I met you."

"And you're afraid I'm going to die?" Bryce asks, the vulnerability in his voice catching me off guard.

I shrug, feeling exposed. "New York's a dangerous place."

"You're worried about me." His lips twitch, a small, understanding smile forming. "That's sweet."

"I thought it was best that I kept my distance at first. But not being around you hurt even more. I thought I could just end what happened, have it be a one-time thing, but that was ultimately more painful. You slept twenty feet away from me, and yet I missed you, Bryce Derrickson." The feeling of not having him in my life crawls up my chest again, the phantom pain seizing me. "I don't want to live in an apartment knowing that the person who I deeply care for is right there and I can't hold him." I swallow hard and blink up at his handsome face. "You. I'm talking about you."

"Yeah, I got that."

I smile, taking another deep inhale. "I don't want to live in a *world* knowing that the person that I deeply care for is just out there walking around, living his life, talking to other people, and that I'm not one of them."

"It's like missing out on a role you were meant for," Bryce says, a familiar thought scrunching his eyebrows. "Sure, the other dancer may do a good job, but every time you watch them on stage, you think *I should be up there."*

"Exactly. I tried to chalk up our dalliance to a one-time, emotion-free occurrence, but I failed miserably because, Bryce Derrickson, I still like you."

"You don't have to keep using my full name."

"I like your full name." I reach out for his hand and rub my thumb over his knuckles. "My feelings for you may have eventually lessened over time, but I know they would never fully go away. Kind of like herpes."

"That is a horrible example. Truly terrible." Bryce rubs my thumb back, his eyes sparkling across the table. "It's a good thing you're cute."

"I don't have much experience with relationships. I'm not even good with people in general, so the fact you've gotten this far with me—I think it's a feather in your cap. I thought I could just have us go our separate ways, but I don't see that being possible. So I want to show you that I care about you ... hence all this." I motion to the table and lights. "You have a beautiful face and terrible taste in music, and I'm definitely falling for you, Bryce Derrickson."

I hold up my wine cooler, and we cheers. With a satisfied smile, I take a bite of my meatball, knowing I've gotten that off my chest.

"Okay, your turn," I say, my mouth full of Luigi's phenomenal food.

"Oh. Okay. Wait ... what?" Bryce scratches his head.

"I just divulged my feelings and explained what happened. I think you should explain, too."

"Explain what?" Bryce huffs.

"Why you ditched me in bed a few hours after we copulated like jackhammers."

"Jackrabbits. And I didn't ditch you. I went to brunch."

"I know brunch is very important to gay men, but sex is also very important to gay men, so I'm a bit confused. Also, I know that's horse shit."

"I have an iron deficiency. I needed the eggs."

I cross my arms, not entirely convinced myself, but also somehow finding all of Bryce's excuses very endearing.

"Okay, fine. I was scared," Bryce says. "I liked you, too. But I'm not good with relationships. Or I thought I was, but guys tend to leave me. Always. They leave. I'm just ... this transitory place."

My heart rips.

"I think it could be something," he continues. "And then boom, they're gone. And I thought that was gonna happen with you, and I got scared. Because I really liked you, too. Like. Still do. A lot. Like a lot, a lot. I like you more than all the other guys combined. You are a good man, Emerson. I do not date good men. I do not have sex with good men." Bryce's eyes go wide, like he's even shocked he's saying all this.

"So I got scared, too. We both got scared. We're even. Our scaredness cancels each other out when you think about it."

I shove another piece of meatball in my mouth. "So you like me?"

"Yes."

"And you want to be with me?"

"Once you learn how to make appropriate metaphors and chew with your mouth closed, yes."

"Okay, it's settled." I twirl some pasta on my fork.

"Wait!" Bryce bolts up from his chair. "This should be a big, dramatic moment! Emerson, we just told each other that we *like* each other. It's a little too early in our relationship to be so nonchalant. This is big!"

He steps toward me and holds out his hand.

"What are you doing?" I ask.

"This is an important moment. I have someone who cares

about me, who is a good person. A *good* person likes me. That does not happen to me. Ever. I mean, not until now. We need to celebrate."

"I mean, I'm assuming we'll have sex again."

"Right now"—Bryce doesn't move away, and I put down my fork—"we need to dance. Dancing is for celebration."

"You've seen me dance."

"I've seen you pretend to dance."

Bryce takes out his phone and pulls up a song. A familiar clapping beat comes on. I've heard it many times come from his side of the apartment.

"Carly Rae?" I ask.

"'Cut to the Feeling,'" Bryce confirms. "Ooh, I trained you well."

Bryce extends his hand further and makes me get up from the table. We walk under the string of lights, the Manhattan skyline all around us—tall buildings stretching to the sky, filled with a million people with hopes and dreams and heartbreaks and love.

A million dreams are happening in the city right now, and we're just two of them. But at this precise moment, that's all that matters.

Bryce pulls me to him, and we sway in a slow dance.

"I don't think this dance matches the tempo of the song," I point out.

"You've never done a slow dance to a fast song?" he asks. "It's like being in the eye of a storm, being calm amid all the chaos. So I want to slow dance with you to this song."

Bryce knows dancing, so he leads the way.

My feet want to go faster. My body wants to move, but he slows me down. That's what Bryce does—all the chaos crammed into my brain, and he keeps me grounded.

He leans his head against my chest, and I hope he can feel my heart thumping along with Carly Rae.

The music swells with emotion and a faster tempo, and yet it makes perfect sense to dance slow. Somehow, it all works. Carly Rae and slow dancing. Me and Bryce.

As the song charges up, Carly gets fully into it.

It's the best dance I've ever had. Dare I say, the best dancer I've ever been.

I tip Bryce's chin up to me, and run my fingers across his cheek. We kiss—a deep kiss full of warmth and all the emotion slow dancing to a fast Carly song about dancing on the rooftop on an actual rooftop can provide.

"Well then," I say.

I feel his growing erection digging into mine.

"Maybe after dinner we can do something else."

"Oh, Em." Bryce gives me a loving but patronizing laugh. "We're gay. I suggest we do that first. The meatballs can wait."

TWENTY-TWO

BRYCE

"BUT WHAT ABOUT THE FOOD? The lights?" Emerson asks as he walks over to a strand sloping between two pipes jutting up from the roof. "I strung fairy lights."

"And this fairy couldn't be more appreciative." I place the foil lids on top of the takeout containers, snapping them into place. "But right now, I'm not interested in meatballs."

"You want some sausage?"

Yes, the joke is cringe, but also ... "Exactly."

Emerson's eyes catch mine, shimmering from the twinkling bulbs. "We can eat after." There's gravel in his voice.

He begins loosening his tie, and without thinking, I shout, "Stop! We're not doing it here." I motion to the concrete floor. "On the filthy roof. Let's go down to the apartment."

He nods, abandoning his full Windsor knot. "It's only nine steps."

My eyebrows jut up as I tilt my head.

"What? Didn't you know that?" He shrugs. "I counted on my way up. For fun."

"For fun." I smile, shake my head as I quickly pack the food in

Luigi's brown paper bag, grab Bobo's leash, and lead the way down to 6A.

Sensing the playful energy, Bobo trots a little faster than I expect, and between his leash and the takeout bag, I stumble down the last few steps.

"Are you okay?" Emerson's right behind me, his firm hands under my arms as I fall back onto him. "I got you."

"Yes. Fine. Or I will be." My body resting on his sends a jolt of electricity through me. "Once we're inside. And naked."

He laughs, a booming chuckle that echoes in the hallway and makes my insides all gooey. We stand, using each other to balance, and head into the apartment.

He goes straight for the bedroom, but I need to get Bobo settled first. "Be right back."

Emerson gives me a soft kiss on the mouth, perhaps a tease. A taste. An appetizer. Then he pats my ass as I walk into the living room, Bobo trotting happily beside me, tail wagging like he's got all the time in the world. I'm not sure what he's expecting, but tonight will not be like all the other recent nights. I ease my hand along his back while leading him to the sofa.

"All right, buddy," I say, nudging him onto the cushions. "It's all yours again. Just like old times, huh?"

He looks up at me with those big, brown pleading eyes, as if he knows what I'm saying. I'm not sure if he's happy about the current situation, but he lets out an enormous sigh, curls into a massive mound as the worn fabric of the couch creases around him.

I glance over at the bedroom door. Emerson's probably already naked and lubed up. It's just us tonight, no interruptions.

I give Bobo one last scratch behind the ears before I head toward the bedroom, knowing he'll be right here, comfy, just like he always has been. A part of me feels guilty for leaving him behind, but I know he's fine. He's always been the best at making any place home.

After a quick pit stop in the bathroom, I barge into the bedroom, ready for action. "Okay, let's f—"

But I stop when I see Emerson standing by the bed, fully dressed, head down, and his right leg turned inward as if he's lost.

"What's wrong?" My voice feels too soft, like I'm afraid to break whatever fragile silence hangs between us. But something urges me to step closer, to close the distance, to understand what's going on in his head.

He doesn't immediately respond, but lifts his head slowly, eyes meeting mine with a look I can't quite place. It's not fear, exactly, but there's hesitation—like he's unsure whether to trust me. His gaze falters for a second, and I can see the conflict in his eyes. The usual spark is dimmed, replaced by something more fragile, more vulnerable. A knot tightens in my stomach, and I take another cautious step forward, barely daring to breathe.

For a moment, he doesn't speak, just stands there, still, like he's battling something. And then, finally, his lips part, but the words are quiet.

"I ... I want this to be different."

"Different?"

"Than last time."

A knot tightens in my chest as the reality of what he's saying sinks in. My thoughts flash back to the last time, the rushed, frantic sucking and fucking—impulsive, almost careless. It was incredibly hot, but certainly not ... deep.

"Oh. Of course. I mean, last time we were horny jackrabbits. This time we'll be ..." I trail off, searching for the right words, trying to lighten the moment. "We'll be turtles. Wait, are turtles sexy? Besides the Teenage Mutant Ninja variety, of course. That's a given. But actual turtles." I take his hand in mine. "We'll be more ... intentional. Slower. Thoughtful. There's no rush, right?"

He looks at me, eyes searching, and there's something new there—a flicker of hope, a longing for what we could be, something that isn't just physical. Something deeper.

"Not only during ... this." He points to the bed. "I mean how we are. Together. In this apartment. Living together. How we communicate. I want it to be better. All of it."

Oh. He's not just talking about the sex. He's talking about the whole damn thing.

"I want that too." I plant a gentle kiss on the back of his hand.

"And another thing." He pulls my fingers up to his mouth, returning the kiss. "I want to make sure I do things ... well. Please you."

My heart gives a little lurch, because of course he's concerned about me.

"Okay. Let's agree to talk more. I mean, communicate. Sure, out there." I nod beyond the bedroom. "But also, in here."

He nods, a small, tentative smile pulling at his lips. And for the first time in a long while, I feel like we might just have a chance at getting it right.

"Now," I say. "Let's get these clothes off."

His mouth blooms into a bigger, brighter smile, and he nods, immediately returning to undoing his intricate knot.

"Wait." I peel off my blazer, realizing I have much less clothing to remove than him. "Would you mind leaving it on? Just the tie."

Emerson's eyes widen, and he shrugs. "Um, sure. Whatever you want."

Carefully, he lifts the tie and unbuttons his shirt. It's a little tricky getting his white undershirt off with it on, but he's a trooper. The minute his soft sandy chest hair comes into view, my fingers tingle at the prospect of getting lost in it.

Once we're both naked, except for his tie, we stand by the bed, the light from the window giving me the perfect opportunity to simply take him in. After the opera, everything was so quick.

Tonight, we're taking our time. And that starts with simply appreciating him.

"Fuck, you're sexy," I say.

He fiddles with the blue and red striped tie around his neck. "I am?"

"Emerson, yes. You're a big, beefy farm boy. But you're also a nerdy professor. It's a total win-win situation."

He removes his glasses, placing them on the nightstand.

"Well, I am a professor. And a farm boy. Or was. I mean, yeah, this body was built by hard work."

"You're ... gorgeous." I move next to him, grasping his tie.

This time, he doesn't ask questions. He simply lifts my chin and delivers a kiss that sends more blood to my semi-hard cock, causing it to poke at him. We're smashing swords, and I'm careful not to tug on the tie too hard as I pull him closer.

"Now." I plant a kiss on his chin. "I'm going to appreciate all this."

Keeping the silk wrapped around my palm, I move down to his chest. The hair tickles my lips as I kiss and lick, paying attention to both nipples until I figure out he favors the left and lingering there.

"Oh, that's nice," he says. "I like that."

"Yeah, I got that," I mumble into his chest. "How about your stomach?"

I head down, the hair funneling into a trail toward his dick. My mouth brushes over his soft skin, and he shudders, a soft laugh escaping from his lips.

"Now, will you sit on the bed for me?"

He nods, doing as I ask.

"And toss me a pillow, please."

With the pillow on the hardwood, I kneel between his legs, again appreciating the view I didn't take the time to fully admire last time.

"Fuck, your cock is beautiful."

"Okay, I've definitely never heard that before." He's leaning back on his elbows, legs spread wide, and yeah, he has no clue what he's packing.

"Well, take it from me. It is. Long and thick. But not too thick. Or veiny. Which is handy since I'd like to be able to walk after this. It's an ideal dick. And it fits you."

He's watching me talk. Watching me study him. Without breaking eye contact, I kiss the head, licking around the tip before taking it in, sucking gently at first.

"How do you do that, Bryce? I've never had anyone ... Oh, oh."

I swirl my tongue over the entire head before running it down right to the base of his shaft, lingering there as my free hand massages his balls.

"Fuck, Bryce. Fuck."

Slowly, opening the back of my throat, I take more in. It's work to keep my mouth open so wide, but damn, he's worth it. When my nose brushes against his soft pubic hair, he lets out a whimper. A fucking whimper. My lips do their best to curl into a gentle smile. I bob up and down, but not too fast. Tonight's theme is Savoring Emerson, and I intend to honor that.

As I find a rhythm, the silk of Emerson's tie brushes against the back of my neck. He's leaning over, his hand moves under me, reaching for my dick, but it's too far.

"Bryce, I want to ... let me ... please."

Pulling off, I sit up straight on my knees and tug on the end of the tie, forcing his face closer.

"Tell me what you want."

He nods toward my waist.

"Emerson. Tell me what you want."

He licks his lips, taking a deep breath as we stare into each other's eyes.

"Your cock."

"Where?"

"In my mouth. Please."

"Of course." I stand between his legs and pull his chin up so our gazes stay locked. "And you asked so politely."

"But ... I've never ... well ..."

His face flushes, and he avoids eye contact, fidgeting with his hands as a nervous smile creeps across his lips.

"Do you need some help?"

He nods, and my insides almost melt from his sweetness.

"Fuck, you're handsome," I say. "Now, think about what I did to you. What did you like? What felt good?" His brow furrows in concentration as he nods slowly, a glimmer of understanding lighting up his eyes. "Now try that with me."

I move a little closer, and Emerson takes my dick in his hand, studying it. He's so close, his warm breath colliding against the precum coating my tip, making every nerve even more sensitive.

"Will you tell me if I do something wrong?"

"Of course." I push myself a little closer, and he rubs the head against his lips. "But, I'll also tell you when you're doing well. Like that. That feels amazing. Rubbing it against your lips. Your whiskers tickle in the best way."

"How about this?"

He takes my cock and brushes the head against his cheek, and getting lost in his beard is a new sensation. A shiver rushes through my body as a connection to Emerson emerges within me, unlike anything I've ever experienced.

"Yes, just like that. Now, take the head in your mouth."

And then, like a star student, he takes me in, replicating much of the tongue action I gave him minutes ago.

"There you go," I say. "You're doing that just right."

I glance down, waiting for a reaction, but he's too lost in blowing me. His eyes fixed on my dick as he takes more in.

"Don't rush. Take your time. And remember, you can use your

lips. Your tongue. Go up and down the shaft if your throat needs a rest."

He pulls off, gasping for air.

"Well, this is fucking delicious."

Laughter spills out of me, and then, to make it worse, or maybe better, he buries the head in his whiskers again.

"Do you want me to fuck your beard?"

"I don't know. Is that a thing?"

I shrug. "We can make it a thing. Lie back."

Emerson does as I say, and I carefully climb up, taking his hands and moving them above his head, gently wrapping his wrists with the tie. Those fucking sexy armpits come into view, almost glaring back at me, and I'm done for.

"Hold still, for a second." I lean over, burying my face in his right pit, sniffing his manliness with my entire soul.

"I showered," he says. "Right before you came up to the roof."

"Mmmh. Yup." He smells like the mountain spring soap he bought for the shower, but there's a tinge of his sweetness underneath. I'm ready to dive right in.

I run my tongue from the bottom of his pit to the top, then skate over to his collar bone. Emerson dips his chin down so our noses almost touch.

"Hey there." His voice trembles the slightest bit, and I remember what we were about to do before his underarms distracted me.

"Hey." I push the tip of my nose on his. "Is your beard ready for my dick, Professor?"

He nods quickly, and yeah, I'm definitely done for.

"Stay right here, and ..." I place my cock on his beard, and slowly thrust back and forth. "There we go."

He gently rolls his head from side to side, and the entire underside of my dick comes to life as it brushes against his whiskers. Emerson's staring at me, and fuck, my insides bubble, watching him study me. The professor has become the student.

"Now," I say. "Stick your tongue out."

He nods quickly, and the warmth of his lips adds to the prickling from his beard. The combination is wonderful as I rock back and forth against him.

"That's it," I say. "Just lie back and enjoy it."

When he lifts his head at just the right angle and my cock slides into his mouth, my shoulders drop at the gratification of being back inside him.

"Oh, damn, that feels amazing, Em." His tongue swirls around the head, and my eyes strain to stay open, but I keep my gaze locked on him. "Yup, do that with your tongue again. Just like that."

When he lets out a little gagging noise, I pull out, my cock dripping with his saliva as I return to fucking his beard.

"Don't hurt yourself, Professor."

This elicits a smile as he uses his tongue to wipe a bit of saliva from his lower lip.

"This is fun," he says, and something about the directness and simplicity of his words brings a massive grin to my face.

"So much fun," I reply. "And we're just getting started."

I unwrap his wrists and drop the tie next to Emerson's head. He moves a hand to my balls, and with a thrust toward his nose, his fingers shift back, grazing my ass as his eyes sparkle.

"Do you want to play with my hole? Get it ready for your farm-boy nerdy-professor cock?" I reach back and wrap my fingers around him. "You're so fucking hard."

"Can you reach the condoms?" He nods toward the nightstand.

"Yes, but I'm not quite ready. And I wanted to chat about that." My dick continues to get lost in his beard as his fingers play around the perimeter of my hole, and I gently stroke him. "I know we were in a rush last time, so we didn't discuss it, but I'm on PrEP. Regularly tested, and well, I'm good to go without."

"Oh. Well, I haven't been with anyone in … years." He smiles, his whiskers somehow finding a new way to pleasure me.

"So, if you're okay with it, we don't need to use them." My eyebrows rise.

He nods then runs his tongue along the underside of my cock for good measure.

"But first, Professor, if you're game, I have another way you can get me nice and ready for this." I give his cock a gentle tug.

"Bryce, I'm game for anything with you."

"Okay," I say, carefully turning around to face his dick. "Have you ever heard of rimming?"

He laughs, but I can't see his face. "Yes, I'm aware."

"I thought your beard might feel …"

And before I can finish, he grabs my hips, yanks me back, and rams his tongue inside.

"Easy there. It's not ice cream, and you don't have to share."

He pulls back. "Sorry. Sorry, I …"

I turn around, catching his eye. "No need to apologize. I just don't want you to hurt yourself." With a quick pat to his firm chest, I grab the lube from the nightstand drawer.

"Now, while you do … Oh!" He surprises me with how deep his tongue gets. "Yowsers, didn't realize I was dealing with Gene Simmons from KISS."

Emerson pauses, his whiskers tickling the skin on my ass. "Who from what?"

"Never mind. I can teach you about eighties glam rock another time."

With the lube in hand, I warm a little between my palms and apply it to his dick. The light from the street filters in, and I take another moment to appreciate just how spectacular he is from this vantage point. I spread the lube all over him, and he thrusts into my grip. Finally, my fingers dab a little right below his balls. For later.

I'm not sure if Emerson has ever rimmed before or if he's just outstanding out of the gate, but he's got me very ... ready.

He yanks my waist down, flicking his tongue deep inside me. "Are you gunning for extra credit there, Professor?"

Panting as he pulls back, his warm breath on my hole sends a shiver right up my back to the nape of my neck. "Sorry, just enjoying myself."

"Never apologize for A+ ass-eating."

I lift my leg and turn around, moving my mouth to his, and he blinks tentatively. Men are always unsure if I'll want to kiss after, but it's my ass, and I always provide a clean workspace.

With a nibble at his lower lip, I pull his tongue in my mouth, moving back and positioning his dick right where I want it.

"Now, Professor, are you ready to rail me?"

He nods quickly, and I dip back down to taste his lips. Before I push back, I grab the rogue tie next to his head, wrap it around his neck, and take the end in my left hand. "Something to hold on to."

I lower myself on Emerson Grant's gorgeous cock. With a deep inhale, I take him in.

"One second, Professor." Another breath. "Let me just acclimate."

When I finally open my eyes, he's staring up at me. And that look. That's when I know it for sure. Emerson is nothing like all the other guys.

"Okay, Professor, ready to fuck me?"

"Absolutely."

And with that, he thrusts up, holding my hips as I tug gently on his tie. After a minute, the pleasure takes over, and I drop the silk fabric, moving my hands to his chest. I tilt my head back, and honestly, the pleasure, the intimacy, the connection with him—this might be the most satisfying sex of my life.

"You good?" Emerson moves a hand to my stomach, rubbing it, perhaps for good luck.

"Yeah, just enjoying the ride."

A smile peeks out from his beard, and he resumes. With one hand resting on his chest, the other moves back, massaging his balls as my index finger takes an expedition south.

I catch his gaze, and there's nothing telling me to stop, but of course, I'm a gentleman, and want to check. "This okay?"

"I've never really ... but with you, yeah." He lets out a focused breath. "Go ahead." His palm massages my thigh. "I'm putty in your hands." He plunges deep, and with permission granted, my fingers swipe some of the lube from his balls and head for his hole.

I don't go past the second knuckle. I'm not trying to send the man into orbit. We need to work up to more. But even with half of a finger, the expression on Emerson's face shifts into overdrive.

"Holy fuck, Bryce. That. Whatever you're doing. Holy crap." He makes the cutest circle with his lips and blows a deep breath out. "Just keep doing it. Please."

His head pushes back into the pillow. He's too handsome. Too kind. Too sweet. I can't stand it, and I abandon his ass to lean forward and kiss him.

The moment our lips touch, his dick pops out. Oops.

We both laugh, mine more of a giggle to his deeper chuckle.

He takes my face in his hands, holding me close, and I'm not sure if it's the light hitting his face just right or something else, but my heart gallops like it's about to burst out of my chest.

"I'm close," I say. "Can you fuck me a little more?"

"Bryce, I can fuck you a lot more."

There's more laughter, and then I move back, his cock sliding right back in like a dancer slotted into place, finding its perfect positioning.

"All right, Professor. Ready?"

He nods, his smile morphing into a smirk as he pounds away.

My body shakes with each thrust, and the first hints of my orgasm come knocking.

"Soon." I'm panting now, lost in ecstasy, and so ready to share this moment with him. "Use my hole, Professor. Please."

Something shifts in him, maybe knowing I'm close, that he's doing this to me, and Emerson holds me in place, driving up harder than before. And then it happens. I'm on the edge. About to freefall. Each plunge of his cock sends ripples of bliss through me. The first shot lands right on his beard, but I'm too far gone to pause and make a joke. The subsequent blasts coat his furry chest. And when the final spasm rips through me, I slouch over him. But Emerson doesn't stop.

"Are you close?" I ask, using a little of the cum on his chest to play with his nipple.

"I think so? Maybe."

And then, remembering the delight on his face when I fingered him, an idea forms in my head. "Hang on, then." I lie next to Emerson, moving my hand between his legs and finding his hole. "I'm going to finger you while you jerk yourself off. Okay?"

He's already stroking himself. "Yeah, please." I glance down, and he's leaking precum. He's so fucking close.

My finger finds his entrance, already lubed up from before, and instead of adding another finger, I simply go deeper. Swirling until he lets out a deep, guttural moan.

"Oh, Bryce, what the fuck, what, wh ..."

"Just enjoy it, Professor." I slope in to nestle my face in his neck, kissing and sucking as his body tenses up.

"Don't stop." He's breathing heavily. "Keep doing that. All that. Fuck, Bryce, I'm close. Now. Don't stop."

As thick, warm ropes of cum blast over his chest, I plunge my finger all the way in, doing my best to give him a taste of what it might feel like with another finger. Or my dick. All in time.

He's moaning, gasping, the release splitting him in half. I move up to kiss him, capturing the last whimpers of his orgasm until he's finished and we're lying quietly, softly kissing.

"How was that?" My head rests on the pillow next to his.

He doesn't reply, but with my hand on his rising chest, I confirm he's alive.

"That good, eh?" I ask.

"I've never ... Not like that, anyway." He turns to face me. "You're amazing."

"You're not too bad yourself, Professor. And if you're interested, I can think of some extra credit projects you could work on later."

"Oh. Yeah. Definitely interested. I need all the credits I can scrounge up."

With another kiss, he moves to sit on the edge of the bed.

"Where are you going?"

"I'll be right back."

Emerson quietly stands and disappears into the dim light of the living room. A murmur of movement reaches my ears, but I can't place what it is. I listen, my heart a little heavier with the anticipation of his return.

Moments later, he slips back into the room, his presence like a sigh of relief. "Bobo's asleep," he says, a gentle smile tugging at his lips. "I just wanted to give him a little goodnight kiss on the head."

I shift, making room for him, and he slides back into bed. My head tucks into the crook of his neck as I curl against him. A feeling, something new and delicate—I can't quite name it, but it's special and radiates through my entire body. I open my mouth to say something, but then my lips close. We don't need words now. Just the quiet of the night, the warmth of our bodies, and the city noises outside lulling us to sleep.

TWENTY-THREE

EMERSON

AFTER THE NIGHT on the roof, I guess you could say Bryce and I are officially a couple.

I'm nervous because I'm not used to being part of a couple, but it's easy with him. Not much has changed between us. We still make each other laugh, talk about each other's days, and have meals together. We walk Bobo. And there's the sex. It's fantastic, and it all feels effortless.

Each day when I return home from class, Bryce and I have dinner and take Bobo for a long, meandering walk. I could get used to a life like this, and maybe I will, because my big interview is coming up in a few days.

Sheena added the daylong meeting to my calendar this morning after my lecture. My heart skipped a beat when I saw the notification pop up. This is it—my shot to get in with the University of New York. Permanently.

"It's not like a regular interview," I tell Bryce over Chinese takeout the next night. "It's an all-day affair. First, I have to give a lecture to a panel of graduate students and faculty. Then, I meet one-on-one with three tenured faculty members. Then Sheena.

That's the one part I'm not worried about." I pull my lips in and swallow. "And finally, the dean."

"Jesus, that's a lot of talking, even for me."

I give up on chopsticks one minute into the meal, but Bryce continues to fight the good fight. At this point, he's stabbing pieces of his chicken and shoving them into his mouth.

"I'll be questioned extensively on my research and work history." I twirl lo mein onto my fork, yet my appetite begins to fade.

"Bring a jug of water so your mouth doesn't get dry. Oh, we can do vocal exercises in the morning to perfect your enunciation, too." He piles three more pieces of chicken on his chopstick like they're kebabs. "We should also do some stretches to engage your core. You don't want to be slouching."

"Holy crap. This is it, Bryce." The panic hits suddenly, like an attack of appendicitis. "This day is going to determine my entire future. I can't only survive this gauntlet of interviews—I need to thrive."

Bryce presses his fingers together, a sly smile on his face.

"Why are you smiling?" This isn't the reaction I was expecting.

"It's a final callback," he says with a knowing grin.

"What's that?"

"Actually it's more than that. It's a final callback plus chemistry read." Bryce puts down his chopstick. The wheels are turning in his head. "Actors go through multiple auditions to get a part, until they reach the final callback. This is the big one with all the stakeholders present. The director, the producers, and the more famous co-star, with whom they'll have to do a chemistry read to see if they spark together. You need to show them how chemistratible you are with the department."

"Chemistratible isn't a word."

"Give it time. I'm in the process of making it catch on." Bryce moves my takeout container to the coffee table.

Admittedly, I'm not the most ... chemistratible person out there. But I landed a guy like Bryce, so maybe there's hope.

"Whenever we have a big audition coming up, what do we do?"

"We practice," I say.

"So all we have to do is practice here. Now, a final callback is different from an audition because you have to impress on a new level. They already know who you are. They already like you. But it's about whether they *love* you. You gotta make them fall in love with you. And I'm not just talking about putting on a tight pair of pants with no underwear and suggestively crossing and uncrossing your legs during the interview, because that won't work here."

"Did you actually do that during an audition?"

Bryce lets out a laugh that doesn't answer my question. "Most quote-unquote 'tricks' won't work here. You need to form a genuine love connection. Fortunately, I know you're very capable of that."

He gently tugs at the tip of my beard and gives me a wink.

"So you want me to flirt with my interviewers?"

"Oh, Emerson. You can't even flirt with a gum wrapper, and that's why you're so endearing." He pats my head. "You flirt with intelligence. When you're into a subject, your whole face lights up. Like *Turandot*. You gotta show them what you know, and they're going to fall in love with you." Bryce pats my knee. "So we practice. Make sure you have good answers filed away that illuminate your intellect."

Once again, Bryce manages to make sense. I can't be stumbling through those important questions. I can't stutter when discussing my research, nor can I afford to go off on tangents or ramble. I must be succinct. "They'll ask me about my work history and what I'm working on. Why this department, why this university? They'll ask how I can really make an impact here. Because as much as it's about helping students, it's about getting out research, getting published, and building a name for myself, which will reflect nicely on the university."

Academia is such a game. Is it really about talent or smarts? I don't know. But there's no use in questioning that. Bryce is right. This is a final callback, a chemistry read, and I've got to make them fall in love with me—because I don't want to leave New York and the guy who I'm in love with here.

Love. I'm in love with Bryce.

"Bobo, I've given you four pieces of my chicken," Bryce says to a whimpering dog.

"Bryce. I ... I ... love you."

"Are you trying to get some chicken too?" He holds up a chopstick skewered with meat.

I wait for him to connect the dots.

"Wait, what did you say?" He blinks a few times, then shakes his head. "I wasn't ready. Say it again." He puts the chopstick down, licks his palm, and smooths it over his hair. "Okay, ready."

"I love you, Bryce Derrickson."

"You do?"

"I do," I repeat with a nod.

Bryce's eyes linger, soft and open. There's a slight parting of his beautiful lips, like he wants to speak but isn't sure what to say. And then he takes a deep breath, and the words come out.

"I love you too. So much. I didn't want to be the first to say it. But wait, maybe I should have. Do you want to take it back? Then I can go first. Take it back." He makes a strange noise, like static, and waves his hand in front of my face.

"Nope. It doesn't matter who said it first. It matters that we both feel it."

Bryce smiles. And yeah, I really do love this man.

"And that's why I have to nail this interview," I say. "If I don't, I'll have to find a job somewhere else. Somewhere not here."

"I mean you don't"—he raises the chicken chopstick, using it to accentuate his point—"have to nail the interview. I mean, you do, I want you to, of course, but Emerson, I don't care if you move to the moon, you're not getting rid of me."

"The moon?"

"The moon. Florida." He shivers. "You know what I mean. I'm only saying don't let the pressure of wanting to stay in the city derail you from the work at hand." He waves the chicken, and Bobo makes a whiny begging noise. "Buddy, I'm hungry. You have dog food. Let me have my human food."

Bobo shrugs and comes up to me.

"Hey, listen to your dad. We're not doing good cop, bad cop this time."

He gets the hint and goes full teenager, choosing to sulk away to the bed.

"Okay, let's do some prep. I'm pulling up an article about questions asked in a professor interview," Bryce says, staring at his phone. "First question: How does your research contribute to the field of music theory?"

"I want to explore contemporary applications of eighteenth-century artists ..." As I talk, I get distracted.

"Bryce, what are you doing?"

Bryce undoes the top button of his shirt.

"Are you hot? Want me to open a window?"

"No. Keep going."

I launch into my interest in Haydn's role as father of the symphony but stop again when Bryce undoes another button.

"I can bring out the box fan," I say.

"No need. Keep going."

I finish my answer, and this time, Bryce doesn't touch his shirt, which was distracting me for multiple reasons.

"Good! Next question: Explain your teaching philosophy."

"That's a ... that's a great question. I believe in engaging students somewhere between where they are and asking them to go one level deeper. You're unbuttoning your shirt again."

Bryce pops open three more buttons, leaving one at the bottom. His chest comes into view.

"You are going to be under a lot of pressure. I am trying to replicate those circumstances as best I can." He undoes the last button and tosses his shirt to the floor. "You will need to work extra hard to maintain concentration and stay on track. Can you do it, Professor?"

I can see the logic in that. I can also see Bryce without his shirt —throwing logic out the window. My pants immediately tighten, but I have to stay focused.

"Okay, next question," I say.

"Good. How do you see yourself fitting into the department?" Bryce asks.

"Well," I begin to go into my answer as Bryce unzips his fly, stands up, and shakes off his pants.

God, his body was meant to be stared at. The David could never. My mind starts to wander to all the things I want to do to him.

Bryce snaps a finger in my face. "Concentrate."

I continue with my answer. I think it sounds good. Bryce seems happy.

"Okay, very nice. Where do you see yourself in five years?"

"Still teaching at the University of New York. Pursuing more interdisciplinary research."

Bryce puts a thumb under his waistband, teasing me. Is he going to take them off? Is he not?

I love the way his stomach hangs slightly over his waistband. There's so much in there, so much to grab. Kiss. Lick. Damn, he's intoxicating.

"You know, I don't think this is working," I say.

"Emerson, you're so close. Don't give up now. If you think

you're nervous and uncomfortable now, just wait. You're getting interview-gang-banged in a few days. The better you are at breathing through your nose, the more successful you'll be." Bryce and I both cock an eyebrow at his statement. "Ah, you know what I mean."

He gets on his knees. I gulp a lump back in my throat.

"Tell me, Professor ... how would you involve students in your research? Would you be ... hands on?" Bryce grabs my aching crotch.

"Absolutely," I say, as all breath leaves my body. My heart immediately jumps into my throat.

"Keep talking, Professor."

He looks up. Those big hazel eyes—so much going on behind them. He undoes my fly, takes out my rock-hard dick.

"Right. I welcome students interested in helping me with research. We can ... dive deep together." I gasp. I'm so hard right now, it's like I have an extra thick chopstick down there.

"Keep talking," he says, as he lowers his beautiful mouth on me.

Somehow, I push through the epic blast of ecstasy lighting up my body. I'm trying to find the academic side of my brain, reaching for it.

"Collaboration is key. I think there's a misconception that our field doesn't require research assistants, so it becomes a self-fulfilling prophecy." I watch as Bryce bobs up and down on my cock, never breaking eye contact with me. I reach up and adjust my hearing aid, and the subtle slurping noises come alive. Gosh, he's beautiful. "We need to actively recruit students to get involved and show them what they can do. Research isn't just about sitting in a lab. Oh my god your mouth is incredible."

Bryce pops up from my lap. "You should refrain from saying 'oh my god' in an interview. It doesn't sound professional. And finally, do you have any questions for us?"

He goes back down, taking every inch of me until my brain short circuits.

"Oh, yeah—"

"I think you should use 'yes.' Academic setting and all," he says.

"Fuck."

"I would avoid cursing, too."

I push Bryce's head back down. His tongue works magic around my head before he runs his lips up and down the shaft. Finally, he darts his tongue under my balls, getting right into that super sensitive spot, and sending me hurtling toward the edge.

"Oh fuck. God." I gasp out helplessly and tap him on the shoulder to let him know I'm about to blow. I nudge him again, but he only speeds up, my cock lodged in his mouth, which is so hot it pushes me to climax.

Bryce swallows like a champ, gulping, moaning, and my eyes damn near roll back in my skull. When I finally finish, he takes one last suck, wipes a bit of cum dripping from his lower lip, and finally chases it with half a fortune cookie. He holds up the slip of paper and reads. "Congrats! You've earned a nap ... and maybe a cookie."

He nods, pops the other half of the treat into his mouth, and swallows. "Good job. How do you think that went?"

To his credit, the words that came out must've been lodged deep in my brain, because if I can pull them up during a time like this, then I won't ever forget them.

"I can't believe I spoke intelligently under such duress."

"Hopefully it bodes well for your interview. Just remember, Emerson, you got this. Whatever happened in the past happened, but each day we're a new person. So give them hell."

We curl up on the couch together naked and being here with him like this, I feel like I've already won the biggest prize in the world.

"Look at us. The dancer and the professor." Bryce moves down and nestles into my chest. "I have my new show. You are on the verge of getting your teaching position. We're really about to have it all, Em."

"That we are," I say back.

And nothing could be better.

BRYCE

A WEEK after Emerson's interview, he was officially offered the position. With a massive grin plastered on my face, we stroll into Pho-nomenal Pizza. It's time to celebrate. Well, more than the perfect pounding he gave me last night.

Even though it's only a few blocks from the Bigby, neither one of us has been here. It's tucked away on a small side street I don't frequent with Bobo because there are no trees or fire hydrants. I'd never heard of it, and Portia insisted we try it.

The name alone makes me question why I agreed to meet here, but then the decor hits me. I'm immediately engulfed in the vibrant atmosphere. The walls are adorned with colorful anime murals, creating a playful yet nostalgic vibe. The fusion of Italian and Asian cultures is clear—a blend of rustic wooden tables paired with elegant paper lanterns that sway gently from the ceiling. Featuring tailored black outfits accented with silk sashes, the wait-staff dart around like well-dressed ninjas.

Who thought this was a good idea? Portia, of course.

"Okay," Emerson says, his eyebrows raised as he glances at the menu. "Is this a joke or ..."

"Nope," I say, unfolding my kitten origami napkin. "Only Portia would know about this place. Vietnamese pho meets pizza. A soup-to-slice fusion." I shrug. "You really can get anything in the city."

Emerson gives me a side-eye. "Have I entered some alternate universe?"

"Wait until you meet Portia. This is just how she operates."

I spot her by the door, wearing a pale blue scarf wrapped tightly around her head, and wave to her. She scurries over as if she's on a caffeine binge, her bright scarf flowing behind her like a classic Hollywood actress late for her call time.

"Bryce! There you are! And you brought Hot Prof!" Portia calls, too loudly. A few heads turn, but nothing fazes her. She's too busy applying a fresh coat of lipstick as she joins us.

I lean over to Emerson. "You'll get used to her. Mostly. Maybe. Just roll with it."

She sits down with a huff, kisses my cheek, and I introduce them. I watch Emerson try to figure out how to shake Portia's hand when she leans her cheek in for a kiss. After he delivers one, she returns it, leaving a bright red mark on his face.

"Bryce, darling. This one is fit to be tied."

I pat Emerson's knee under the table. "He sure is."

"Well, I skipped Pilates for this. And my chakra cleanse. But all the kids are raving about it. Apparently the food is pho-nonemal." She winks at me. "So, Emerson, I hear you've secured a permanent position at the University of New York." She applies more lipstick, presumably to replace what she's painted on our cheeks. "You locked that down quickly. How does it feel? You must be very proud."

Emerson, ever the professional, takes a beat before answering. "Well, it feels great, actually. But I don't think 'locked down' is the right phrase. More like 'I've finally reached the promised land of tenure.'"

"Oh, sure," Portia says, nodding as if she completely under-stands. "I get that. It's how I feel whenever I walk into the first-class lounge at the airport."

I glance at Emerson, who's trying not to laugh.

"Oh! I have the best news to share," she says. "Well, best news for me. You'll likely be neutral."

"Do tell," I say.

"Whitney sprained her ankle during rehearsals. Guess who has two thumbs, flawless skin, and got cast to replace her?" Portia points at herself.

"Justice prevails. That's fabulous." I reach across the table and squeeze her hand in excitement.

"I'm assuming we don't like Whitney?" Emerson asks.

"I swear I'm not usually this petty," she tells him. "But trust me, she deserves it."

The waitress arrives, and we order—Portia gets a cocktail called a Wasabi Fizz and some bizarre combination of pho and Hawaiian pizza, Emerson goes with the classic Pho-Roni, and I settle on something that looks like the bastard child of a Margherita pizza and a steaming bowl of soup. The food arrives, and despite everything, it actually smells incredible. I take a bite and ... okay, okay, as usual, Portia is right. It's surprisingly scrumptious.

Between bites, we chat about Emerson's new gig, his excite-ment, and the relief of it all. He's been working so hard for this.

"I'm just excited to not have to deal with adjunct professor paperwork anymore," Emerson says, wiping a tiny drop of broth from his chin. "I never thought I'd get so giddy about research opportunities and regular office hours."

I run my fingers over his thick thigh. "Don't forget the benefits."

Portia leans in with a smile that can only be described as

mischievous and unhinged. "Does that mean, like, unlimited salad and breadsticks?"

I shake my head. "No, I mean a steady income and health insurance. You know, basic needs."

"Meh," Portia says. "Doctors these days are extremely over-rated. Clean living is where it's at." She lifts her fancy drink.

Emerson snorts, trying not to choke on his food. I can't help but chuckle at the absurdity of it all.

Just then, my phone buzzes on the table. It's Preeti. *Gulp.*

I look at Emerson. "I'll be back in a jiff. Work stuff. This is important."

Or could be. I step outside, the cool evening air hitting my face as the city zooms by.

"Bryce," Preeti says immediately, her voice sharp. "I need you. Now."

"For the last time, I can't have sex with you. For multiple reasons."

"I'm actually being serious. The network ordered *Queers in the Headlights* straight to series. Ten episodes. They loved the pitch so much, they want this on the air by December. They think it could be great counterprogramming to all the December reruns and holiday specials."

"Ten episodes?"

"Yep. It'll be about three months of work with the possibility of more if the show does well."

I clutch my chest in amazement. Finding steady work as an actor can feel as impossible as searching for love on dating apps.

"When do we start?" I ask.

"I need you to take the first flight out here in the morning."

"Out here? Where's here?"

"LA."

I guffaw into the phone. I wonder if Preeti can see my eyes bulging out. "I thought we were filming in New York."

"We were, but the network got tax credits, so we'll be filming the first season in LA. Depending on how things go, future seasons might go back to New York. LA is great! You can work on your tan and recreate the opening montage from *Clueless*. I'll be your Dionne."

"LA." Not even the thought of imagining my life as a Noxzema commercial can quiet the unease piling up inside me. This is the opportunity I've been waiting for, the one that could change everything. I look up at the sky, letting the rush of emotions wash over me. But there's a pull in my chest, a weight I can't ignore.

Emerson. Bobo. What I have here. What I've finally found. Built. Emerson's handsome face floats into my head. I've never had something so steady. Something so real. He's such a good man.

"Preeti ... I need to think about this."

"Bryce, I need an answer now. Because if you're not in, I need to pivot."

I nod my head. Shooting schedules can't be adjusted for people like me so far down on the call sheet. Preeti extended a lifeline getting me this gig, but she can't hold it forever.

"Do you want it or not?" she asks. The million-dollar question.

I stare down the street, the lights of the city blinking back at me. I think about what I have, about what I could lose.

I close my eyes and utter the only response possible.

"Yes."

Preeti rattles off some details about an email, flights, and packing lists, and we hang up, my mind racing. I walk back into the restaurant, my feet suddenly heavy. I take a seat again, trying to look casual, but my stomach coils like a rope pulled too tight.

Emerson looks up, sensing something's off. "Everything okay?"

I nod, forcing a smile. "Yeah. Everything's ... fine."

Portia, ever the observant one, raises an eyebrow. "You look like my mum whenever she walks into a kitchen with Formica countertops."

I let out a half-laugh, trying to shake off the unease.

"No. No. I'm just ... hungry. Let's eat."

Emerson gives me a curious glance but doesn't press. Instead, he raises his glass. "To new jobs and adventures," he says, smiling. "To us!"

"To us," I repeat, raising my glass too. But inside, I'm already thinking about LA. And everything I'm about to leave behind.

EMERSON

THERE'S something on the tip of Bryce's tongue as we walk home, but he refuses to say it. Though we haven't been together long, I can already spot his tells. The corners of the lips lift, but they're hiding something.

"Isn't it a beautiful night out?" he ponders. "The city feels so alive."

Bryce would never say something that generic. I stop walking, nerves building in my stomach.

"Okay, what is going on with you?"

"Me? I'm fine. I'm strolling with my boo in the greatest city in the world." The words sound pleasant, but the panic in his eyes and added sweat beading at his forehead say otherwise.

"You sound like a tourist. A straight tourist. From a square state. What happened? Are you all right?" Concern floods my brain. I'm wired to immediately scroll through the top five hundred worst-case scenarios.

"I'm fine."

I plant myself on a neighbor's stoop in protest. "I'm not going anywhere until my actual boyfriend shows up."

"Excuse me. Did you just call me your …"

"Boyfriend," I repeat. "Is that okay?"

Bryce's eyes are all puffy, but I can't tell if he's happy, sad, or both.

He's staring at me. Silent. And now I'm truly starting to worry. But then he nods, lets out an exasperated sigh, and collapses next to me, fainting onto the steps. "I'm fine, Emerson—my boyfriend." He takes in a huge gulp of air. "I'm actually fantastic. Ecstatic. On cloud freaking nine. The guy I'm in love with called me his boyfriend." He bats his eyelashes at me, and my fingers twitch, wanting to touch his face, but I don't. "And I just received the biggest professional break of my life. My dreams are coming true. Isn't it wonderful?" He throws his head into his hands and sobs.

I rub his shoulder, concerned yet confused. I realize I need to acclimate to dating someone prone to drama. As someone who grew up in the Midwest, my only experience with men showing emotion was while watching football games.

"Bryce, talk to me. Whatever it is, we'll get through it together. Or celebrate. I'm not sure which."

I pull his hands away, revealing watery eyes. Oh, he was actually crying.

"That call at the restaurant? It was Preeti offering me a job to choreograph *Queers in the Headlights* in Los Angeles."

"Oh my goodness, well that's amazing news …"

"I have to leave tomorrow morning." He shakes his head gently. "And I'll be gone for three months."

Suddenly, Bryce's histrionics make sense. This is huge for him. All of his hard work is paying off, and I'm so proud of him. This could take his career in an exciting new direction.

West. Three thousand miles west.

That's the direction he'll be going. For three months.

My elation evaporates.

"That's fantastic." I stretch my lips into a big grin, and I don't care how painful it is. Bryce isn't the only one who can act here. "Bryce, this is wonderful!"

"God, you're upset."

"No. No, I'm not. This is huge. We need to celebrate!"

I pull him into a hug, which allows my strained smile to take five. "You're doing it. You're making your dreams come true. I knew you were destined for big things."

"But what about us?" Bryce scooches back from the hug. Instead of joy, his gorgeous features are drooping with worry, fear, and sadness.

I know what it's like to strive for a professional goal that seemed forever out of reach, until one day, it's yours. Bryce deserves to be radiating happiness in this moment. I'm hit with a wrecking ball of guilt for giving him a forced smile.

"Nothing's going to happen to us," I assure him, confidence growing in me. "You should be crying tears of joy."

"We just got together, and now I'm leaving. It's like I'm transporting my art project before the Elmer's Glue dries, and it all falls apart. I'll be covered in glue, popsicle sticks, and glitter." Bryce wipes away a tear. "True story."

Even in the bowels of sadness, Bryce still finds a way to make me laugh.

"We are stronger than Elmer's Glue. We're Gorilla Glue at the very least."

"Three months is a long time."

"It'll go by like that." I snap my fingers.

"Because of the time change, we won't get to talk much."

"I'll stay up later."

"So you're not worried?"

I let out a sigh. Bryce also doesn't deserve someone who paints a happy face over everything. "Worried isn't the right word. Am I thrilled about being apart? I am not. But I know we can make it."

"You think?"

"Look, relationships get tested all the time. For some people, those tests happen months or years in. Our test is happening sooner. It doesn't mean we'll fail it." I pull Bryce close, and he melts into my arms. "Bryce, you have this amazing opportunity. If you stay behind because of me, all that will do is foster resentment. You need to see this through." I pull his hand up for a kiss and give it a squeeze. "I've never felt this way about anyone. And a three-month work trip isn't going to change that."

"You say that ..." Bryce scrambles back down to the sidewalk and paces in front of the stoop. I want to comfort him, but neurotic Bryce is too adorable not to watch. "But New York is filled with oodles of gay men. And they all go to the gym."

"Gym bodies are notoriously weak. I doubt any of those guys could last five seconds performing one of your dance routines. You have real muscle." I check out his chest stretching his T-shirt, and yep—under the cuddly exterior is solid gold.

"What about all the guys jogging shirtless in the park?" he asks.

"Oh, they're just showing off."

"Half of the gay guys on this island have a farm-boy fetish. They're going to be throwing themselves at you the minute you mention riding a tractor."

"I actually rode a thresher, but that's beside the point."

"What about your students? Everybody wants to sleep with their professor."

"I'll bore them with treatises on Beethoven."

"You're not worried at all?" Bryce asks.

"Should I be? What about you and the LA gays, huh? They can't resist a guy from New York City." I stand up and take a step down the stoop.

Bryce crosses his arms. "Technically, I'm from Pennsylvania. Plus, they're all hopped up on Red Bull and erectile dysfunction meds. Pass."

"You might love California so much that you decide to stay." I take another step down.

"And abandon New York? Not a chance."

"You'll ditch me for yoga on the beach and kale salads and post-brunch hikes." Another step. The distance between us closes.

"Those all sound like medieval torture devices."

"You're going to become a world-famous choreographer and live in a *bungalow* in West Hollywood." I take the final step onto the sidewalk. Our lips are barely an inch apart. "And one day, while in a hot tub with a bunch of lithe twenty-two-year-olds, you'll have a vision of this nerdy professor you used to know. Eddie? Emilio? What was his name again?"

I sweep Bryce into my arms for an epic kiss that takes both of our breaths away. He moans lightly into my lips as I pull him closer and savor the heat of his body.

"So we're going to be okay?" he whispers.

"It's only three months. If we can handle six flights of stairs, we can handle three months apart."

Bryce kisses me again. He gazes into my eyes and smiles. Try as he might, I can sense the fear and anxiety bubbling under the surface of his sunny exterior. That's the beauty and the curse of a dramatic, highly expressive boyfriend.

I take a deep breath, and then his hand. "Let's go home."

TWENTY-SIX

BRYCE

I'M wide awake at an ungodly hour, moving around the apartment as if my body hasn't processed the fact that I'm about to board a plane and leave my life here for *three months*.

Gulp.

Emerson helped me pack last night between kissing me and doing everything he could to calm my nerves—including a blow job my dick will write poems about. I'm packed. I've got my suit-case, my backpack, and I think I've remembered all the essentials—phone, charger, toiletries, and ... oh yeah, the signed, framed photo of Queen Carly Rae, which I obtained by waiting outside of the Hammerstein Ballroom until almost three a.m. in the pouring rain. Zero regrets.

I'm standing in the kitchen, trying not to fall asleep on the counter while Emerson meticulously makes coffee like he's conducting a symphony. He's so much more put together at 4:30 in the morning than I'll ever be. Oh, who am I kidding? He's more put together than me at any time of the day. This must be why he looks like someone who could be a contestant on a dating show.

"Don't forget your mini toothpaste," he says, holding up a tiny tube like it's the Holy Grail. "You want to make sure your mouth is fresh and cavity free."

"I can always buy toothpaste in LA," I mutter, rubbing my eyes. "I'm sure they sell it along with the kale smoothies everyone drinks. Do you think they even have pizza there?"

"They have pizza everywhere," Emerson says. "Sure, it might be cauliflower crust and fake cheese, but ..."

"Blasphemy."

"I'll ship you pizza. And Luigi's meatballs." He abandons the dripping pour-over and pulls me into a warm hug. "I don't want you starving."

"You'd do that for me?" I bury my face in the crook of his neck. Even before the sun's up, Emerson smells like heaven.

"Babe, I'd do anything for you."

I heave an enormous sigh. How am I leaving this man?

"Ugh!" I smash my face deeper into him, trying to muffle my frustration.

"Bryce. We've been over this. It's okay. Three months, and you'll be home."

"It's not okay. It's never okay." Tears stream from my face, and I'm kind of surprised my body is able to produce moisture before coffee. "Guys always leave me, Emerson. Always. I'm not used to someone sticking around. And now, I'm the one leaving. And I'm leaving *you*. The most perfect guy."

Emerson's face softens, a gentle smile gracing his lips. How does he make me feel like the most delicate flower, carefully protected within a vibrant bouquet? "Bryce," he says, and hearing my name from his lips makes my heart do this little flip-flop. "I'm not going anywhere. You're not getting rid of me that easily."

I blink rapidly. "You're not?"

"No. You're going to LA, and I'm staying here. I'll take care of

Bobo," he continues. "He'll take care of me. We're both staying right here." He pokes my chest right near my heart and kisses my forehead. Every atom in my body lets out a collective sigh. "And we'll keep each other company until you get back. We'll talk, we'll text, we'll video chat. I've always wanted to try cybersex. I have no idea how it works, but we'll figure it out. Together. We'll make it work."

"I know we will." I swallow thickly. "But I'll miss you."

"You'll miss me," Emerson repeats, smiling like he knows exactly how much I'll miss him. "And I'll miss you. But that's how we know this is real." He captures my lips in a delicate kiss, and I can't help but let out a little moan. "Come on, your car is going to be here any minute."

Emerson grabs Bobo's leash, and even though it's way too early to go outside, he trots over, and the three of us head downstairs.

The street is eerily quiet this early. They say New York is the city that never sleeps, but maybe between four and five in the morning, only the rats are awake.

I pass the leash to Emerson, and for reasons I can't quite explain, it feels as though I'm relinquishing a piece of myself—like I'm entrusting him with more than just my dog, but with a part of my very soul.

I look over at Bobo, who's staring at me with those big, sad eyes like he understands the weight of the situation too. His tail thumps against the sidewalk as I kneel to give him a quick kiss and head scritches.

"Hey, buddy," I say, feeling my throat tighten. We've never been apart for so long, and the realization of how badly I'm going to miss him crashes into me. "You're in charge now. Be a good boy for me, okay? Keep an eye on Emerson while I'm gone. Can you do that for me?"

Bobo gives me a woeful little whine and sniffs my hand. I swear, he knows something's up. "Remember how much I love you." I give him one last kiss, taking a deep inhale of his corn chip fur.

The car pulls up, and Emerson puts my bag in the trunk and walks back over, standing in front of me. He reaches out and runs a hand through my hair, his touch soft and reassuring. "I love you, Bryce," he says, his voice thick. "My home is right here." Again, he pats my chest, this time tapping along with my heartbeat. "And I'll be right here waiting on you."

I try to smile, but honestly, it's too hard.

"I love you too," I say quickly, then add, "in a 'no, really, you're the most amazing man I've ever met, and I'm going to miss you a lot, but I don't want to cry in front of you again' kind of way."

Emerson laughs softly, his eyes lighting up with an affection that only deepens as he leans in. His lips meet mine with a tenderness that speaks volumes, and in that single kiss, there's a connection so powerful it says what all the words in the universe never could—we're going to be okay.

And suddenly, all the nerves about leaving don't feel so heavy. It's still going to suck, but I know I have something to come back to. Something real.

The car honks. The driver's got that look on his face—the look of someone who wants to get to the airport on time. But also someone who really hopes they don't have to hear me talk for the next forty-five minutes about how much I'm going to miss my hunky boyfriend.

Emerson opens the car door, and I study him one last time before getting in. Yes, he's hot, but underneath that hotness is a good man. A really good man.

I give him the kind of wave that feels like I'm trying to etch his face into my memory. I don't want to forget the way he looks, the way Bobo's sitting next to him, both of them in their own little bubble, waiting for me to come home.

As the car pulls away, I glance back at them one last time.

Emerson's standing there, waving, and Bobo's right there by his side. It's the kind of image that, if I let myself linger too long, might break me into a thousand pieces, but it also gives me a little piece of hope to hold on to for the next three months.

I *can* do this. Yes, I have an incredible man by my side, but more than that, I have me. I am enough. I've got this.

EMERSON

BOBO and I've gotten into a good routine in the three weeks since Bryce left for LA. Fortunately, if I leave my hearing aid on, I can usually hear Bobo a few seconds before I see him, so the apartment never feels that empty.

On a cool fall day, the first of my official tenured role, I walk into my department building with Bobo in tow and into the hallway with professors' offices. It's eerily quiet. As soon as I step into my now permanent office, my coworkers yell, "Surprise!"

Alarmed, Bobo emits a single loud bark. He's popular with my officemates, and they all crowd around to pet him. I can't help but wonder how much did my hiring hinge on my work, and how much hinged on getting to see Bobo regularly?

Will hands me a cupcake. A whole box of them sit on my desk. Professors and office staff gather around.

"Congratulations on joining the department," Will says. "Permanently."

"You've earned it." Sheena peels the wrapper back on a cupcake. "We're lucky to have you."

"I'm excited. It feels right being here." I scan the room. "I'm honored to be a part of such a prestigious team."

"So, where are you going to live?" Will asks.

"Any luck on extending the apartment?" Sheena adds.

"I'm planning to stay," I say.

Bobo abandons the orgy of hands touching him and gallops over, smashing his head against my leg.

A warm feeling fills my chest at the thought of Bryce.

"It's a great apartment," I say. "I'm excited to keep living there, although it's feeling kind of empty right now."

"When does Bryce get back again?" Sheena asks.

"Three months." I kneel down, and Bobo gives my beard a giant lick. "Well, technically two months and one week."

"But who's counting?" Sheena smiles and takes a bite of her treat.

It's weird. A few months ago, I'd never met this person, and now my life feels extremely empty without him. All these things I used to do on my own with no problem—now that Bryce isn't there, it just doesn't feel the same. I never thought I'd be one of those romantic people, but here I am. I shrug.

"He'll be home right in time for the holidays," Will says.

"That's right. Maybe I'll do some decorating."

"So, what will you do to pass the time?" Will procures a cupcake with purple flowers iced around the perimeter.

"Bobo and I have dinner together, and we go on walks." I cradle Bobo's giant face. "So many walks, right, boy?"

I let out a sigh.

"What is it?" Sheena asks.

Sheena is busy running the department and keeping tabs on her family. I haven't wanted to bother her outside of school. I didn't want to admit to my colleagues that I didn't have any other friends here. That was kind of a bleak thought. While I love spending time with Bryce and Bobo, I don't want to be one of those people who just has a boyfriend and no one else. That would drive Bryce and I apart, or to murder-suicide. In a city of millions of people, a lack of friends feels more acute.

"I'm just hoping to expand my social circle." I attempt to make it sound less pathetic than it is. Does it work? Judging by everyone's pity looks, not so much.

"Emerson, I'm sorry, you know—" Sheena begins, but I interrupt her.

"You're busy. And we're not in grad school anymore. You've got a family."

"Well, you have me," Will says.

"You're my TA. You're going to flee the nest quite soon."

"Emerson, how did you meet Bryce?" Will carefully takes the cupcake from its wrapper.

"Through very odd circumstances."

"You got to know him by putting yourself out there. That's really all you have to do. Just keep putting yourself out there, and you'll make friends."

"You're right."

"Bobo, no!" I pull him away from the cupcakes and put them on the top shelf of a tall bookcase. "Believe me, buddy, I want you to have these cupcakes as much as you do. I just don't want to clean up the mess that will happen if you eat them."

***

AFTER THE CELEBRATION AND SCHMOOZING, Bobo and I take a leisurely walk home. It's chilly out with fall in full bloom. Trees are changing color. And sure, we have autumn back in Indiana, but it's nothing like here. There really is no place like New York City in the fall. The changing leaves against the buildings—everything feels just so much older and classic, frozen in time. There's a palpable excitement; people know that they're existing in the best time of year.

We stop at the takeout window of a local pizza place. With Bryce away, I don't really cook as much as I should, but I plan to prepare meals for him when he's back. I'm already looking at recipes and menu planning.

We trudge up the stoop and enter the building, but before we even make it past the mail area, I hear someone call out Bobo's name.

Bobo barks back.

"Do you have a friend in there?"

Suddenly, the door to an apartment opens, and a tall, bald man sticks his head through the door.

"Oh, hello," he says.

"Hi," I say.

"Bobo," the mystery person inside squawks.

"I guess Bobo has a friend in there."

Bobo starts barking and pushes his way inside. I follow him into the apartment and find the voice belongs to a parrot. So that's who was squawking at Bryce and me that night after the opera.

"She senses Bobo in the hallway. He has a very unique gait," says the man.

Bobo barks back.

"Should I be worried about him trying to eat her?" I ask.

"He hasn't yet."

A familiar melody wafts through the apartment, as does the scent of delicious, fresh-baked pizza. I adjust my hearing aid, and the music becomes crisper. All my senses come alive.

"Is that ... Tchaikovsky's Fifth Symphony?"

"Good ear," he says. "It's my favorite. It's dramatic storytelling at its finest. From the depths of sorrow to the height of exuberance."

"His use of the orchestra elevates the rich textures of the notes.

Is this the Leonard Bernstein/New York Philharmonic 1974 performance?"

"It's Herbert von Karajan conducting the Berlin Philharmonic. Bernstein's conducting is too brash for my style. Von Karajan's conducting is smoother, more refined."

"I don't think I've ever heard this version." We listen in silence, and he's watching me to get my reaction.

"Excuse me. I have to check on my pizza." He steps away. My nose greedily follows him and the delicious scent to the kitchen, ten times more savory than the quick pizza I picked up. My stomach growls in agreement. "Are you making your own pizza?"

"Yes, I have an indoor pizza oven. I prefer homemade. I don't like going out ... for pizza," he says. "Would you like to join me?"

He asks it almost sarcastically, since Bobo and I have practically moved in at this point.

I glance down at the pathetic slice in the white paper bag.

"I can save this for tomorrow." I place it on a small table near the door. "I'm sorry. Where are my manners? I'm Emerson. I live on the sixth floor."

"Horton. Are you Bryce's new roommate?"

"Bryce!" yells the parrot. She's almost a foot tall, and her body sways back and forth as she speaks.

"I haven't seen him around the building lately," says Horton.

"He's in LA for work for about two more months."

"Bryce!" the parrot yells again. "Fuck you, Bryce! Fuck you!"

"Don't mind Camilla. She also misses Bryce." Horton pets her head as she stares down on us from her perch.

"I'm surprised Bryce likes her company."

"Bryce and her mostly tell each other to fuck off, but it's all in good fun."

"It's good to meet you." I shake Horton's hand. He has pale skin and kind eyes that hint at a deeper story. "And yes, I am

Bryce's roommate. Well, I was. Now we're dating. I mean, we're still living together, but more than roommates."

"Ah. I see. I didn't think Bryce would be into classical music aficionados. Good for him." He smiles, amused. "I can't eat this whole pizza by myself. If you two would like to join me. Bobo can have my crust. I get organic flour delivered. It shouldn't upset his stomach."

Bobo taps his paws on the floor, eagerly awaiting any kind of food. He really has a one-track mind.

"We'd love to," I say. My stomach is as excited as my dog's. "I might have a bottle of wine upstairs we could share."

"I have a Barolo I was going to crack open."

Barolo is infinitely classier than the five-dollar bottle I picked up from the drug store.

"Thank you so much."

"It's good to have company. Eating meals together is a custom since the dawn of time. We should embrace it. The word 'company' comes from the Latin meaning 'with bread.'"

I love that he isn't afraid to nerd out. This will be the first time I'm not eating in front of my computer screen alone since Bryce left.

"Why don't you two go to the table?" Horton shuffles back to the kitchen.

Back in the main living room, I take a beat to look around.

It reminds me of one of those New York City apartments that someone has been living in for at least thirty years, if not more. The layout is identical to ours—Bryce explained all the units are the same—but it somehow seems so different. Every square inch of the walls is covered with pictures and gorgeous artwork. The bookcases are bursting with books. Old books. Two record players. Old maps. Photographs of gorgeous beaches and European cities. There's so much culture and memory bursting out of here. I'm surprised it can all fit into a single apartment.

In the corner of the room, next to the couch, I spot piles of delivery boxes from Amazon, UPS, FedEx, as well as old bags with the Instacart logo.

I don't see any signs of a roommate or partner. I get the feeling that all this stuff is very meticulously placed by Horton.

"So, it's just you in here?" I ask when he returns. Bobo rests on his couch. Horton tosses him a crust.

"Me and Camilla. Just how I like it," he says. He slices the pizza into sixths and hands me a plate with a slice. It's the best thing I've had in my mouth since Bryce's dick. Maybe better? I won't tell him that.

"Wow. This is amazing," I say between bites. I fight my urge to scarf it down.

"How's the weather today?" Horton asks me. He cuts his pizza with a fork and knife.

"It's a beautiful day. You should really get out there—New York in the fall is really something," I tell him.

"Nah, I enjoy it from my window," he says. He pours us each a glass of wine. "Do you play Scrabble? I have a vintage set from the sixties."

"I'd be down for a game. I haven't played in a minute."

Horton lifts his glass. "To new friends."

I clink with my first New York friend. "To new friends."

TWENTY-EIGHT

BRYCE

THE WEEK BEFORE CHRISTMAS, I step into the lobby of the Bigby, my backpack and bag slung over my shoulders, and practically float up the landing. I don't make it past the mailboxes before I hear her.

"Fuck you! Fuck your fucking face! Fuck you!"

Camilla.

"Sorry, we've had the *South Park* movie on repeat and, well ..." Horton leans down, and the bird hops onto his arm. "She really loves the songs."

I laugh because, somehow, being assaulted by a twelve-inch bird seems like a fitting welcome home in the city.

"Anyway, welcome home." Horton bats his eyes, his lips pulled into a barely there smile, and he backs into his apartment. I turn back toward the stairs but pause as he calls out, "Emerson is a great guy. I'm glad he's staying."

Emerson mentioned his Scrabble games with Horton, and my heart swelled knowing both of them had made a new friend. "Me too. Bye, Camilla!"

"Fuck you!"

I step into the apartment, and the familiarity of home wraps around me. I haven't been here in three months, and damn if warmth doesn't take over my body now that I'm back. The thrill of choreographing, dancing, and pushing myself beyond what I believed I was capable of—it was all amazing. I've grown so much, both in my work and in confidence. LA was a whirlwind, and I wouldn't trade the experience for anything, but I'm elated to be back to what matters most.

The place looks different. Familiar, yes, but different. It's clear that Emerson has settled in—his things are scattered about. His jacket hangs over the back of the couch, a few of his books are piled next to the chair, and his bag sits by the door. He's made himself at home. My heart kicks up a notch.

There's a small note propped up on the mantel. I freeze for a second. He's not here. Why is there a note? My heart trips over itself in my chest. We talked this morning. He was fine. Excited to see me. Wasn't he? All his stuff is here. I take a deep breath, step forward, and pick up the note.

Hey babe,

Took Bobo to grab dinner. Should be back in a few minutes.

Can't wait to kiss your face.

Love you,

Em

Of course he's not gone. I chuckle softly, shaking my head. I can't even explain how much I've missed him. How glad I am to be home. Home. With Emerson.

I smile at the thought. Something inside that's been off for the last three months settles. I'm right where I'm supposed to be.

The door opens, and in they come. Emerson's arms are full of takeout bags, and his face lights up when he sees me. Before I know it, Bobo is bounding toward me, his tail spinning like a helicopter blade. I crouch down, laughing as I give him a good rub behind the ears, and he plasters my face with his giant tongue.

"You're home," Emerson says, his voice soft and full of relief.

"Yeah," I reply, standing and reaching for him. We meet halfway, his arms wrapping around me, and for a moment, it's just the three of us, tangled up in each other in the most perfect huddle. "The pack's back together."

"I missed you so much," he murmurs.

"I missed you too." My voice comes out rougher than I expected, and I pull him closer, burying my face in his neck. He's mine. I'm his.

We share a long kiss, slow and full of everything I've been feeling these past few months—longing, love, and the hope that everything will keep getting better, that we'll keep growing together.

"I'm so horny for you." It shoots out of my mouth without thinking. "I know I shouldn't say that, but I can't help it. I've jerked off for three months thinking about you, and well, there you have it."

Emerson pulls back, a mischievous grin on his face. "All in good time. I promise. We have ... well, forever." He spins me around, holding me from behind. "Look. We have a tree. I didn't know if you'd want one, but it's all set up. And, uh ..." He moves over to the tree, reaches into the corner, and it comes to life. "I saved the fairy lights."

"From the roof."

I'm by the window, beside the tree, arms open, ready for him. "It's beautiful. Perfect."

And then, as if on cue, snow starts to fall outside the window, tiny flakes drifting down in the glow of the streetlights. It's peaceful, serene, like something out of a dream.

"It's snowing," Emerson says softly, taking my hand. Bobo lies at my feet as if to anchor me in place. "And now we get to spend Christmas together."

Christmas. Crap. "Listen, about that, I, well, I didn't really have time ..."

"You're my present." Emerson leans over and gives me the sweetest forehead kiss. "And there's an entire week until Christmas. We can shop together."

I nod as tears well up at the corners of my eyes. For the first time in a long while, everything feels right.

"I'm so glad you're home," Emerson whispers, and I pull back to look at him, my heart swelling with a love I've never known.

"Me too," I reply. "Me too."

With the tree sparkling, the snow falling softly, and Emerson beside me, I realize this is where I belong. In the city. With my man and my dog. I'm finally home.

EPILOGUE
EIGHT MONTHS LATER

"BRYCE, are you almost ready to go?" I yell from the bathroom where I put the finishing touches on trimming my beard. I put my hearing aid back in post-shower so I can hear Bryce's response.

However, he says nothing.

"Bryce?"

I strut into the bedroom and find my boyfriend sprawled out on the bed in a T-shirt and sweats.

"Bryce," I sigh.

"I can't get dressed. There's a dog on me."

Bobo lounges across Bryce's legs. He looks up and yawns, then goes back to licking his paw.

"Bobo. Off." I give him a strict nod and point to the floor. Bobo has gotten better at heeding my commands over this past year. Or maybe I've gotten better at giving them, a difficult task when faced with such an adorable dog.

Bobo lumbers off Bryce and jumps to the floor. He rubs against the towel wrapped around me.

"I wish you could come with us," I tell him.

"He can take my place," Bryce says, still prone on the bed with no intention of moving. "Put a bowtie on him. Nobody will know the difference."

I gently shake Bryce's ankle.

"Ow," he deadpans.

"We have to go soon. The opera waits for no one."

"I can sum up what happens. Someone sings a beautiful song in a language we don't understand while their lover dies. The end."

"We're seeing *Die Fledermaus*. It's a farce."

"People in elaborate makeup and costumes trying to be funny while singing? Honey, can't we just go to drag cabaret instead?"

I sit on the bed and give his leg another shake. When I was growing up, my dad used to overturn the mattress when I slept in. Maybe I should do the same here.

"It's a special night. A year ago, you mistook me for a Grindr date, and our love blossomed from there." I chuckle, thinking about the truly odd path that love can take. So long as that path led me to Bryce Derrickson, then it was worth the crazy twists and turns.

"Let's stay in instead."

Bryce reaches out a hand and feels around my face like he's searching for a light switch in the dark.

"What are you doing?" I ask.

"Trying to give you a hand job."

"I'll pass." I politely move his hand away.

"Ugh I'm so tired. I just got home an hour ago, and I was on set until eleven last night going over the choreography for next week's show."

"I'm so proud of you."

"I'm proud of me, too. But working hard is really hard. I have an idea. What if you quit teaching and do finance?"

"I don't think 'do finance' is grammatically correct."

"This is why I'm bad at money. Anyway, you do finance, and

then we'll buy a house in the Hamptons, and I can be a housewife who reads magazines and shops at farmstands all day."

"Baby, you would be so bored. So. Bored."

"Ugh, you're right."

I massage deep circles into his foot. The first season of *Queers in the Headlights* was a big hit for the network and quickly renewed. However, most of the major talent involved realized that filming in LA didn't have the same energy as filming in New York. They couldn't do on-the-street segments because there were no pedestrians in Burbank, for one. They missed the grungy, scrappy downtown vibe that had birthed the show. With the improved clout, Preeti and the producers got them to move production back here.

Just as I was about to psych myself up for a long-distance relationship, I learned that Bryce wasn't going anywhere. His days on the show are long, but he gets to come home to a home-cooked meal and lots of snuggly couch time with me and Bobo. My heart still skips a beat when I hear him lumber up the stairs and jiggle his key in the lock.

Bryce tips his head in my direction. He cocks an eyebrow. "What?"

"What do you mean, what?"

"You're looking at me."

"Because I like what I see." I used to think that my work was enough to sustain me. I had passion for classical music and my research. I had ambition. But I realized how hollow these desires were without love in my life. Having someone who gets me enriches my life in new ways. With Bryce, I don't have to work hard. I don't have to try or strive. I can just be me.

I lean down and kiss his salty lips, peer into his wide, warm eyes.

"I love the opera, thanks to you, but I'm going to fall asleep," he whispers.

"You can rest on my shoulder." I push a lock of hair away from his face.

Bryce reaches between us. "Someone's excited for the opera."

He wiggles his eyebrows as he goes to town rubbing something.

"Bryce, you're stroking one of Bobo's chew toys."

He grabs the phallically shaped toy in question, a bright blue, rubber object. "Oh."

"Let's get dressed." I pat his leg and toss the toy onto the floor.

"Fine." Bryce drags himself to sitting up. He wipes exhaustion from his eyes, and for a second, I feel bad for forcing my boyfriend to go to the opera. But then I remember that Bryce has a huge capacity for finding his second wind. Once we get to dinner, he'll perk up. And being around all the operagoers at the Met will wake him up even more. He's very much an extrovert energized by being social. I am so not that, but I'm glad I'm dating someone who is or else I'd never leave the apartment.

He trudges to the closet and picks out an outfit. I walk over to the wardrobe crammed in the corner of the room and pull out my clothes for tonight. I play some Wagner in the background as we get dressed.

"You know, it's cruel and borderline homophobic to get naked in front of me and not do anything about it," he says.

"That will come later." I loop the tie around my neck.

"Or we could come now." He gives my butt a squeeze right before I put on my pants.

As much as I would like to have my way with Bryce on the bed, we really are pressed for time. I tried to give him as much time as possible to rest before we had to leave.

I wait in the living room with Bobo as Bryce finishes getting ready. A few minutes later, he emerges looking gorgeous in a blazer, slacks, and sparkly boots. You can't turn down the volume on Bryce Derrickson no matter how hard you try.

"I'm ready." He gives me a halfhearted thumbs-up.

"Before we go, I want to show you something." A smile sneaks onto my face. "It's on the mantel."

I point to the envelope.

"What's that?" Bryce's face turns a curious shade of white.

"Open it and find out."

"I'm not big on surprises. Remember the anxiety attack I had while watching the finals of *Drag Race*?"

"Open it." I stay in place. My eyes try to assure him as much as possible that it's a good surprise. Bryce has been burned in the past with surprise breakups. My goal is to eventually make him fall in love with surprises.

Bryce opens the envelope. He scans through the document, crinkling his brow. "I'm confused. There are a lot of words on this. What is it?"

"It's a new lease agreement. As of this month, I've officially and permanently taken over the lease."

"No more Anthony?"

"No more Anthony. I made Carl put your name on the lease this time." I walk up to Bryce and get on one knee. I take a pen from my front pocket and hand it up to him. "Bryce Derrickson, will you co-sign this apartment lease with me?"

He throws a hand over his heart. Tears well at his eyes.

"There's nobody on this earth that I would rather live in over-priced real estate with," I say. Forget about rings, in Manhattan, real estate is the real romance.

"This ... you're staying ..."

I get up and pull him close to me. He has been through so much. I want to protect him from all future heartache. "Bryce, I'm always staying. And if I ever leave this apartment, you're coming with me. And you too, buddy." I double-pat my leg to signal Bobo over. He nuzzles into his favorite spot, the gap between our legs.

"I love you," Bryce says in between kisses.

"I am truly so proud of what you've accomplished, and what you're going to accomplish. I am so lucky I get to stand next to you." I wipe away his tear.

"And I'm proud of you, Em. You're one of UNY's most popular professors."

"Just according to Rate My Professor." I give a modest shrug. Bryce also found pictures of me lecturing on a Hot For Teacher Instagram page. I am nicknamed Professor SLG (Slutty Little Glasses). Bryce assured me any attention was good attention, and I assured him that I am only hot for him.

"We should go. Opera. Arias and all that." Bryce looks up at me, his eyes two deep wells of emotion and hope. I could stare into them all day. And lucky for me, I get to.

I pull him closer with one hand. Bobo nuzzles deeper into the space between our legs. Their warmth radiates in my heart.

There we are, one happy family.

BIG BOYS SMALL SPACES: THE SERIES
BY A.J. TRUMAN AND M.A. WARDELL

Marshmallow Mountain: Data and Marsh's story is out now!

Cut to the Feeling: Bryce and Emerson's is out now.

Untitled Book 3: Horton's story coming in 2026.

ALSO BY A.J. TRUMAN

<u>South Rock High</u>

<u>Ancient History</u>

<u>Drama!</u>

<u>Romance Languages</u>

<u>Advanced Chemistry</u>

<u>Single Dads Club</u>

<u>The Falcon and the Foe</u>

<u>The Mayor and the Mystery Man</u>

<u>The Barkeep and the Bro</u>

The Fireman and the Flirt

<u>Browerton University Series</u>

<u>Out in the Open</u>

<u>Out on a Limb</u>

<u>Out of My Mind</u>

<u>Out for the Night</u>

<u>Out of This World</u>

<u>Outside Looking In</u>

<u>Out of Bounds</u>

<u>The Combacks Series</u>

<u>Gross Misconduct</u>

ALSO BY M.A. WARDELL

<u>THE TEACHERS IN LOVE SERIES</u>

Teacher of the Year - Marvin and Olan's story is available now!

Mistletoe & Mishigas - Sheldon and Theo's story is available now!

Napkins and Other Distractions - Vincent and Kent's story is available now!

Husband of the Year - Marvin and Olan's series finale coming November 2025.

Stirring Spurs - What if he didn't have to quit you? Boone and Wylie's cowboy romance is out now!

Peaches and Pucks - Darius and Harry's hockey romance coming in 2026.

Download free bonus stories!

https://www.mawardell.com/freebies

ABOUT A.J. TRUMAN

A.J. Truman writes books with humor, heart, and hot guys. What else does a story need? He lives in a very full house in Indiana with his husband, kids, and cats. He loves happily ever afters and sneaking off for an afternoon movie.

www.ajtruman.com

Want to stay in touch and be the first to know about my new books? Join my mailing list The Outsiders today and instantly receive a free short story at www.ajtruman.com/outsiders.

For exclusive content, join me on Patreon.

ABOUT M.A. WARDELL

M.A. Wardell lives near the ocean with his husband and cats. When he isn't writing, he's snuggling those cats, reading all the rom-coms, walking to unravel plot points, and taking long hot baths. He loves playing matchmaker on the page and has many more stories planned.

For more information, visit https://www.mawardell.com/

Purchase signed copies here!

For access to exclusive content and merchandise, join me on Patreon.

www.ingramcontent.com/pod-product-compliance
Lightning Source LLC
Chambersburg PA
CBHW021042310726
48969CB00006B/1770